Touched by a Gladiator

MARISA CHENERY

CONTENTS

CHAPTER ONE

Present Day

Petra Holtz lifted the long narrow box that sat on the passenger seat of her older model black Toyota Camry and then cradled it in her arms while she used her body to shut the door. She blew her bangs out of her face and headed for the front door of the large mansion. Having the air conditioning in her car break down on a hot summer day in Los Angeles was not fun. And having to ride around in said car for what seemed like hours just to pick up a package for her boss had not made Petra's day. As the personal assistant to a wealthy real estate investor, it was part and parcel of her job.

She managed to open the heavy oak door of the mansion without dropping the box and breathed a sigh of relief when the cool air inside washed over her heated skin. Petra hoped whatever it was that Mr. Dunn had sent her to pick up was worth it. The man at the out-of-the-way

1

antiques store already had Mr. Dunn's purchase boxed up by the time she had arrived so she hadn't seen what it was.

Knowing at this time of day her employer would be sitting outside in his massive backyard, drinking coffee while he read the real estate section of the paper, Petra headed to the living room and out the French doors. Mr. Dunn sat at the glass and wrought-iron patio table just as she had predicted.

Walking toward him, Petra slowed her steps and took the time to straighten her skirt and fluff her hair. Mr. Dunn—who was in his late sixties—held firmly to the belief that a person should be impeccably dressed at all times. She'd started working for him a year ago and she had yet to see him wear anything but a suit and tie. Even now, with the day one of the hottest of the summer, he sat under the shade of the patio table's large umbrella with his suit jacket on. She thought he had to be roasting.

She put a smile on her face when she reached him and placed the box on the glass patio table next to him. "Here's your purchase from the antiques store, Mr. Dunn."

He gave her a curt nod. "Very good. I'll open it, then you can take it to my study. It should go on the new shelf I had installed."

"Okay."

Petra had to admit she was a little curious as to what was inside the box. That it had warranted Mr. Dunn having a shelf installed in his study just for it, said it was one of his pricier purchases.

Mr. Dunn made short work of opening the box and pulled open the flaps. He pushed the top layer of packing material aside. Petra peered inside to see what looked to be a wooden sword. To her it didn't look like much, but from the large smile he wore he was obviously pleased with his newest acquisition.

"So what do you think of it, Petra?" Mr. Dunn looked up at her.

"Uh, it's a nice looking wooden sword."

Mr. Dunn shook his head and chuckled. "This isn't just any old wooden sword. This is a replica of an original ancient Roman rudis. A very, very old replica."

"What exactly is a rudis?" History hadn't exactly been her strong suit in school, and she knew next to nothing about Roman history.

"A rudis was presented to a gladiator when he was set free. If he was lucky enough to survive to reach that point."

"Cool." The only knowledge she had of ancient warriors was from the movie *Gladiator* that stared Russell Crowe, and she had a feeling it hadn't been that historically correct, though it did make for some good watching.

"Yes, it is," Mr. Dunn replied. He pushed the flaps of the box closed. "Why don't you take this inside while I finish up here?"

"All right."

Petra picked up the box before she headed back through the French doors, grateful to be inside the air-conditioned mansion. She walked to the study and then crossed the room to put what she carried onto Mr. Dunn's large mahogany desk. The shelf for the rudis had been installed on the wall kitty-corner from it. She grabbed the top layer of packing material to take hold of it. She jumped when a jolt of energy shot through her fingertips where they had come in contact with the wooden sword. *That was strange.*

Thinking she couldn't have somehow shocked herself with static electricity when she had touched it, Petra reached inside the box and lifted the rudis. She took a step away from the desk, intending to place it on its shelf when another jolt went through her. Only this time she had to blink her eyes when she thought she saw something forming directly in front of her.

Petra cradled the wooden sword in one arm while she used her other hand to rub her eyes. She had to be seeing things. She blinked again, but whatever it was didn't go away. What appeared to be a small circle of swirling mist hovered in front of her. It grew until it was the size of a large beach ball.

Frozen in place, Petra gasped when the mist cleared. What looked to be a room made out of stone appeared. And chained to the wall, completely naked, was a very large, very muscular man. He stood with his blond head bent. She couldn't stop her gaze from running all over him. The man had a killer body without an inch of fat on him anywhere. She took in his well-defined, hairless chest and washboard abs. Petra swallowed when she reached his cock. It hung flaccid between his well-muscled thighs, and even in that state it looked big.

A thick wooden door she hadn't seen at first opened. A woman walked through and pulled back the material of a shawl-looking garment she wore from her head. The door shut behind her when she slowly crossed the room to the chained man. Once she reached him, she pulled off the shawl, revealing what looked like a toga-styled dress underneath it and ran her hand down his chest. The man lifted his head.

All the air left Petra's lungs in a whoosh. The man was drop-dead-want-to-screw-his-brains-out-all-night-long gorgeous. He had a square jaw, high chiseled cheekbones and firm lips. There was a faint scar that ran from the corner of his left eye down to his cheek, but it did nothing to take away from his good looks.

The woman stepped closer and kissed the side of the man's neck while she took his flaccid cock in her hand. She pumped it up and down as she placed kisses at the base of his throat and down his chest. Petra swallowed. Unable to look away—feeling as if she were locked in some kind of waking dream—her body started to respond as the man's cock hardened. An ache built between her legs, causing wetness to pool.

Petra knew she should be freaking out at seeing whatever the hell she was seeing, but she couldn't get herself to do anything other than stare like a sick peeping tom. As the woman moved lower down his body, the man let his head fall back against the stone wall behind him. His throat worked and he closed his eyes. The sight of him standing there chained, naked, obviously enjoying what the woman was doing to him turned Petra on. Her fingers itched to reach out and stroke that deliciously muscular body. She'd always had a weakness for muscular, tall men, especially blonds.

The woman sank onto her knees before him and took his now engorged shaft into her mouth. The look of pure pleasure—and the husky moan he made at the same time—had Petra's nipples tightening beneath her lightweight sky-blue blouse. Wetness leaked into her panties, causing a moan of her own to push past her lips.

As if he had heard her, the man straightened his head and a pair of blue eyes locked gazes with her. Shocked that he actually seemed to see her, Petra gasped and let the rudis fall out of her grasp. The window—or whatever it had been—suddenly disappeared as quickly as it had appeared.

Petra stood with her chest rapidly rising and falling while she tried to pull herself together. *What the hell had just happened?* Had the scene with the chained man and the woman going down on him been real? She didn't think she'd totally lost her mind and saw things that really weren't there.

Feeling more than a little rattled, Petra bent to pick up the fallen rudis. When her fingers came within a scant inch of it, a small jolt of energy shot through them. No, she wasn't going to touch it, at least not with her bare hand. Going back over to the desk, she grabbed some of the packing material and placed it over the rudis before she picked it up. She quickly placed it on its shelf.

Petra gathered up the rest of the packing material and empty box. She looked over at the rudis one last time before she left the study. Whatever had happened, the sight of the man in the throes of passion would be forever etched in her brain.

* * * *

Fourth Century Rome

Euric rolled onto his back and stared up at the stone ceiling of his cell. The Roman woman — who had come to take her pleasure from him — had long since gone. She had just been another woman to come to him so she could boast later to her friends that she had been with one of the gladiators who fought at the *Amphitheatrum Flavium*. Being one of the mob's favorites did have its quirks. Nothing more than a slave, he took what pleasure he could from this life when the opportunity presented itself.

Even though he had found release with the woman, he still lay unable to sleep on his bed. Something had happened this night while he had been otherwise occupied. The other woman — the one who he had seen in the strange window-like circle that had appeared in his cell — he found he couldn't stop thinking about her. He had found himself drawn to her when he'd heard her moan and their gazes had met. He'd had a split second to take in her long, light brown hair that hung around her slim shoulders and dark green eyes — along with full kissable lips — before she gasped and the window had disappeared.

Euric had no idea what had caused the window or the woman to appear in his cell, but he hoped they would come again. Hopefully the next time he would be alone. He had not minded that she had obviously seen what the

Roman woman had been doing to him. From the flush on her cheeks, he knew she had found it arousing. With a life as a gladiator, being self-conscious about your body did not last very long.

He closed his eyes and tried to settle himself enough to find sleep. The next day would be a full one of training at the *ludus – Ludus Magnus*, the school where gladiators were trained as well as barracked. He was to have his second match out of the three a year he fought in a week's time. Euric didn't have to worry about losing. He was a mob favorite and had enough skill not to be defeated easily, but that did not mean he did not have to keep himself in top fighting form. He had vowed long ago he would not end his life on the sand of the *Amphitheatrum's* arena.

* * * *

Present Day

Petra arrived at her small apartment three hours after the incident in Mr. Dunn's study. Feeling too hot to cook, she'd picked up some sushi on the way home. Kicking the apartment door closed behind her, she put her take-out food on the kitchen table before she went to the bedroom to get out of her skirt and blouse. After she pulled on a tank top and a pair of shorts, she smoothed her long hair back into a ponytail. She wished she could dress like this for work. She would have been a heck of a lot cooler.

After she returned to the kitchen, she sat at the table. While she ate her sushi, Petra found her thoughts drawn to what she'd seen when she'd held the rudis. She couldn't get the man's face out of her mind. Every time she thought about him, she started to become aroused. Yes, she didn't have a boyfriend right now, but this dry spell hadn't been all that long. She shouldn't be lusting after a man who didn't really exist. She hadn't sunk that low yet. At least she hoped she hadn't.

Still, Petra couldn't stop remembering how the chained man had looked with his head thrown back, his face a mask of pure pleasure. She squeezed her legs together against the ache that built in her pussy. She gave her head a shake. She had to stop this. She couldn't explain what had happened in the study. As far as she knew, it wouldn't happen again, but that didn't stop a small part of her wishing it would.

She'd just finished eating when the phone rang. Petra stood and went to pick up her cell phone that sat on an end table in the living room. "Hello?"

"Hey, Petra."

"Hi, Lia."

Lia was Petra's best friend and had been since high school. Now both twenty-five, they pretty much knew all the ins and outs of one another. That being the case, Petra knew what Lia would ask next, and that she would have to disappoint her.

"So? Are we still on for dinner and a movie tomorrow night?" Lia asked.

Petra cringed. Yup, she'd been right. "Ah, sorry, but I'm going to have to cancel."

"Why?" Lia didn't sound exactly pleased.

"Mr. Dunn decided to go on a last-minute business trip out of the country and he leaves tomorrow morning. He'll be gone for a week. He wants me to house sit again."

"Aw, come on, Petra. We planned this a week ago. You know how hectic my schedule is. It's just an evening out. He'll never know."

Petra sighed. Lia was right about her schedule. As an ER nurse, Lia worked such long hours they sometimes had a hard time getting together. "I can't, Lia. Mr. Dunn wants me to stay in the mansion during the evening and at night. I could lose my job if he happened to call and I wasn't there."

Lia huffed. "I don't understand why the old codger wants you to stay there. It isn't as if anyone could really break in with all the security you told me he has."

"He has a lot of expensive antiques. I guess he feels with me there someone would be less likely to break in if they knew the mansion wasn't empty. I know Mr. Dunn can be a bit particular at times, but I enjoy working for him. I really don't have any complaints about him."

"Fine," Lia said. "I won't push, but I want you to promise me that once the old fart gets back we'll reschedule."

Petra chuckled. "Mr. Dunn is hardly an old fart. And I promise."

"I'm going to hold you to it. I've got to run. I have to start my shift at the hospital in an hour. Have fun house sitting."

"I'll call you in a couple days."

"Sure. Catch you later."

After Lia hung up, Petra cleared the kitchen table and then went back to the living room. She turned on the TV and changed the channels until she hit one that snagged her attention. On it played the movie *Gladiator*. Thinking it was a bit of a coincidence when she'd thought about it earlier that day, she settled down to watch. She'd only missed the very beginning, but she'd already watched it a few times so she was able to easily pick up the storyline.

It wasn't until the scene where the emperor's sister came to visit Russell Crowe's gladiator character in his cell at the gladiator barracks that Petra sat up straighter and really focused on the TV. Something about that scene had her comparing what she'd seen in Mr. Dunn's study. Just like the chained man, Russell Crowe's character was chained to a stone wall, except he wasn't naked and he had some chain length to move around with. And the woman's character with him — dressed in ancient Roman clothing —

reminded her of the woman who'd come to the chained man. Even her style of dress sort of matched the woman's in the movie.

Naw, it couldn't be. It just had to be another coincidence that what Petra had seen in the study seemed so similar to one that was supposed to of taken place in ancient Rome. Yes, the rudis was a replica of a real Roman rudis, but there was no way in hell it'd allowed her to catch a glimpse of the past. It wasn't possible. Only crazy people and those who believed in weird paranormal things like that would think she'd looked through a window into the past. She just didn't believe in the paranormal, psychic stuff. She was the type of person who needed to see physical proof before she bought into it.

Watching the rest of the movie, Petra couldn't shake the idea that maybe, just maybe, she'd seen something that had taken place centuries ago. She told herself to knock it off, that thinking she was able to see into the past would make her a loony toon, but she couldn't get herself to stop. By the time it grew late and she decided to go to bed, she figured there was only one way to prove it—she needed to touch the rudis again and see if the window or portal thingie opened again. It was either that or let it drive her completely crazy.

* * * *

Early the next morning Petra hauled a suitcase filled with enough clothes for a week out to her car and then drove to Mr. Dunn's mansion. Even though she'd be staying there until her employer returned, she planned to stop by her apartment each day to pick up her mail. Being allergic to anything with fur, and a well-known plant murderer, she at least didn't have to worry about those two things during her absence.

After she arrived at the mansion, she went inside,

dragging her heavy suitcase behind her. Petra found Mr. Dunn waiting impatiently at the front door. He smiled when he saw her and helped her with her luggage.

"I really appreciate that you can house sit on such short notice, Petra," he said. "I promise the next time I go away, I'll be sure to give you advanced warning."

"It's okay. I really don't mind."

She really didn't. Staying at the mansion would be like a luxury vacation for her. With a maid and a cook on the premises, Petra wouldn't have to do much, except whatever paperwork Mr. Dunn wanted her to handle.

"Good. You can have the same guestroom you used the last time you were here. I had the maid get the room ready. I left some papers that I need scanned and emailed on my desk in the study. I'll call you when I have something else for you to do. Other than that, make yourself at home and I'll see you in a week."

Petra opened the front door for Mr. Dunn when he picked up his brief case that sat on the floor in the foyer. His black limousine was parked idling just outside. "Thanks. I hope you have a productive week."

He smiled. "It should be."

Mr. Dunn walked outside and climbed into his limousine. Petra stood in the open doorway and watched it drive down the long driveway. Once it disappeared from sight, she shut the front door. Deciding the first thing she should do was take her suitcase upstairs, she grabbed it and manhandled it to the bedroom that would be hers during her stay.

When she had stayed there the first time, Mr. Dunn had given her the choice of the five guest bedrooms. She'd ended up picking the one that had French doors that opened onto a balcony facing the beautifully landscaped backyard. There was a small wrought-iron patio set out on it as well. Petra had enjoyed drinking her morning coffee out on it in her bathrobe each morning. She planned to do it again this time around.

The inside of the bedroom appealed to her as well. The king-sized bed with its carved oak headboard had a deep ruby-red jacquard comforter on it with matching sheets. The walls had been painted a pale sky-blue and the floors had been covered in wall-to-wall thick royal-blue carpeting. The room itself was the size of her kitchen and living room put together. It also had its own bathroom with a shower and tub. No, staying there was far from being a hardship.

Suitcase now taken care of, Petra headed back downstairs, making a beeline for the study. Practically the whole night she'd had dreams of the chained man. In them, she'd taken the place of the woman who'd been with him. Petra had been able to run her hands all over his delectable body while she licked and kissed every inch of him. The chains had fallen away, and he'd been able to do the same to her. He'd stroked and kissed her until she'd begged him to take her. Of course she'd woken up just before she'd gotten the final prize. She'd come awake horny as hell, and frustrated to boot.

Once inside the study, Petra found herself having second thoughts about touching the rudis. What if she touched it and nothing happened? Or better yet, what if she touched it and something *did* happen? She wasn't normally this indecisive, but now that she was in the same room with it she felt nervous. She really did want to see the chained man again, but he couldn't be real. Or could he? All she knew was just the sight of him turned her on.

Deciding to take things slow and easy, Petra made a point of not looking at the rudis as she walked by it and went over to the desk. She forced herself to concentrate on the paperwork Mr. Dunn had left her. She'd work on getting some of it done, then she'd pick up the rudis.

While Petra worked, her gaze kept drifting over to the wooden sword. A few times, she had to stop herself from getting up and going over to it. Gritting her teeth, she pulled her gaze off it for the hundredth time and centered her attention on sending out the paperwork she'd scanned into Mr. Dunn's desktop computer.

As soon as she hit send, Petra was on her feet and walking over to the shelf that held the rudis. She couldn't take it. One way or the other, she had to see if she could see the chained man again. If it didn't work, at least it wouldn't drive her crazy anymore. She'd chalk up the first incidence as a fluke, or a temporary breakdown on her part.

With hands that shook slightly, Petra reached for the rudis. Same as the other day when her fingertips came within mere inches of it, a jolt of energy shot through them. *So far so good.* She took a deep breath and picked up the wooden sword in both hands. She turned away from the wall to look at the empty space to the right of her when she caught something forming out of the corner of her eye.

Petra's heart beat faster when a misty circle formed and once again grew until it was the same size as before. She held her breath once the mist cleared. Instead of seeing the chained man, the window cleared to show her the same stone room, but this time it appeared to be empty. She saw the empty chains hanging on the wall and the same thick wooden door. Wanting to see the rest of the room, she unthinkingly reached out to touch the edge of the window and pushed to the right. Much to her surprise, the scene inside shifted in the same direction, giving her another angle.

She shoved at the window until she came to a single bed barely covered by a thin blanket. The mattress looked to be nothing more than a large sack that had been stuffed with some kind of filling and sewn together. It didn't look very comfortable. With no sight of the man, she shifted her point of view again. The only thing she found was a small scarred wooden table that sat pushed up against one of the stone walls. After making a complete circuit with no sighting of him, Petra felt more than a little disappointed.

Crap. She'd gotten herself all worked up for nothing. Petra put the rudis back on its shelf, and the window closed. Well, it hadn't entirely been a waste of time. At least she now knew the day before hadn't been a one-shot deal. She'd seen the room the chained man had been in. He just didn't happen to be inside it. There was always next time, and there would be a next time. She returned to the desk to finish some more of the work Mr. Dunn had left for her. She'd try again later. Even though a sane woman would be more than a little freaked out to find herself able to open a window to what could possibly be the past, she felt nothing of the kind. Obviously, she'd lost all sense.

* * * *

Fourth Century Rome

Euric wiped the sweat out of his eyes. He had been on the training ground of the *ludus* for the last two hours, taking part in sword practice with the rest of the gladiators under his *Lanistae* — the man who owned the school. All of them were considered his *Lanistae's familia gladiatorial*, or simply put, they were family members who the *Lanistae* had power over, including life or death.

Having defeated his sparring partner, Euric lowered his *sica*, a wooden curved sword. As a Thracian-type gladiator, he fought with a real *sica*, wore a helmet that covered his entire head, carried a small round shield and wore thigh-high greaves on his legs while in the arena. His armor was considered light compared to the heavily armored Samnite-type gladiator who wore a helmet with a visor and fought with a spear instead of a sword.

Euric walked to the bucket of water sitting on the edge of the training ground for the gladiators to refresh themselves, picked up the wooden ladle and drank from it. He still had more than a few hours of training to go before they would be given their evening meal and he returned to his cell. Today the thought of being locked inside his for the duration of the night didn't bother him. He hoped the strange window would appear, enabling him to have another glimpse of the woman. He found he could not stop thinking about her.

"So, Goth, are you ready to be defeated when we fight in the upcoming *munera*?"

Euric returned the ladle to the bucket and then slowly turned around. Calix—a Roman who had voluntarily chosen to become a gladiator—stood smirking at him. Euric did not know what reason Calix had for basically selling himself into servitude, but it would not have surprised him to learn Calix had done it so he could take part in the games. The Roman was one of the more blood-thirsty of the gladiators in the *familia*. Standing at six-foot-three—the same height as Euric—Calix was one of the taller fighters. His dark brown hair was cut short and his brown eyes had a cruel edge to them. He was also as muscular as Euric, which put their strength at just about equal. Neither of them was a *tiro*—a beginner. Calix was a *primus palus*, or first sword, while Euric was a *secundus palus*, or second sword. If Euric defeated Calix during their fight, he would be classed a *primus palus*, knocking Calix down a place in status.

Euric being a Visigoth—one of the tribes from Germania—Calix liked to remind him of his captive of war status every chance he got. Not that it really bothered him since he was proud of his heritage.

"It may be you, Calix, who will be defeated."

Calix snarled his lip. "Oh, I will be the victor. And if I had my way, I would have the mob give the thumbs-down. I would love nothing more than to end your miserable existence."

Euric refused to be pushed into a fight by the Roman's insults. Calix was full of hot air. The man—even though he was a slave the same as Euric—looked down his nose at all the gladiators who had been captured in battle. Euric kept his gaze on Calix, but remained silent.

Obviously realizing Euric would not be drawn out, Calix stalked to the middle of the training ground. Euric winced for the much smaller man, a *tiro*, the Roman started to beat with his wooden sword.

Euric was not going to lie to himself. He wanted nothing more than to be the one to defeat Calix. The Roman needed to be taken down to the dirt. And fighting Calix meant Euric would be one step closer to gaining his freedom. If he continued to be the mob's favorite, he could very well be given his rudis. Having fought in many *muneras* over the last two years since he had become a gladiator, he felt he had more than earned it.

Pulling the round collar of the plain knee-length tunica he wore away from his sweaty skin, Euric headed for his next sparring partner, another *tiro*. Unlike Calix, he did not start to beat the man down. No matter how competitive the life of a gladiator was, he could not bring himself to treat the newer members of the *familia* with disdain. Having once been in their place, he knew some would be lucky to live to fight in more than a couple *muneras* before they lost their lives.

Settling into the motion of swinging his sword, he focused all his attention on the task at hand. Even though he had a high status in the *familia*, it did not mean he could afford to become lax. How well he fought—as well as his good looks—helped to keep him a favorite. And Euric intended to keep it that way.

CHAPTER TWO

Petra managed to resist touching the rudis for the rest of the day. From time to time her gaze was drawn to it while she worked, but now that she knew the window would open again, it didn't seem to pull at her quite so much as it had earlier. She even got through eating the dinner the cook, Sally, had prepared for her.

Once the maid and cook left for the day, Petra dressed in a tank top and shorts before she returned to the study. Confident it would work, she crossed to the rudis, picked it up and turned to face the center of the room.

She smiled when the misty circle appeared. Once the window cleared, Petra found herself looking at the chained man again. Except this time he wasn't chained. He lay on top the bed while he stared at the ceiling. He wore a coarse, off-white, short-sleeved tunic that seemed to barely reach his knees. It was belted at the waist by what looked to be a length of slim rope.

Petra ran her gaze over his body. Even though what he

wore no man she knew would be caught dead in since it'd be considered effeminate, the man looked nothing of the kind. With his arms bent and his head resting on his hands, his large biceps bulged with well-defined muscle. He exuded pure testosterone and complete maleness, even right down to the sandals on his feet.

Taking a deep breath, Petra looked back up at his face. So far, he hadn't acknowledged she was there. It made her wonder if she'd imagined him looking right back at her the day before. She hoped not, because if she was going to accept that this was really happening, she wanted at least to be able to communicate with him.

Petra swallowed before she said, "Hello?"

The man's blond head jerked her way. He quickly sat up and turned to face her. His blue-eyed gaze latched on to her when he said something she didn't understand. His deep voice went right through her to her pussy, making it clench.

With a groan, Petra shook her head. "I don't understand you." He said something else in what sounded an awful lot like Latin, which she didn't know either. "Sorry, I don't know how to speak Latin."

Frowning, he stood and came closer to the window. Now wasn't that just great. She somehow was able to see into the past—she was sure of it now that she saw what the man wore—and she wasn't able to communicate with the one person she had contact with. It'd make for a frustrating conversation.

Petra touched the center of her chest. She slowly said, "Petra."

She pointed to him, hoping he understood she wanted to know his name. His gaze left her face and settled on her chest where she'd pointed. Her nipples grew taut beneath her tank top when a look of definite interest formed on his face. Petra's heart beat a little faster. That one look made her body stand up and take notice. The image of what he had looked like the last time she'd seen him—naked and aroused—shot through her mind. Desire surged through her, causing her body to respond.

Before her brain led her off to fantasy land, staring at the man standing on the other side of the window, Petra took a deep breath and pointed in her direction once again. "Petra. My name is Petra."

His gaze lifted to her face. This time he seemed to catch on to what she was doing. He touched the center of his wide chest, and said, "Euric."

Now they were getting somewhere. He wouldn't understand her, but she said it anyway. "Nice to meet you, Euric." He must have liked that she'd said his name, because he nodded and gave her a smile that just about turned her body to mush.

Unable to tear her gaze away, Petra stared at his mouth. She wondered what it'd feel like to have it pressed to her skin—preferably while he licked and kissed her entire body. When the smile he wore slowly faded, she forced herself to look Euric in the eyes. What she saw there had her heart beating even faster. Her chest rapidly rose and fell with each breath she took. His eyes had dilated with arousal. The look he gave her promised hours of hot, wild sex that would leave her begging for more.

Lost in a sexual haze that swirled around them, Petra took a step closer to her side of the window and reached out to touch Euric. He lifted his hand at the same time. When their hands came in contact with the window, they both jumped back. Petra hissed and shook hers. Obviously, touching the window hadn't been such a good idea. It'd given her one hell of a shock. Looking at him, she realized he must have gotten the same jolt since he shook his hand as well.

"I guess whatever this thing is it doesn't want to be touched," Petra said.

Euric chuckled. "It would appear not."

They both froze. Petra met Euric's gaze through the window. He'd understood her, and she him. He'd spoken in Latin, but somehow her brain had instantly translated it into English. The same must have happened to him, because he stood with a shocked expression on his face.

"You understand me now, don't you?"

Euric nodded. "Yes."

"Okay, that's weird. Well, I guess we won't have to rely on sign language anymore."

His face grew serious. "What is causing this window to appear?"

Petra shook her head. "I don't really know. All I do know is that when I touch this the window forms." She held up the rudis she had in her hands.

A look of longing appeared on Euric's face. "A gladiator's rudis. I hope to earn one of my own. How did you come by yours?"

Oh god. She'd been right. Euric was a gladiator. She now understood the chains and what the woman had been doing there with him. In ancient Rome, some gladiators had the same status as present-day movie stars. They used to have groupies of Roman women—some even from the aristocratic levels of society—who'd sleep with them just because they were gladiators. Obviously, Euric didn't mind sleeping with the willing women who came to his cell. Petra, on the other hand, didn't like the idea of some strange woman using him just to say she'd slept with a gladiator. Not that it was any of her business what he did.

"It's not exactly mine," Petra said. "The man I work for owns it. So you're a gladiator? You don't look Roman."

Euric scowled. "That is because I am not. I am Visigoth. The Romans captured me in Germania. I did not choose to become a gladiator and fight in the *muneras* at the *Amphitheatrum Flavium*."

Petra may not know much about Roman history, but she knew the *Amphitheatrum Flavium* was now called the

Colosseum. She'd done a little research on the Internet about it after she'd first watched the Gladiator movie. For some reason, the original name had stuck in her mind. Holy crap. She was now standing face-to-face with an honest-to-god gladiator who fought in the Colosseum.

*

Euric had watched Petra's eyes widen when he had said he was a gladiator. Obviously, she knew what one was. He had not been so sure, considering her world looked so much different. Just as if he were looking out a regular window, he saw most of what was on the other side, which gave him a good view of her. The chamber she stood in looked more luxurious than one he figured would be found inside the emperor's palace. There was dark red carpet beneath her bare feet while the walls had been painted dark green. Some of the furnishings he recognized, but they were in a style he had never seen before. Some, he had no clue what they were.

He skimmed his gaze over Petra's body. She was scantily clad in what looked to be very short leggings and a top that just modestly covered her chest. He doubted any Roman woman would dare to walk around in public in what Petra wore. Not that he found anything wrong with the outfit. The short leggings showed off her slim, long legs while the top did nothing to hide the shape of her more-than-a-handful breasts. Euric could almost picture what it would feel like to have her long legs wrapped around his waist while he pounded inside her.

Euric's cock hardened even more beneath his tunica. Now that he had been able to look his fill of Petra, he found he was more than a little attracted to her. He had no idea where she was, who she was really, but that did not stop him from wanting her. And she wanted him as well. When her gaze had locked on his mouth—and her face

21

had flushed with arousal—he wanted nothing more than to reach through the strange window to see if her skin felt as soft as it looked. As he had touched it, receiving a strong jolt of power in return, he had not been pleased. The only good thing that had come from that was they now understood each other. When Petra had spoken earlier, he'd had no idea what language she had used. It was one he had never heard before.

Petra leaned even closer to the window. "You're truly a gladiator?"

There was awe in Petra's voice. Wherever she was, obviously the women there were just as enamored of gladiators as Roman women. "Yes." He gave her a smile that had earned the favors of more than one Roman aristocratic woman. Much to his satisfaction, Petra's cheeks flushed a becoming shade of pink while she stared at his mouth. "Have you ever been to the *munera*? Do you enjoy watching the gladiator fights?"

"What?" Petra pulled her gaze away. "The *muneras*? You mean the gladiator games? No. I've never seen a real-life gladiator before, let alone talked to one. There haven't been any for a very, very long time."

He frowned. "If there are not any more gladiators, then how did the man you work for come by his rudis?"

Before Petra answered, mist slowly filled the window. Euric heard her call his name, but it sounded very faint as if she were a great distance away. He was not ready to let her go yet. He had so many questions to ask her. Wherever it was she lived, it had to be very different from the world he knew. He smacked the window with the flat of his palm as the mist grew thicker. This time he received no painful jolt, but it felt as if a layer of something cold and hard separated him from her. Just before it completely blocked her from sight, he heard Petra yell that she would try again, then the window disappeared.

Euric stood in the middle of his cell, waiting for the

window to reappear for a very long time, but it never did. Assuming Petra could not get it to open, he took off his tunica and then slipped into bed. Disappointment washed through him. The short time he had spent talking to her had not been enough. Seeing her through the strange window had been the bright spot of his day. Even though she had known what he was—a gladiator and a slave—she had not looked down her nose at him. In her presence, he had all but forgotten where his life had taken him.

* * * *

Petra shouted, "No, no, no," but it didn't stop the window from shrinking and then disappearing altogether. Why had it suddenly closed? It wasn't as if she'd dropped the rudis again. She still held it firmly in one hand.

Determined to get the window to open again, Petra gave it a shake. "Come on, rudis, do your stuff." Nothing happened.

Not to be put off so easily, she placed the rudis back on its shelf. Just like a computer when it froze and had to be forced to shut down, she counted to sixty. She had no idea if it would work, but always waiting a full minute before she turned her computer back on seemed to work with it. Once the sixty seconds were up, Petra reached for the rudis and touched it with her fingertips. No jolt of energy shot through them. She wrapped her hand around the wooden sword's pommel and picked it up. Still nothing. With the hope that if she waved it around it would jump start it, she swung it in front of her. All that did was make her look like an idiot.

"Damn, damn, damn. Don't do this to me." Holding the rudis in front of her face, she said, "I want to see Euric again. Don't you know it's impolite to cut people off in the middle of a conversation? Didn't your mother teach you any manners?" Petra snorted. "Of course she didn't, because wooden swords don't have mothers."

She had to be losing her mind. There she was talking to a sword made of wood, thinking it actually understood her. She'd even given it a mother as well, of all things. If anyone were to see her now, they'd call the men with the straightjacket to come and take her away.

Not ready to give up, Petra glared at the rudis. There had to be a way to get the window to open again. Maybe it just needed a little encouragement. Thinking of how in genie stories the person who found the lamp had to rub it to get the genie to appear, she rubbed her hand up and down the length of the wooden blade. She gave up after a few seconds when that garnered no response. She guessed a magical rudis wasn't the same as a magic lamp.

That last thought got Petra thinking. If the rudis was well and truly magical, maybe it just needed some magic-type words to charge it again.

She took a deep breath. "Abracadabra." Nothing. "Simon says make the window appear." Zilch. "By the power invested in me, open the window to the past." The rudis remained dead. Frustrated, Petra wrapped her hands around the pommel and shook the wooden sword as if she were choking it. "If you weren't a valuable antique, and my only connection to Euric, I would throw you into the nearest fireplace and set you on fire."

Realizing threats would get her nowhere, she stopped shaking the rudis and shook her head. She really needed to stop talking to inanimate objects.

The sound of the mansion's doorbell ringing broke through Petra's frustrated thoughts. With rudis still in hand, she rushed to answer the door. She had no idea who it could be. Mr. Dunn hadn't told her anyone would be dropping by while he was away and it wasn't as if he had any family. His wife and he hadn't had any children, and she had died a few years before Petra had come to work for him.

Much to her surprise, she opened the door and found her best friend standing on the other side. "Lia? What are you doing here?"

Lia shook her head. "Well, that's a fine welcome." She glanced down at the rudis Petra held. "What are you going to do with the wooden sword? Are you going to stick me with it or hit me over the head?"

Petra lowered her arm and rolled her eyes. "Neither. Knowing my luck, I'd hit you and your thick head would break it. I doubt Mr. Dunn would appreciate me treating his valuable antiques like that, either."

"If it's so expensive, what are you doing walking around with it?"

"Forget about the rudis. Really, what are you doing here, Lia?"

Her friend held up a DVD case. "Since you couldn't go out for the movie, I brought one to you. I'd have preferred to go to the theater and see that new romantic comedy, but this will do."

"I don't know, Lia."

"Why not? Did your boss man say you couldn't have anyone over?"

"Well, no."

"Then there won't be a problem."

Lia crowded Petra until she backed away from the door and walked inside. Even though Lia was only five-foot-three and slim as a reed, she'd take on the best of them. With fiery red hair, and a temper to match when riled, she didn't put up with other people's shit. Add sharp brown eyes that didn't miss anything and you had one tough customer.

Petra sighed and closed the door behind Lia. Her friend's ability to get done what she wanted done held her in good stead while working in the hospital, but when it came to situations like this, it at times frustrated the hell out of Petra. And there was no point asking Lia to leave.

Like a dog with a bone, Lia had her mind set on watching a movie with Petra and she wouldn't let it go.

"Fine, you can stay, but we'll watch the movie upstairs in the bedroom I'm using. It has a DVD player."

"Gee, Petra, don't sound as if I'm putting you out or anything. I thought this would be a good compromise. My schedule at worked was changed. If we don't do this now, we won't be able to get together for another three weeks."

"I'm not complaining. Not really. I just don't know what Mr. Dunn would say about you coming over."

Lia crossed the large foyer and headed for the staircase to the upper level while she looked around. "Wow. This place should be featured in one of those magazines that do those write-ups about houses of the filthy rich. And for your information, you worry too much. Your boss won't even know I was here." She had already gone up four steps before she stopped and turned her head to look back at Petra. "Well? Are you coming or are you going to stand there all night?"

Petra shook her head and chuckled. "You win, as usual. I don't know why I keep hanging out with you."

"You love me, that's why." Lia continued walking up the stairs.

Once inside the guest bedroom, Petra turned on the TV sitting in the wall unit against the wall across from the foot of the bed and stuck in the DVD while Lia made herself comfortable. She hit play. The movie trailers flashed on the screen. Petra climbed onto the bed next to Lia and placed the rudis on her lap. She couldn't bring herself to put it back in the study. As long as she held on to it, she felt as if she had a connection with Euric. She was acting like a ninny, but after talking to him, she felt even more drawn to him. Of course she had to have a crush on a man who had to have died well over a thousand years ago, and one she had no chance of having a relationship with.

Petra gave herself a mental shake. *A relationship?* Where

had that thought come from? Now that would really be called a *long* distance romance. Yeah, Euric seemed to be attracted to her as much as she was to him, but that didn't mean it'd go past that stage. Christ, they couldn't even touch. She'd seen Euric hit the window and his hand hadn't gone through it.

Lia nudged Petra with her arm. "Okay, what's with the wooden sword, slick? Are you trying to start a new fashion statement?"

Petra shrugged. "I just like it."

"I can see that." Lia's gaze shot down to where Petra's hand stroked the wooden blade. "If you keep doing that, you'll wear a hole in it."

"Ha ha." Petra forced herself to put her hands at her sides with her palms flat against the mattress. "Oh look, we're finally at the main menu. I'll start the movie."

Lia reached over and took the rudis off Petra's lap. "It is a nice sword, I guess. It'd be better if it was a real one instead of a wooden one."

Petra quickly took it from her, afraid the window would open for Lia. She didn't want to have to explain to her friend what it was. It'd be better if she kept it as her little secret.

"Give me that." She breathed a sigh of relief when a window didn't suddenly appear.

Lia gave her strange look. "Possessive much? It wasn't as if I was going to keep it. I just wanted to look at it."

"Sorry. I didn't mean to be grabby. Mr. Dunn just got this yesterday. I don't want anything to happen to it."

Mr. Dunn had nothing to do with her reaction, and Petra well knew it. She didn't want to risk anything happening to it for an entirely different reason. She had a feeling if the rudis ended up getting broken, she'd no longer be able to see Euric.

"You really are a worry wart," Lia said. "I won't touch your precious sword again. Or I should say your boss' precious sword. You better watch it, though. You may find yourself squatting on the floor hunched over, stroking it while you call it your precious."

Petra rolled her eyes and laughed. "Yeah, right. I see you're in fine form this evening. How about we watch the movie before you get any worse?"

After the movie ended, Lia left once she made Petra promise to call her at the end of the week. Petra had to admit that having Lia over had been a great idea, and the rented movie had turned out to be a good one. When Lia and she got together, it was never a dull moment.

Once Lia drove away, Petra locked the front door and made sure the security system was on. She walked to the middle of the foyer and looked at the rudis in her hand. She really should put it back in the study, but she wasn't ready to part with it. Realizing how pathetic she must look—becoming attached to a piece of wood—she went upstairs.

Petra changed into the oversized t-shirt she slept in and then crawled into the bed with the rudis. She shifted to lie on her side and put it on the pillow next to her. With one hand resting on the wooden blade, she closed her eyes and went to sleep.

* * * *

Fourth Century Rome

Euric awoke to the sound of someone mumbling. He rubbed the sleep from his eyes, thinking that couldn't be right since he was alone inside his cell. Gladiators never shared, for obvious reasons. He turned his head to the side and looked toward the middle of his cell. What he saw put a smile on his lips.

Heedless of his nakedness, he got out of bed and went to stand in front of the window that hung suspended above the floor. Petra was stretched out on an enormous bed fast asleep. She held the rudis in one hand against her chest. Her other arm rested on the pillow above her head. She mumbled something unintelligible in her sleep.

With Petra fast asleep, Euric used the opportunity to look at her. He had spent the night dreaming about her. He had not been this attracted to a woman in a very long time. The last time was before his enslavement, when he had lived in his tribe in Germania. Even though he had slept with his fair share of Roman women since he had become a mob favorite, all those encounters had left him feeling hollow. They just gave his body release with no emotional attachments.

Petra was different. Even if she were able to come to him as the others had, Euric had a feeling he would not want to give her up. Staring at her now while she slept, he longed to touch her. He wanted to run his hands all over her, memorize every curve of her body. His cock ached to be inside her. Theirs would be no quick joining. He would take her again and again until neither one of them could move.

Euric groaned at his wayward thoughts. They were not doing him any good. He looked down to see is cock standing up straight from his body. He needed to stop thinking about Petra in that way. It would never be possible. Whatever this window was, it kept them apart.

Not sure how much time he had have before his *Lanistae* unlocked his cell door, Euric decided he had better wake Petra. "Petra." She mumbled again but did not wake up. He called louder, "Petra."

This time she stretched and said in a sleepy voice, "It's too early to get up. Let me go back to sleep."

Euric chuckled. "Do all women where you come from lie in bed all day?"

Petra quickly sat up. "Euric! You're back." She threw off the covers and swung her legs over the side of the bed so she faced the window. "When did it open again?"

"I do not know. I woke up and there it was."

She held up the rudis and gave him a guilty look as if he had caught her doing something she should not. "I slept with it. When I couldn't get it to open after it closed last night, I got a little worried it wouldn't work again."

He grinned. "Would it upset you if you did not see me again?"

Petra blushed. "Maybe a little." She stood and walked over to stand in front of the window. Her gaze ran down his body and stopped when it reached the juncture of his thighs. "Ah, Euric, you're naked and very... You know." Her gaze shot back to his face.

Euric did his best not to smile. "Aroused? I told you I was sleeping, and it is the morning."

He let his gaze roam over the garment Petra had worn to bed. It showed more of her legs than what she'd had on the night before. It sort of resembled a tunica, but it was much baggier and shorter. Euric's fingers itched to grab hold of the bottom of it and slowly push it up to see what her naked body looked like underneath it.

His cock jerked in response to his thoughts. Petra quietly moaned. "Is something the matter?" he asked, trying to keep his voice from betraying his amusement.

Seeing where her gaze had landed once more, he was pretty sure he knew what Petra's problem was—she liked what she saw and wanted more. That just made Euric's cock harden even more.

Petra seemed to give herself a shake, then she put her empty hand over her eyes. "Euric, could you please put something on. Seeing you like that is distracting, to the say the least."

"You find my nakedness disturbing?" Euric could not quite keep the humor he felt out of his voice.

Petra's hand dropped and she gave him a hard stare. "You're doing this on purpose, aren't you?"

He swept a hand in front of his body. "I normally sleep naked. Do you know so little of men that you do not know we awaken most mornings in this condition?"

"Of course I know that," she shot back. "I've had a few boyfriends."

Euric frowned. "You have seen men you consider friends naked?"

"No, that isn't what I meant. A boyfriend is what we call in this time the men single women date."

"Date?"

"Date as in woo. I think that's what you'd call it."

Something Petra had said before had him stiffening. "You said in your time. What do you mean?"

Petra's face grew serious. "What is the date where you are, Euric?"

"I am not sure of the exact date, but it is the first month of summer."

"What year is it?"

Euric looked at her with confusion. "It is the year 324. You do not know this?"

"No." Petra's gaze locked with his. "I'm not from your time, Euric. I'm from the future. In your time I haven't even been born, and won't be for a very, very long time. It's the year 2015."

The year Petra told him was more than a bit of a shock. "Then how is it possible we can see each other?"

She shrugged. "I wish I knew. We in the future can do a lot of things the people in your time can't, but time travel isn't one of them."

At that moment, Euric heard a key being put in the lock of his cell door. "You must close the window, Petra. My *Lanistae* has come to let me out for the day."

She gave him a look of longing. "I'm going to let go of the rudis. That should make the window close. I wish we had more time, but I promise to try to get the window to open again later."

Euric nodded. He wished they had more time together as well. The longer he spent conversing with Petra the more he wanted to be with her. "Do it. Now." He heard the lock turning.

Petra held the rudis over the bed and opened her hand to allow it to fall out of her grasp, but the window remained open.

"I don't understand," Petra said. "The first time I saw you and dropped the rudis the window closed. I thought I had to hold it to keep it from closing."

It was already too late for Petra to try something else to get the window to shut. The door to his cell swung open and his *Lanistae* stepped inside. He was an older man who at one time had been a gladiator himself, and a longstanding mob favorite. After he had been given his freedom, he had set up his own *ludus*. His *Lanistae* looked around the small space. Surprisingly, he did not seem to notice Petra or the window hovering above the floor.

"Have you now started talking to yourself, Euric?" his *Lanistae* asked as he eyed him up and down. He obviously did not expect an answer, because he said, "Get dressed. I want you fed and out on the training ground."

"Yes, *Lanistae*."

Seemingly satisfied, the older man left Euric alone in his cell, leaving the door open.

Euric turned to look at Petra. She stared back as a look of relief flashed across her face. "I can't believe it," she said. "He didn't seem me."

"I noticed." He waved his hand at the window. "It is not as if this would be hard not to see. I have a feeling I am the only one who can."

"What did he say to you? I couldn't understand him."

"You could not? You should have been able to. I am speaking in Latin right now as he did."

She shook her head. "I knew he was speaking in Latin, but from the look of things, I can only understand you for some reason."

Euric crossed to the other side of his cell and then took his tunica off the hook in the wall. He pulled it on before he tied the rope belt around his waist. He turned back to Petra. The way her gaze quickly jerked up to his face, he had the feeling she had been eyeing his backside while he was dressing. He bit back a smile.

"I have to leave. My *Lanistae* — he is the one who owns this *ludus* and me — told me to hurry up. He wants me on the training ground. I have a fight in a few days, and he wants me to be in top fighting form."

Petra's face went white. "You have a fight soon? You aren't going to die, are you?"

Euric chuckled. "There is always a chance I will meet my death every time I step into the *Amphitheatrum*, but I doubt that will happen. I am one of my *familia's* best fighters. I am also a favorite of the mob. I do not see my death in the immediate future."

"Do you like being a gladiator? Having to fight all the time?" Petra asked softly.

He shook his head. "No, but it is not as if I have any choice. I m a slave, Petra. I long for my freedom like any man here. Only my skills as a warrior have kept me alive for the last two years. I do not find watching men pitted against each other for no other reason than to thrill a blood-thirsty mob entertaining like these Romans. I dream of the day I can return to my tribe."

Petra held her hand up with her palm facing the window. She did not touch it, but that did not stop Euric from putting his palm against it on his side.

"Be careful, Euric."

"There is no need to worry today. We practice with wooden swords. Only during the *munera* do we get the real ones." He met her gaze with longing coursing through him. "Come back, Petra, and give me something to look forward to."

"I promise."

After letting his hand fall to his side, Euric turned and walked out of his cell. He did not look back to see if the window had closed or not.

CHAPTER THREE

Present Day

Petra watched Euric walk away. Once he was gone, the window filled with mist and disappeared. She sat on the bed and looked at the rudis that lay next to her. She brushed a fingertip down its length. It felt how a normal wooden sword would feel. No jolt of energy surged when she touched it. Touching it obviously was no longer a necessity to get the window to ancient Rome to open. She just hoped she could get it to appear when she wanted it to.

Now that she was up, Petra decided she might as well get ready to face the day. She crossed the room to the en suite. She used the toilet and then brushed her teeth before she turned on the water in the shower. While she showered, she couldn't stop thinking about Euric having to fight a few days from now. The *muneras* were so brutal compared to what modern times would allow. She couldn't imagine what it'd feel like to walk out into the Colosseum and know it could very well be the end of you.

To live with that hanging over a person's head day in and day out would drive someone crazy.

After her shower, Petra dressed in a lavender-colored t-shirt and gray shorts. Since Mr. Dunn was away and she just had work to do on his computer, she figured she could dress more casually. No one but the maid and cook would see her, anyway.

Before she headed downstairs, Petra retrieved the rudis from the bed to return it to the study. It wouldn't do for the maid to notice it missing when she came to dust the study and think it'd been stolen.

Since the cook wasn't due to arrive until that afternoon, Petra had a quick breakfast of yogurt and toast. Not much of a tea or coffee drinker, she settled for a glass of orange juice.

Petra picked up the rudis off the center counter island where she'd sat to eat and headed for the study. She put it on its shelf and then went to the desk to boot up the desktop computer. While she waited, she looked through the paperwork still remaining. What Mr. Dunn had left for her would probably only take her the morning to finish. If he hadn't sent her anything more to do overnight, she pretty much would have the rest of the day for herself.

Once she checked her work email that Mr. Dunn had had set up on his computer for her use, and finding no new work from him, Petra launched the web browser. She went to a search engine and typed in fourth century Rome. Constantine was the sole emperor of Rome after he'd finally defeated his rival, Maxentius, back in 312 AD. Apparently during their last battle near the Tiber River while trying to flee, Maxentius ended up being pushed into it when he tried to cross a bridge of boats and drowned. Constantine had his body dragged out of the river and Maxentius's head cut off so he could bring it to Rome to parade through the streets. Petra shuddered. Constantine sounded like a lovely person. Not.

She did a search about gladiators. From what she read, they were better treated than the average slave, but the possibility of death still hung over them, especially if they happened to have been condemned to be a gladiator. Those men who'd been sentenced to the sword were supposed to be killed immediately or at least within a year of their sentence. She felt a little better about Euric's situation when she read that most gladiators only fought three times a year and didn't fight to the death in the majority of cases since it was costly to replace them. It still wasn't a life she wished on anybody.

After closing the browser, Petra got down to work. She spent the next three hours working on the last of the paperwork. That done, she left the study and headed for the kitchen. She'd heard the maid and cook arrive earlier. She found the cook, Sally, writing what looked to be a shopping list.

"Hey, Sally. Just letting you know I'm going out for a few hours while I swing by my apartment."

Sally, a woman in her late forties, looked up from her list and smiled. "Do you want me to make you something for lunch before you go?"

"No. I'm fine. If I get hungry, I'll just grab something from my apartment. I'll be back in time for dinner."

"Is there anything you want in particular?"

Petra smiled. "Why don't you surprise me? You put my cooking to shame any day. If I could afford you, I'd steal you away from Mr. Dunn."

Sally laughed. "There is no chance of that. You know I'd never leave him. Without me here, I don't think the man would remember to eat."

What Sally had said about Mr. Dunn was probably true. When he got working on a new real estate deal, it tended to become his sole focus. And that Sally would never voluntarily leave him spoke to his character as an employer. Everyone he employed was treated as if they were a part of his family. Petra guessed in some way they were since he had none of his own.

"You take good care of him, Sally. Well, I'm out of here. If you need me, I'll have my cell phone on."

Sally waved Petra away. "Take your time."

Petra left the kitchen and then hurried up to the guest bedroom to get her purse. A few minutes later, she was on the road headed for her apartment. After she parked her car in the underground parking garage, she rode the elevator up to the lobby and stopped to collect her mail from her mail slot. She then took the elevator to the ninth floor and let herself into her apartment.

She shut and locked the door behind her and then walked into the small kitchen while she looked through the stack of mail she carried. Most of it was junk with a couple bills thrown in. Petra put her purse on the kitchen table before she opened the first bill.

Turning around, she looked up from the bill and just about jumped out of her skin. In the middle of her living room, hanging suspended above the floor, was the window.

Dumbfounded to see the window that allowed her to see Euric actually in her apartment, Petra slowly walked toward it. This just seemed to get stranger and stranger. The rudis wasn't anywhere near the vicinity of her apartment, but there was the window. And she hadn't even tried to get it to appear. She'd decided she'd wait until after Sally and the maid had left for the day. If they weren't able to see it, she didn't want them to think she was a crack pot talking to herself.

Once she stood in front of it, Petra sucked in a breath. Euric lay naked on his stomach on his bed while another man massaged oil into his back and shoulders. After doing her research that morning, she knew massage and medical care were given to all gladiators to keep them in peak condition. Their training regime was supposed to be so rigorous they were given regular massages to loosen their aching muscles.

The sight of Euric stretched out on his bed with his skin shining with oil had Petra staring with longing. Even though there was nothing sexual about the massage, seeing him like that started to turn her on. Her breasts grew heavy and her nipples tightened. The man had a gorgeous body. She ached to explore every inch of it and run her hands along all those hard-looking muscles. Her gaze settled on his ass. It was just as muscled as the rest of him. She bet she could bounce a quarter off it, it was that tight looking. Actually, she wanted to grab it in both hands and give it a good squeeze, preferably while he was stretched out on top her, plunging his cock deep inside her.

The man who massaged Euric finished up and then left. Euric didn't move. He had his face turned toward the cell wall so Petra couldn't see it, but she had a feeling he was asleep. His longish blond hair laid spread across his thin pillow. She wanted to run her fingers through it while he kissed her senseless. She could almost feel his firm lips moving over hers. She sighed. She'd never get to know what it'd feel like to have him really kiss her.

Euric stirred on the bed. Not wanting to startle him, Petra called quietly, "Euric, are you awake?"

He turned his head in her direction and gave her a smile that made her knees go weak. "Petra. I did not think you would come again so soon."

"Neither did I. It just appeared on its own." Euric got off the bed and came to stand in front of the window. Petra bit back a moan. "You do realize that I think I've seen you naked more times than I've seen you with clothes on. It's starting to become a bad habit with you."

With a shrug, Euric said, "I am not ashamed of my body."

"I didn't think you were." If *Playgirl* saw him now,

they'd have him signed up to be their centerfold in a snap.

Euric's heated gaze swept the length of her body. "I would like to see you without your clothes on." He then said in a deep, husky voice, "You have seen me naked and I think you should return the favor."

Petra's breath hitched. She wasn't that bold. If they were somehow able to touch, take things a little further, then maybe she'd let him see her naked. Stripping to give Euric a peep show wasn't something she was confident enough to do. It wasn't as if she was unhappy with the way her body looked—she did Pilates and yoga a couple times a week—it was when it came to sex she was on the shy side. She had a hard time bringing herself to do anything daring, even after she'd known a guy for months.

"I have made you uncomfortable," Euric said. "That was not my intention."

She gave him a small smile. "I know. It isn't your fault. It's mine. It takes me a while to work up to the get-naked stage with a man I find attractive. I usually need a few good make out sessions before I feel comfortable doing something like that."

"What is a make out session?"

Petra couldn't stop the blush that heated her cheeks. "Lots of kissing and touching. That sort of thing."

"I would like nothing more than to kiss and touch you, Petra."

She met his gaze and swallowed. She easily saw the stark hunger on Euric's face. No man had ever looked at her like that, as if he wanted to devour her. As if he wouldn't survive for another minute longer if he didn't get a taste of her. An ache built in her pussy and her blood pumped faster through her body.

Stepping closer to the window until her nose almost touched it, she said quietly, "I wish you could, Euric."

Petra let out a startled yelp when the window suddenly grew bigger. Its shape changed from a circle to that of a large rectangle. The bottom stretched down until it almost touched the floor. The top lifted toward the ceiling so it stood taller than Euric's over-six-foot height. The sides widened to double the size of a doorway. Looking at him through it, she could almost fool herself into thinking he actually stood before her with nothing separating them. All she had to do was just reach out and touch him.

Acting on her thoughts, Petra reached out. Instead of meeting a barrier, her hand passed through the window and settled on Euric's chest. Petra quickly pulled it back. "Oh! I think I just touched you."

His wide chest rose on a deep breath. "You did." Arousal flared in his eyes. "Do it again."

Petra reached out once more and placed her right hand over Euric's heart. It thumped at a rapid pace beneath her palm. His skin felt warm and smooth. She pulled away again.

"See if you can touch me."

Euric lifted his hand, but when he tried to reach out for her, he came up against an invisible barrier. His lips thinned. "I cannot."

"Then I guess I'm only allowed to reach over into your time."

"Put your hand on me again," Euric said in a strained voice.

More than happy to oblige, Petra reached through and placed her palm on his chest. Euric placed a hand over top hers. His chest rapidly rose and fell as he briefly closed his eyes. When he opened them, his pupils had dilated with desire, the black taking up much of the blue iris.

With her other hand, she stroked the side of Euric's jaw. The muscle there jumped when he moaned softly. Her body liquefied with her own desire. She wanted this man, and now that she was able to touch him, she wanted him even more. Her lips parted as she breathed at a rapid pace. His gaze settled on her mouth when she ran the tip of her tongue along her suddenly dry lips.

Still holding her hand against his chest, he took a half-step back. More of her arms passed through the window to his side. When he went to take another, Petra stiffened, realizing what he intended to do.

"Stop, Euric. I can't."

He froze in place. "Why not?"

"If I go into your time and the window closes, I may never be able to get back."

Euric groaned in frustration. "I want more than this, Petra. You do not know what you have come to mean to me. When I am around you, I can forget I am a slave. You make what I have to live with easier to endure. In your arms, I know I would feel like the warrior I once was."

His admission sent a wave of pleasure surging through her. She hadn't realized her visits had made such an impact on Euric. Of course she really didn't know what life was like for him in his time. Knowing the logistics of it wasn't exactly like living it. She didn't want to deny him — Petra hungered for Euric's touch — but she couldn't risk taking that final step into his time. It didn't mean she couldn't have a little taste.

Petra leaned forward so the upper half of her body passed through the window. "This is as far as I'm willing to go."

Euric didn't need any urging. He threaded his fingers through her hair at the back of her head and brought his lips down to hers. His kiss started off tentative and gentle, but as he swept the seam of her lips with his tongue and she opened them to let him in, it became more demanding. He kissed her as if he'd never get enough of her.

She lifted her arms and wrapped them around Euric's neck. He pressed closer so her taut nipples rubbed against the hard muscles of his chest. Petra moaned into his mouth as he twined his tongue with hers and then gently sucked on it. Arousal beat at her senses, causing her pussy to grow wet with hunger and need. One kiss and he set her body on fire. Hot desire thrummed through her veins, heating her from the inside out.

While Euric moved his lips moved hers, devouring her, he lifted his hand and covered her breast through her t-shirt. His thumb brushed back and forth across the tightened peak of her nipple. Her sex clenched as a wave of pleasure shot down from her breast to where she ached with need.

Petra pressed her breast tighter into Euric's hand. "More," she said against his lips.

"Yes," he replied with a husky groan.

Euric bunched the front of her t-shirt in his hand until he had it lifted high enough to expose her breasts. Once he encountered her lacy bra, he released her lips only long enough to take a quick look at it before he claimed her mouth once again. Shoving his hand inside her bra, he squeezed her breast before he took her nipple between his thumb and index finger, rolling it between them.

He continued to play with her nipple as he left her lips and moved to the side of her neck. He licked and sucked her skin, moving down the slim column of her throat. Euric let go of her hair and used that hand to hold the bunched material of her shirt to her chin. He yanked aside the cup of her bra, bent his head and circled her taut nipple with the tip of his tongue before he opened his mouth and sucked it inside.

Petra nearly went on her toes when Euric sucked. Each pull of his mouth caused her pussy to clench and grow even wetter. She moved her hands to the tops of his shoulders and dug her nails into his skin. A low, whimpered moan escaped her lips. God, she wanted him. Her body was more than ready to have his cock moving deep inside her.

They went still when the sound of voices just outside Euric's cell door reached their ears. He released her and quickly pushed Petra away. She straightened, returning to her side of the window. They stared at each other, breathing as if they'd just run a marathon. She looked down his body to find his cock fully erect, thick and full. She wanted to scream in frustration.

Euric was the first to break eye contact as he turned away. He snatched up his tunic off the end of the bed and pulled it on.

Petra straightened her bra and t-shirt. "You have to go again, don't you?"

He turned around and nodded. "Yes." His gaze raked her body. "That was our first make out session. I intend to pick up where we left off when we see each other again."

Euric gave her a look filled with such naked lust Petra trembled and her arousal shot up another notch. Unable to think around her pounding need, she silently nodded. Once he turned to walk away, the window closed, leaving her alone in her apartment, longing for a man she could never have.

* * * *

Fourth Century Rome

Euric left his cell and headed with the other gladiators to the large room where they were given their meals. His body had yet to calm down. If the others noticed his erection beneath his tunica, they wisely kept it to themselves. He was in no mood to put up with any ribbing—good-natured or otherwise. That one taste of Petra had only made him ache for her even more. Touching, tasting the real Petra was far better than what he had imagined it would be like.

After he got his wooden bowl of food, Euric went and sat at the end of one of the long tables. He used his spoon—also made out of wood—to push his meal around.

It was a mixture of barley, oatmeal, beans and ash with some dried fruit thrown in. They were never given any meat. There were days he longed to sink his teeth into a juicy hunk of roasted venison. His mouth practically watered just thinking about it.

Euric groaned to himself when he noticed Calix walking to his end of the table. The Roman sat on the bench next to him. Euric purposely focused his attention on the bowl in front of him. He hoped Calix would get the message that he wanted to be left alone, but the Roman did not.

"What is the matter, Goth? Do you think you are too good to sit with the rest of us?"

No, Euric thought. *That would be Calix.* He continued to ignore him, which seemed to annoy the Roman.

"You really are a barbarian. You sit there ignoring your betters."

Euric knew better than to respond to Calix's goading, but the brief make out session — as Petra had called it — had left him edgy and out of sorts. Calix's words seemed to prick his nerves more than he could tolerate.

He turned his head so he looked at Calix, and said, "I hardly think you are better than I am. In or out of the *Amphbitheatrum*."

Calix's face turned red as he jumped up from the bench and launched himself at Euric. Knowing full well there would be a price to pay for brawling, Euric did not care. As he and Calix rolled over the bench and onto the floor, Euric gave as good as he got. He heard a satisfying crack when his fist connected with Calix's jaw. He grunted in pain when the Roman managed to ram his fist into Euric's stomach.

Before they could get any more strikes in, they were forcibly separated by the guards who were never far away when the gladiators were released from their cells. Not that very many fights broke out, mostly because the punishment was usually swift and severe.

Notified of the commotion, the *Lanistae* entered the room and looked between Euric and Calix. "What is the matter with you two? You both have been a part of this *familia gladiatoria* long enough to know this kind of behavior will not be tolerated in my *ludus*."

"Euric started it, *Lanistae*," Calix quickly replied. "I was only trying to defend myself."

Euric ground his teeth together while he fought to keep his mouth shut. There would be no refuting Calix's claim. It did not matter that the guards had more than likely seen Calix start the fight. The *Lanistae* always took the Roman's side. Euric would not be the first gladiator to suffer punishment in Calix's stead.

The *Lanistae* gave them each a hard stare before he spoke to the guards who stood on either side of Calix and Euric. "Lock Calix in his cell for the remainder of the day and the night. Put Euric in the punishment cell for the same amount of time."

As the guards led them away, Euric wished he could get his hands on Calix again. He would have gotten a lot of satisfaction from smashing the arrogant Roman's head into the nearest wall. It would have been a small compensation for what he was about to endure.

The guards led Euric to the end of the row of cells and then opened the door on the last one. It was about half the height of the rest. He had to bend over to enter as the guards pushed him inside. There was no room for him to stand at his full height, and with his arms outstretched, he touched either side of the walls. The space was so small there was not even enough room for him to stretch out on the floor. Given no tallow candles for light in the windowless cell, when the door closed behind him, he was plunged into total darkness. Sitting on the floor with his back against one of the walls, he knew he would find no rest during the long hours of his confinement.

CHAPTER FOUR

Present Day

The rest of the day passed slowly for Petra. After she returned to the mansion, she sat outside and read while she sipped on some flavored water until it was time for dinner. With no work left for her to do, she had to do something to distract her thoughts from Euric.

Petra put her book on the patio table and touched her mouth with the tips of her fingers. She still felt Euric's lips moving over hers. And the taste of him was still on her tongue. She wanted his inside her mouth while he held her close again. Like a teenage girl with her first crush, she couldn't stop thinking about him. She yearned to be with him with every particle of her being. She was being a total head case, but she couldn't make herself stop. If he lived in her time, she could quite easily see herself following him around, being jealous of any woman who happened to look his way.

He didn't live in her time, and she had no idea how a relationship between them would work. And who knew how long the window that allowed them to see each other would last. Petra wasn't controlling it, at least she didn't think she was, nor was Euric. Each time it closed, she couldn't help wondering if that would be the last time she saw him. She didn't want what little they had to end—not today, not tomorrow or even a month from now. She'd finally found a man that, given time, she could have strong feelings for, and she had no control over her fate. It sucked the big one.

Petra picked up her book and empty glass before she headed inside the guest bedroom. Looking at the clock on the bedside table, she saw it was time for her to go downstairs for dinner. With the empty glass in hand, she went down the stairs to the kitchen. Sally was just putting a plate of steaming food on the island for her.

Petra sat on the stool and bent her head to smell the grilled steak, steamed rice and grilled mixed vegetables Sally had cooked. "Yum. This smells delicious."

Sally smiled. "I hope you like the steak medium, because I refuse to cook one well done. That's a good way to ruin a perfectly good cut of meat."

"Medium is how I like it," Petra said with a chuckle. "I agree with you about the whole well done thing."

As Petra picked up her fork and knife and cut into the juicy steak, Sally leaned her elbows on the island and rested her chin on her hands. "All right, out with it."

"Out with what?"

"I noticed when you came back from your apartment that you were looking a little down. Did you have another run-in with that brother of yours?"

Petra shook her head. "No."

She put a piece of steak in her mouth and chewed. To say she and her older brother didn't normally see eye to eye was a bit of an understatement. Even though they didn't get along, it didn't stop her brother, Chad, from butting into her life. Everything she did he had to criticize.

The only decision she'd made that he hadn't thought was a colossal mistake was when she'd taken the job as Mr. Dunn's personal assistant.

"Are you sure? You know it's better to get it off your chest than keep it bottled up inside."

"You know I'd tell you. Actually, Chad has been pretty good lately. After the last time he decided to lecture me on how I should improve my life, I went and talked to my dad. He basically told Chad to butt out or else he'd cut him out of his will. Not that my parents have a ton of cash, but Chad wouldn't want to be left out of anything."

'Well, if it isn't your brother, it has to be another man. A new boyfriend perhaps?"

"Perhaps."

"I knew it. Come on, give me details."

"There isn't all that much to say. I just recently met him."

"So what's the problem?"

"Let's just say he doesn't live around here."

"A long-distance relationship, huh? How far away?"

"He lives in Rome."

Technically, that was where Euric lived, but there was no way in hell she was going to tell Sally he also happened to live over a thousand years in the past. Even though the older woman was the most down-to-earth person Petra had ever met, she'd look at Petra as if she were out of her gourd.

"The time difference must be a pain in the ass."

"You don't know the half of it," Petra said before she ate some of the rice.

"Any chance of him coming here for a visit? Or you going to Rome to see him?"

Petra swallowed. "No. Euric is kind of stuck in Rome for the time being. I'd go to him, but I don't think that would be a good idea right now." Getting stuck in the fourth century held no appeal to her. To be honest, the thought of it was downright scary. Life was so much harsher and brutal then.

"Euric? That doesn't sound much like an Italian name."

"It isn't. Euric is originally from Germany."

"You're falling for him, aren't you?"

Petra shrugged. "I guess. I don't know. It's still too early to tell, but I know he's on my mind all the time. I miss him when I can't talk to him. He's the first thing I think about when I get up in the morning and the last thing when I go to bed at night. I sound pretty obsessive, don't I?"

Sally chuckled. "No. You sound like a woman who may have found her man. I was the same way when I first met my hubby. I knew he was the one. Luckily for me, he felt the same way. We ended up getting married two months after we met. Twenty-five years later, we're still together and are madly in love. Honey, if Euric is the one for you, you'll make the long-distance relationship work. It may take a little more work, but you'll get it figured out."

"I wish I felt as confident as you, Sally. And I wish it was that simple, but it isn't."

Sally straightened. "Try not to let it stress you out. I have to run. It's hubby's and my date night tonight."

"Then why are you hanging around here? Go. I'll see you tomorrow. Have fun."

"I plan on it." Sally picked her purse off the counter and gave Petra a wave before she left the kitchen.

Petra finished eating and then put the half piece of steak she couldn't eat into the fridge. It was still fairly early in the evening and she really didn't know what to do with herself. While she'd been talking with Sally, she'd felt on edge, as if something wasn't quite right. The feeling seemed to increase every time she thought about Euric. She had no idea why she felt as if something was wrong with him. She just did. It was stupid really, but she couldn't shake it.

Not sure when or even if the window would open for her again, Petra decided to return to the guest bedroom and watch some television. She switched it on and sat on the bed. Switching channels to find something good, she moved one of the pillows against the headboard behind her back.

Finally finding something that interested her, the feeling of wrongness increased. It got so bad Petra found she couldn't concentrate on the TV. She kept looking at the middle of her room, hoping the window would suddenly appear.

Unable to sit still any longer, she got up and paced. Petra told herself to snap out of it, that there wasn't anything wrong with Euric. Her imagination was just playing tricks on her. She was by no means physic, and she didn't believe in all that hocus pocus. Now that she could see through a window into the past, she had a feeling she'd have to seriously reconsider her stand on everything paranormal.

Her nerves stretched to the breaking point, Petra stopped her pacing, and with her hands on her hips, she faced the middle of the room. "All right. I've had enough. Window, whatever you're called, show me Euric. Now."

When it didn't appear, she decided maybe demanding it to open may not be the best thing. She took a deep, steadying breath and tried again.

"Please, can I see Euric? I promise I won't be rude anymore." Petra let her mind focus on Euric and how desperately she wanted to see him. "Please."

As if she'd turned on a switch, the window formed in front of her. It once again took on its large rectangular shape. Petra frowned as the mist cleared and she saw nothing but black. She couldn't see a thing. No Euric, no cell, no nothing. If she'd been inside the darkness, she bet she wouldn't even be able to see her hand held up in front of her face.

Hoping the window would at least allow her to talk to Euric since it was no longer allowing her to see him, Petra called, "Euric? Are you there?"

"Petra?"

"It's me." Euric's voice had sounded strained. "Are you all right? I can't see you. The window has decided not to let me see anything."

She heard Euric shift around before he spoke. "You are seeing all that there is to see."

"I don't understand. All I can see is black."

Euric made a sound that sort of sounded like a chuckle, but it had no humor in it. "I have been locked in the punishment cell, Petra. There are no windows and candles."

"What happened?" She heard Euric shift closer while she spoke, as if he were following the sound of her voice.

"My opponent in the upcoming *munera* has never really taken a liking to me. He decided to take exception to the way I was sitting while I ate my midday meal. He started a fight."

"Is he in a punishment cell like you?" Feeling pissed off on Euric's behalf, Petra hoped the other gladiator got it worse than Euric had.

"No. The *ludus* only has one punishment cell. He was just sent to his own for the remainder of the day and the night while I get to sit here in the dark."

The absolute black on the other side of the window was starting to get to Petra. Even the light from her side didn't penetrate the absolute darkness. "Well, that sucks."

"Suck on what?"

"I mean, that's terrible." Petra had to remember Euric wouldn't know modern slang. Even if her words were being instantly translated for him, he'd only get the literal meaning. "You got the shitty end of the stick."

Euric gave a short burst of laughter. "That, I do understand."

Petra heard a loud rumbling pass through the window. "Euric, is there something else in that cell with you?"

"Not unless you count my empty stomach," he said with a laugh.

She started to back toward the bedroom door. "Hunger pangs I can fix." For Euric and the window's benefit, she said, "I'll be right back. Don't go anywhere."

Spinning around, Petra hurried out of the room and then ran down the stairs to the kitchen. She grabbed her leftover steak out of the fridge and put it, and some leftover mashed potatoes she found, on a plate. Once she had it in the microwave to heat, thinking Euric could be thirsty as well, she took a bottle of water out of the fridge to go along with the food. She took a fork and knife out of one of the drawers, the plate out of the microwave, and with the water bottle held in her other hand, she headed back upstairs.

Petra was halfway up the stairs when she realized Euric wouldn't be able to see the food to eat it. Going back down, she headed once again to the kitchen and then opened the drawer that held a bunch of odds and ends. She fished out the small LED flashlight she remembered seeing in it one day when she'd scrounged around for something. She stuck it into the front pocket of her shorts, then carried the food and water up to the guest bedroom.

She breathed a sigh of relief to still see the window when she stepped into the room. "I'm back," she said.

Petra put what she carried on the floor and then straightened. She reached into the darkness to see if she could see exactly where Euric was in the cell. Instead of touching warm skin, her hand hit cold stone.

"Euric? Are you still there?"

"I'm down here."

Petra looked at her feet where his voice had come from. "Can you stand? I have something for you."

"Not unless I want to bash my head on the ceiling. It is

a punishment cell, Petra. Part of the punishment is its uncomfortable size."

She dropped to her knees next to the plate of food and reached through the window again. This time she touched Euric's arm. He put his hand over hers.

"This won't do at all," Petra said.

After pulling her hand back, she took the flashlight out of her pocket and aimed it at the spot Euric would be. She turned it on. He held up his hand in front of his face as the flashlight's bright light hit him and chased some of the darkness away. Now able to see the dimensions of the cell, she didn't know how he stood to be in such a small space in total darkness. She would have been a basket case if she had to spend more than five minutes in there, and he had to spend hours.

Euric squinted against the light. "What kind of candle is that?"

"It's what is called a flashlight. It doesn't need a flame to work. It uses something called batteries to make it light up." Petra put the hand that held it through the window. "Here, take it. I have something else for you." Once he took the flashlight—and spun it around in his hand to examine it—she put the plate of food and bottle of water through the window as well. "I know it isn't much, but it was all I could find."

Euric propped the flashlight on his lap and picked up the plate. He looked at the fork and knife, but didn't bother to use them. He picked up the piece of steak and took a big bite from it. He moaned while he chewed. His face took on an expression of ecstasy. He wasn't doing it to be sexy, but it made delicious shivers run through her. He continued to moan in pleasure as he took another bite and chewed. If Euric kept it up for very much longer, Petra was pretty sure she would have an orgasm without even having him touch her.

"Good, huh?" Her voice sounded low and breathy. She

cleared her throat.

"I haven't had a piece of meat since I was taken in battle."

He hadn't had a piece of meat in two years? A man Euric's size and musculature needed lots of protein. "What do they feed you?"

Around a mouthful of potatoes, he said, "Grains, beans, dried fruit and ash."

"Ash? That's disgusting."

"The Romans believe ash fortifies the body."

"Whether it's supposed to be good for you or not, you won't catch me eating ash any time soon."

"It isn't as if I get to pick what I get to eat."

Petra fell silent and let Euric finish his meal. Once he picked up the water bottle and flipped it upside down, trying to figure out how to get the water out of it, she took it from him and unscrewed the cap. She watched his throat move as he drank from the bottle.

She picked up the plate and brought it back to her side. Petra put her hand on Euric's heavily muscled thigh while he drank more of the water. She hated the idea of him being trapped inside the small dark room. His life was rough enough as it was, and he didn't need to have to endure this on top of everything else. If only she could take him away from it all.

Sitting up straighter, an idea flitted through Petra's mind. She could pass through the window and Euric couldn't, but she'd been able to pass the plate, water bottle and flashlight over to his side. And she'd been able to bring the plate back to her side as well. Maybe he hadn't been able to reach through the window because she hadn't been touching him at the time.

Petra lifted her hand off Euric's thigh and picked up his hand that rested on the ground next to him. She linked their fingers together and then pulled them toward her. A large smile of victory formed on her lips when his hand appeared on her side still held firmly in hers.

Meeting his surprised gaze, she said, "Come to my time, Euric. You can be free."

*

You can be free. Petra's words echoed inside his mind while he looked down at their linked fingers on her side of the window. *You can be free.* The thought of being a free man, no longer a slave, made his heart beat a little faster. He had spent the last two years dreaming about it.

Now that he was offered a chance to see his dreams realized, Euric found himself hesitating. He knew nothing about Petra's time. It could be worse than what he had to endure now. And then there was the knowledge that if he passed through the window and it closed behind him, he would never be able to return to his tribe.

Euric sadly shook his head. "I cannot, Petra, for the very same reason you will not step through to my time. At least here there is a chance I can return to my tribe and see my family again."

Petra's fingers tightened around his while she pleadingly looked at him. "And there is a chance you won't survive to receive your rudis. You could be cut down during the *munera* coming up or the ones after it. In my world, you'd be safe."

"I know nothing of your world, Petra. This is the only one I know."

"So you'd much rather be a slave in a time where most people die before they reach old age?"

"We all have to die at some point."

"Why risk it when you're still so young. You have years to live, Euric."

He chuckled. "I would not have ever made *secundus palus* if I was not the warrior I am. I am not lacking in sword skills. I make no easy target during the *munera*. And

I am hardly so young. I have seen seven and twenty summers."

"Twenty-seven is hardly old, at least not in my time. I'm twenty-five. You would be considered a man reaching his prime. People live to be in their eighties or nineties, sometimes into their hundreds."

Euric saw how upset Petra was getting when he did not back down from his decision to stay. He pulled on her arm until her head and part of her upper body came through the window. He only meant to kiss her to distract her, but when his lips settled on hers, he was lost.

He put the flameless light and the container that had held the water Petra had given him on the ground next to him before he went to kneel in front of her. She shifted so she kneeled as well. He cupped the back of her head and kissed her deeply. She let go of his hand and put her arms around his waist. Euric sucked her tongue into his mouth, savoring the taste of her, when she reached down and took his ass in her hands. She dug her fingers into it and urged him closer.

Their bodies met in the middle of the window, suspended through times. Pressed together from chest to thigh, the feel of Petra's soft body against his hard one, made Euric moan. He felt as if he had died and gone to the Christian's heaven. Wrapping an arm around her waist, he ground his hard cock against her soft belly.

He lifted his head and stared at Petra. The sight of her flushed face and parted lips — swollen from his kisses — made him ache to have her under him while he pounded inside her pussy. He shifted his hand from the back of her head to the side of her face and stroked his thumb across her soft cheek.

"Let me see your body. I need to touch you. Make me forget where I am just for a little while."

Petra's gaze never left his as she let go, pulled her top over her head and threw it to her side of the window.

Euric let his gaze fall to what she wore over her perfect breasts. He had no idea what it was called, but he liked seeing her wear it. The material was sheer enough he saw her dusky nipples through it, which were taut, begging him to suckle them.

Petra moved her hands to the front of her chest and then somehow unfasten what covered it. As the material parted, giving him his first real view of her breasts, she slowly pulled the straps that held it up down her arms and off. The piece of clothing fell onto her top when she let it drop.

She ran a hand up his chest and along the side of his neck to the back of his head. She pressed on it, urging him toward her breasts. "Touch me, Euric. Take what you want."

With a groan, he placed his hands on her waist while he circled one of her taut nipples with his tongue. Petra arched her back, pressing her closer. Euric opened his mouth and sucked her nipple deep inside. While he sucked, the sound of her moans filled his head, causing his cock to harden even more.

Skimming his hands down her sides, Euric reached the top of the short leggings Petra wore. He shoved his hand down the front of them and found she wore something else underneath. It had the same feel as the piece of clothing she had worn on her chest. She rocked her hips against him as he shoved his hand down farther and encountered her material-covered sex. Wetness had leaked from her pussy through to the cloth.

After releasing her nipple, Euric moved to give the other the same undivided attention. Petra shifted her hands to the tops of his shoulders when he followed the seam of material between her legs with his fingers. He pushed them beneath it until he found what he sought.

A loud groan rose out of his chest as he traced the line of Petra's pussy and found her wet and ready. Her inner muscles clamped down around his finger when he pushed it inside her core.

He moved from her breast and kissed the side of her neck. "You are wet for me."

"I love how you touch me, Euric."

Euric gently bit her neck, then ran his tongue over it. "I am going to touch you until you scream my name."

He pumped his fingers in and out of her slick opening. Petra's breathy sighs and moans pushed his arousal higher. Euric had to fight the need to take her down to the floor and plunge inside her. He was not about to make love to her on the hard dirt floor of the punishment cell, even if they could manage to keep each other in their own time while doing it. For now, he would only taste and touch.

Petra clutched his shoulders when he used his thumb to circle her clit while he worked her with his fingers. She was so wet his cock throbbed to be inside her instead. Pumping faster, he pushed her closer and closer toward climax. Once he felt the first small flutter inside her core, Euric knew she was there. He stroked his thumb over her sensitive clit. Her cries of pleasure while she came filled his ears. Her inner walls rhythmically clamped down around his fingers. He continued to move them in and out until the last wave of pleasure hit her.

She brought his head down for a slow languid kiss. After she pulled away, she said, "It's your turn. I get to give you as much pleasure as you gave me."

Euric did not move as Petra swiftly undid the belt around his waist. She took hold of the hem of his tunica and pulled it up his body. With some help, she got it over his head and off. He threw it on the floor behind him.

Petra took his mouth in a heated kiss while she molded her hands to his chest, tracing the lines of the muscles she found there. His cock throbbed in time with the blood surging through his veins. He wanted to feel her touching him all over. A moan pushed past his lips as she shifted from his mouth to place kisses along the line of his jaw.

Her hands moved from his chest and down across his stomach. It quivered when she stroked him there. "Touch me lower, Petra," he groaned.

She nipped his chin. "I plan to. I've been dying to explore every inch of you. I've dreamed of having you spread out on my bed while I lick and kiss all the interesting parts of your body."

Euric moaned. His heart beat so fast he wondered if it would beat right out of his chest. "I do not think I would survive it."

"Oh, you'll survive it, Euric. A big, strong gladiator like you can't be brought down by a small amount of pleasure."

"Your mouth on me," he said roughly, "would by no means be a small amount of pleasure."

He lost all ability to speak, let alone think, when Petra wrapped her hand around his straining erection and squeezed him. His hips jerked as he pushed his cock harder into her hand. She pumped it up and down his hard length, eliciting another moan from him. The feel of her pleasuring him did not compare to any of the other women's attempts when they came to his cell. Only with Petra did he come alive.

He put his hands on her waist while he pumped his hips. Each stroke brought him closer to orgasm. She squeezed him tighter and slid her hand up and down his shaft faster. His release rushed up to meet him. With a loud moan, he came and jets of his seed pumped out of him.

Euric leaned his forehead against Petra's. "The next time I do that I want to be inside you, but it will not be now. Not while I am stuck in this cell."

Petra released his now-flaccid cock. "I want it too, Euric. Somehow we'll make this work."

* * * *

Petra returned from cleaning up in the en suite with a warm, wet cloth for Euric to use. While he washed up, she pulled on a pair of yellow pajama boxer shorts that had pink teddy bears on them and a matching yellow baby-doll t-shirt she'd taken out of her suitcase. Once she was dressed, she turned back to the window to see he had already put his tunic back on.

He ran his gaze down her body before he looked her in the face. "I do have to say I like what the women in your time wear."

"These are my pajamas, the clothes I sleep in."

"If I was sleeping in your bed, you would not be wearing those for very long."

A shiver of pleasure went through her. The thought of Euric slowly taking off her pajamas made her body tingle with awareness. She still felt his hands stroking her, pleasuring her, bringing her to release.

"And I doubt we'd be getting much sleep," she said huskily.

He gave her a knowing grin. "No. Sleep would be the furthest thing from my mind."

Petra resisted the urged to wave her hand in front of her heated face. Euric was turning her on again. The climax he'd given her had been pretty close to mind-blowing, but it hadn't been quite enough. Touching him, bringing him to his own release while he moaned in pleasure, made her ache to have all of him. Since they couldn't do anything more than heavy petting, she had to let things cool down. She didn't want to get herself worked up for nothing.

She reached through the window and took the wet cloth from Euric. "I'll just get rid of this."

Inside the en suite, Petra rinsed, then hung the cloth on

the side of the sink to dry. She looked at her reflection in the mirror. Her lips were still puffy from Euric's kisses and her cheeks were colored with a slight blush. She looked like a woman who'd been thoroughly pleasured.

After returning to the bedroom, she went and sat on the floor next to Euric. She put her hand through the window and linked their fingers together. "I think I'll sit here with you for the rest of the night. I don't like the idea of you in that dark cell all by yourself."

"I would like that. Having you near me, I can endure just about anything."

Petra shifted closer until her thigh came up against his and she rested her head on his shoulder. "I understand why you don't want to come to my time, but I still wish you would."

Euric reached up and stroked her cheek. "I know. Tell me about your time, Petra."

"All right. The cities are a lot bigger than what you'd be used to. There are more people since they live longer and the infant mortality rate isn't as high."

"What is the city called that you live in?"

"I live in Los Angeles, in California. It's in the part of the world that in your time even the Romans hadn't discovered."

"Does Rome still exist?"

"Yes. It's bigger now as well, though some of the buildings from your time have survived to mine. The *Amphitheatrum* still stands, but we now called it the Colosseum. Parts of it are missing. There was a big earthquake in 1349 that knocked the outer south side of it down, and the wooden floor is no longer there. I'm sure if you were to see it you'd recognize it."

Euric turned and kissed Petra's forehead. "So the *Amphitheatrum* still stands, but it is no longer used for the *munera*?"

"No. Not for years and years. Now it's a huge tourist

attraction. Thousands of people go to Rome to see it."

"How far away is Rome to where you live?"

"Very far. Rome is on the other side of the world."

"Have you ever been there?"

Petra shook her head, then shifted so she smiled up at Euric. "No, but I'm thinking I'll have to go now since I'm very well acquainted with a certain gladiator." He didn't smile back as she'd expected. She lifted her head to better study his face. He looked somber. "What's the matter, Euric?"

He gave her a half-smile. "I was just thinking that if you do go to Rome, I will already be long dead."

That was a sobering thought. To her, Euric was very much alive, but in actual fact, in her time he would have died well over a thousand years ago. It made Petra's chest ache thinking about it. The idea of losing him after she'd just found him made her throat tighten. The more time they spent together the more she wished he could be hers for all time.

CHAPTER FIVE

Fourth Century Rome

E uric waited for the guards to let him out of the punishment cell. They would come for him soon.

During the night, Petra had stayed with him as she had said she would. They had done a lot of talking, and he had learned more about her world. He had a hard time believing some of the things she had told him actually existed. When she had gone and gotten something called a laptop computer and shown him, he could not refute what she had told him. The computer itself had fascinated him. Seeing the still and moving pictures that had played inside it had been astounding.

At one point, the small flameless light, a flashlight, had gone dark. Petra had quickly taken it and replaced what she called the batteries with new ones and the light had come back on. She had also showed him the small metal cylinders she had removed from the flashlight. Euric had no idea how they made the light work. They had not looked like much when he had held them.

They had also come to the conclusion that whatever time of day it was on his side of the window it was the same on Petra's. She had been quite surprised that it was. She tried to explain something called a time difference, but she had lost him in the end. The only part of it he had understood was when she had explained that since Rome was on the other side of the world from where she lived, if it was morning in Rome, it would still be the middle of the night in Los Angeles. Euric had a feeling the world of the future would be a strange and complicated place.

When Petra started to get sleepy, she had taken a pillow and blanket off the bed in her room and shared them with him. Sitting with the pillow under their heads and the blanket over their legs, they had fallen asleep, leaning against each other. Unable to sleep for long, Euric had spent most of what remained of the night watching her.

Once dawn's light filled Petra's room, Euric had gently shaken her awake and told her she had to go. He would be released soon, and he wanted none of the guards to see the things from the future she had shared with him.

After Petra had removed everything but the flashlight, she had pulled him into the middle of the window where their times met and passionately kissed him. Even though he yearned to stay with her, Euric had been the first to pull away. He had handed her the flashlight and then the window had closed, leaving him alone in the small pitch-dark cell.

Having spent the night with Petra, and able to see because of the flashlight, the dark seemed to close in around him. Euric realized if not for her, he would have had a hard time handling being locked inside the punishment cell. The dark and cramped space would have played tricks on his mind.

The sound of a key being put in the cell's door told Euric his time of isolation was now over. A guard threw open the door and moved aside for Euric to step out. Since this cell faced the wide-open space of the training ground, which was open to the sky, he had to squint against the bright sunlight as he straightened. The guard walked him to his own cell where his *Lanistae* waited.

Once the guard left, his *Lanistae* turned to Euric and gave him a hard stare. "I expect better from you in the future, Euric. You and Calix will fight tomorrow in the *munera*. Stay away from him until then or I will have you forcibly kept away."

Euric had to bite his tongue on the rush of words that threatened to spill out of him. He had no problem with staying away from Calix, but the Roman would be the one to seek him out. His *Lanistae* should be warning Calix away from Euric, not the other way around.

"Yes, *Lanistae*," he said tightly.

His *Lanistae* nodded, obviously satisfied Euric would do as he had been told. "Good. Just because you were in the punishment cell does not mean I do not expect you out on the training ground this morning with the others."

"Yes, *Lanistae*."

With that said, the other man walked out of the room. Euric left shortly after to eat his morning meal. Luckily for him, Calix was not sitting at one of the long tables when he arrived. Once he finished eating, he went out to the training ground to join the other gladiators.

Calix stood with two others, talking loudly enough for everyone around him to hear. As Euric walked by, the Roman boasted about how he would have the mob cheering for him during the *munera* the next day. Euric did not even bother to look at the smug bastard.

The Roman must have spotted him, because in an even louder voice, Calix said, "I am going to beat the Goth so badly he will know why I am *primus palus* and he is not." Calix laughed.

Euric did not bother to turn around. He picked up a weighted wooden sword and swung it in front of him.

Tomorrow's fight would be one he looked forward to. Making the overblown Roman bleed would more than make up for the time he had spent in the punishment cell. Defeating him would be even better.

Euric spent the next two hours in sword practice while Calix spent more time bragging than swinging his wooden sword. Overconfidence would be the Roman's downfall. Calix could brag all he wanted, but when it came time for Euric to cross swords with him in the *Amphitheatrum*, the Roman would not find him so easy to defeat.

* * * *

Present Day

Petra had crawled into bed after the window had closed between her and Euric. Once again, she'd had no idea how it'd known to close, or if she or he had been controlling it. She'd been surprised it'd remained open for the entire night.

After a couple hours of deep sleep, Petra woke up feeling a little more rested. She stretched, then smiled when she thought of the night she'd spent with Euric. It'd been more than nice. Usually when she was first getting to know a man, she sometimes found herself at a loss for words. That hadn't been the case so far with Euric. She felt comfortable around him. She didn't feel as if she had to put on an act either. She could just be herself. And the fact he blew her socks off every time he touched her just had her falling for him even more.

Using her laptop to show him some of her world had been an experience she soon wouldn't forget. The wonder that had played across Euric's face when she'd showed him clips of cars and airplanes had put the things she found normal in her everyday life in a different perspective. To him, they were things he never would have thought existed until she'd shown them to him.

Petra hadn't shown him so much of her time in the hopes that it would keep Euric distracted from the fact that he was locked up in the punishment cell. She'd had an ulterior motive. She still hadn't given up hope that she'd somehow be able to convince him to pass over into the present day. She'd seen the look of longing on his face when she'd told him if he did he would be a free man.

Petra got out of bed and went to the en suite to shower and brush her teeth. Once she was dressed, she went downstairs to the kitchen. Since Sally wasn't due to arrive until later in the day, Petra opened the fridge and took stock of what was inside it and the freezer. Seeing the way Euric had enjoyed her leftover steak, and the fact that he really hadn't eaten a half-decent meal in years, she decided she'd get Sally to cook her a big dinner. Petra found a small roast in the fridge, thawing. Obviously, Sally had to have already planned to make it, which fit in with Petra's plans. When she went to her apartment that afternoon, she'd do a little shopping of her own. A nice bottle of red wine and some rich chocolate cheesecake would round off the meal she planned to serve Euric.

Her evening plans all sorted, Petra ate a bowl of cereal and had a glass of orange juice before she went into the study. She'd just started the desktop computer when the phone rang.

Hearing Mr. Dunn's voice on the other end, she asked, "How has the trip been so far?"

"Very productive. I emailed you a couple things last night. Did you get them?"

"Let me check. I just started the computer." Once it finished booting up, Petra checked her work email. Sure enough, there was one from Mr. Dunn sitting in her inbox. "Yup, I got it."

"Good. I want you to see if you can find out how accessible this property would be and whether the people would be willing to take a lower offer. The estate agent's number is listed in the email."

"I'll get right on that."

"I suggest you do that as soon as we hang up because of the time difference."

"The time difference?" Petra opened the email and found herself looking at a picture of an Italian villa situated near Rome.

"The property is in Italy. And since they're nine hours ahead of us, you don't have much time before the estate office closes for the day."

"I'll make the call."

"Oh, and ask the estate agent if the owners will be in favor of pushing up the closing date. The villa is empty, so I really can't see them having much of a problem with it closing in a couple weeks."

Petra grabbed a scratch pad of paper and quickly wrote down what Mr. Dunn wanted her to ask. "Will do. Is this going to be one of your investment properties? Italy is pretty far away."

"Not this one. This is for my personal use. I've had my eye on this property for a while, and now that it's on the market, I intend to snap it up before anyone else can. Once you've spoken to the agent, email me with the information."

"I will."

After Mr. Dunn hung up, Petra punched in the phone number for the estate agent's office in Italy. The woman was more than happy to answer her questions, especially when Petra told her Mr. Dunn was willing to close on the property within the next couple weeks. She'd even given Petra the lowest price the owners were willing to take.

It turned out the villa was located on the outskirts of Rome, close to Tuscany. It was also a mile from Lake Bracciano, which had gotten its name from the medieval town of Bracciano that had its own historical castle. The city of Rome was twenty miles away, which was where the closest airport could be found. Once Petra got off the phone with the Italian estate agent, she typed all the information in an email and then sent it off to Mr. Dunn.

After going on the Internet and following the link the estate agent had given her to see more of the property, Petra clicked through the pictures posted of the grounds and inside the villa. She saw why Mr. Dunn was so keen on purchasing it. It'd make a perfect Italian getaway. She sighed. It wasn't as if she could ever afford to stay in a place like that. If she ever went to Rome, she'd be lucky if she could afford to stay in a four-star hotel.

The more Petra looked at the villa the more it reminded her of Euric. If she ever got him to come to her time, this was the Rome she wanted him to see. A Rome where there were no slaves and gladiators. They'd spend their days touring the historic sites and soaking up the hot Italian sun. The Colosseum would be on the top of the list. Then at night, after they had eaten a large meal of Italian food and drank copious amounts of Italian red wine, they'd make love. She could almost picture it now.

Lost in thought while she stared at the computer monitor, Petra didn't at first hear Sally come into the study. She jumped when the other woman said, "What has you looking all dreamy eyed?"

Petra pointed to the monitor. "I'm just looking at the new property Mr. Dunn is going to buy. It's an Italian villa on the outskirts of Rome."

Sally walked around the desk to stand at Petra's back. She looked over her shoulder at the pictures. "So it finally went on the market. He's been talking about buying that villa for the last year. He figured it'd only be a matter of time before the owners sold it since it has been empty for almost that long."

"It'd be the perfect place to go for a vacation."

Sally chuckled. "You're thinking about a certain

German man who happens to be in Rome, and how you'd love to spend some time with him in that villa."

Petra sighed dramatically. "It doesn't hurt to dream."

"No, it doesn't." Sally laughed backed up when Petra turned the desk chair around to face her. "Are you going to your apartment again this afternoon?"

"Yeah. I'll be back in time for dinner. And speaking of which, I noticed the small roast in the fridge."

"I decided you'd like to have one with all the fixings, even though I'm sure there will be enough leftovers to make another meal out of it."

"Don't be surprised if I eat more of it than you think. I love roast beef, and I tend to make a pig of myself when I get it."

She did love roast beef, but there was no way she'd be able to eat most of it on her own. Petra had to have some reason to give Sally as to why there wouldn't be many leftovers, considering she was going to feed Euric too.

"Aw, to be in my twenties again," Sally said. "I used to be able to eat like that when I was your age, but not any longer." She patted her well-rounded hips. "I'll be sure to make enough roasted potatoes and green beans so you can eat yourself silly. How does that sound?"

Petra laughed. "It sounds as if I'll be doing more Pilates and yoga this week to work off the extra calories."

"Enjoy it when you can, my girl." Sally started to walk away, but stopped and turned back to Petra. "I just thought of something. Why don't you invite your friend over for dinner tonight? What's her name again? Mr. Dunn won't mind if you have some company over."

"Her name is Lia. I think I'll do that. I know she worked a night shift at the hospital last night, so I'll give her a call when I'm at my apartment." Even though Lia would be working again that night, she'd make the perfect stand in for Euric for Sally's benefit. "And while I'm out, I think I'll pick up a bottle of wine and some dessert."

Sally shook her head. "Good thing I won't be eating with you," she said with a laugh. "As is, I'll probably gain five pounds just looking at it."

Petra smiled. "Don't worry, Lia and I won't leave you any of the cheesecake."

"That's just plain mean." Sally grinned. "I'll let you get back to work. I suppose if your friend worked a night shift last night, you'll want to eat a bit later. If it's all right with you, I'll leave the food in the oven to stay warm for the two of you."

"We'll manage on our own. Don't worry about serving us. Just leave when you normally do."

"Then I'm out of here. I have to pick up some groceries so I may or may not get back before you leave."

"Have fun."

After Sally left the study, Petra turned her attention to the computer monitor and her thoughts returned to Euric. She couldn't help but wonder what he was doing right now. She hoped they'd let him out of the punishment cell by now. If she'd been the one stuck inside it, she would have been a basket case before the night had been over. The thought of what he had to endure on a day-to-day basis, so different from her life, made her ache to protect him, to take him away from all the pain and suffering. If only he'd let her.

Telling herself Euric wasn't a lost cause just yet, Petra closed the Internet browser and then worked on the smaller items her boss had sent her with the email about the Italian villa. She still had tonight to wine and dine Euric. Petra wasn't ready to admit defeat.

* * * *

Fourth Century Rome

Glad to be allowed to retire early to his cell because he

would be fighting in the *munera* the very next day, Euric stretched out on his bed to wait for Petra. He had really pushed himself during training and now his shoulders ached a bit from swinging the weighted wooden sword. The massage he had received earlier had helped loosen him, but after he caught up on his sleep, he would be in fighting shape for the munera.

He must have drifted off, because the next thing he knew Petra was calling his name and the smell of roasted meat tickled his nose. His mouth watered when he sat up and saw she stood in front of the window, holding a trencher piled high with food. Euric did not know whether he wanted to kiss her senseless for feeding him once again or pounce on the food.

As he crossed the cell to the window, Petra said, "After what you told me they feed you, I thought we could share a meal together. There is roast beef, roasted potatoes and green beans. As much as you can eat. I also have some red wine to go with it. Plus, there is something sweet for dessert."

Euric did not know what to say. It had been so long since somebody had done something this nice for him. That Petra would go to all this trouble just for him meant more than she could possibly know. Her thoughtfulness made him want to pull her to him and never let go. He wanted to bind her to him so she would never leave him. Make her want him as much as he wanted her. He had never been more tempted to tug her through the window and keep her in his time, but if he did that, Petra would never forgive him, just as he would not want her to bring him to her time without his consent.

Clearing his throat that suddenly felt tight with emotion, Euric smiled. "It smells delicious. You must have spent hours cooking this."

Petra gave him a sheepish look. "Well, I didn't exactly cook it. The man I work for has a cook, so since I'm staying here house sitting Sally makes dinner for me. I just picked up the dessert and wine."

"It still means a lot that you were the one to arrange this."

"Good." Petra handed the plate through the window. "Take this and I'm going to see if I can move the table over here. I figured if I push it halfway through the window both of us can use it when we eat."

Euric took the plate and then Petra went to the other end of the bedroom and tried to heft a low wooden table sitting between two stuffed chairs. It was not all that big, but it looked heavy. By the time she got it over to the window, she was huffing and puffing.

Once she had it close enough, Euric reached out. "Pull my hand through and I will move the table the rest of the way."

Petra straightened and stretched her back. "Good idea."

She took hold of his hand and placed it on the end of the table. Standing at the side of it, she kept hers wrapped around his wrist while he yanked half the table over to his side. That in place, Petra passed him some ruby-red wine in a glass chalice. Euric was almost afraid to touch it. Something that delicate, and made out of glass, no less, would cost a fortune in his world. With great care, he gently placed it on his end.

He looked up to find Petra watching him with amusement lurking in her eyes. "You don't have to worry about breaking the wineglass. It isn't that fragile. And even if you did, it wouldn't be a big deal. It's not from one of Mr. Dunn's—the man I work for—expensive sets. The table is worth more than that wineglass."

Euric shook his head. He sat on the floor in front of the table the same time Petra did. "Only the very rich can afford real glass to drink from."

"Not here," Petra said as she picked up the steel blunted knife and the other pronged utensil.

Observing how she used the pronged one to stab her meat to hold it in place while she cut it and then lifted the cut-off piece to her mouth, Euric tried to do the same. His first couple attempts were clumsy, but after that he managed to get the meat into his mouth without dropping it onto his trencher. He had to admit the pronged utensil made for less mess when eating. The food tasted as good as it smelled. He had to stop himself from shoveling it into his mouth. Taking a sip of the wine, he made a sound of appreciation.

"I guess you like the wine," Petra said after she had taken a sip of her own. "I haven't tried this kind before so I wasn't sure how it'd taste. I'm not much of a wine expert or anything."

"It and the food are very good. I have not had wine in a long time, but I better not have any more than this. Tomorrow I fight in the *munera*."

Petra stopped chewing and quickly swallowed her food. Her concerned gaze settled on his face. "You're fighting tomorrow?"

"Yes. Remember, I told you when we first met that I had a match coming up in a few days."

"I remember, but I didn't think it was so soon."

"I will be fine, Petra."

She put her utensils onto her trencher and pushed it to the side. "I don't think I can eat now."

"You are worried?"

"Of course I am. How else would you expect me to feel? The man I'm starting to care for deeply is about to risk his life for other people's enjoyment."

A large smile formed on Euric's lips. "You care deeply for me?"

A rush of warmth surged through him at the idea that Petra felt that strongly for him. Never before had there been a woman waiting for him, worrying about him, while he fought in the *munera*. Before her, if he died in the

Amphitheatrum, he doubted anyone would have much cared. Maybe except for his *Lanistae*, who would miss the money he would have to spend to purchase another slave to train as a gladiator.

Petra nodded. "Of course I do. I don't let a man do the things I let you do to me if I don't have feelings for him."

All of a sudden, Euric was no longer hungry for the food in front of him. He now had a hunger for the woman who sat across from him. The need to hold her in his arms, smell her woman's scent as he kissed and caressed her, could not be ignored. Keeping his gaze locked with Petra's, he moved his trencher and glass chalice to the side before climbing onto the table.

He knelt in front of the window and pressed his hand flat against it. "Take my hand, Petra, and let me touch you again."

She moved her trencher and chalice to the floor before she climbed onto the table in front of him. Petra lifted her hand and linked their fingers together. Euric shut his eyes briefly, relishing the feel of her touching him even if it was only her hand.

Slowly, Petra pulled him closer until they met in the middle of the window. She cupped the back of his head, urging it down. Her lips met his halfway. Her tongue came out and stroked his bottom lip. With a groan, Euric opened for her and sucked it inside his mouth. He moved his lips over hers, loving the taste and feel of her against him.

His cock hardened painfully as Petra cupped him through his tunica. She stroked his shaft through the material while she left his mouth and nuzzled the base of his throat.

"I want you, Euric." Her warm breath caressed his skin while she spoke. "I want you to make love to me."

"I cannot," he said with a groan.

"Why not?"

"I fight tomorrow. I will need all my strength. No

warrior sleeps with a woman the night before a battle."

Petra dragged her tongue across his skin. "Then don't fight tomorrow."

He half moaned and half laughed when she squeezed his cock harder. "I do not have a choice."

"Yes, you do." She kissed her way up the side of his neck and nipped his earlobe. "Cross over to my time and you'll never have to fight again. We could be together, make love all night until neither one of us can move."

"Petra, I cannot."

"You can. I could save you. My world is a much better place than yours. It isn't as barbaric as yours."

Euric stiffened and pulled back to look Petra in the eyes. "You think I am a barbarian? That is what the Romans consider my people."

She quickly shook her head. "That isn't what I meant. Compared to the people of my time, even the Romans are considered to be barbaric. The *munera* they so enjoy would turn the stomachs of most people I know."

Euric pulled farther away until he was back on his side of the window, then he released Petra. She thought the *munera* was barbaric? They were far from it when compared to the battles he had fought in Germania. Gladiator fights were civilized when put up against some of the atrocities committed on a battlefield. At least on there, fighting to defend his tribe, he fought for a purpose, and he had been good at it.

As Petra tried to reach for him, Euric got off the table and went to stand in the middle of his cell. "If you think Romans are barbaric, then I am even more so. I come from a people who believe how capable a man is with his sword is what makes him a man. From the time I was ten summers old, I have trained to fight, to kill as many of the enemy as I can on a battlefield. The more I kill the better a warrior I become."

Petra gave him a sad look. "You don't have to live that

way. I'm giving you the option to better yourself. To be something more than a warrior."

He shook his head. "Leave it be, Petra."

"I can't," she said. "I don't want you to fight tomorrow. Please, Euric."

"It is what I do."

"It doesn't have to be," Petra said vehemently. She held her hand out to him. "Just take my hand and you can have your life back. You would gain so much more than what you'd be losing."

"I would only be giving up the chance to return to my family and reclaim my status as a Visigoth warrior." As Petra opened her mouth to say something more, Euric cut her off. "Enough, Petra. I need to stay focused tomorrow during my match. I know I will not be able to if you keep pushing me to do something I do not want to do. I think it best that you leave now."

Before she could protest, Euric took hold of the end of the table and pushed it through the window. Petra slid off it and then pulled it the rest of the way through when he hit the barrier. Giving her one last look, he turned his back on her. When he turned around, both her and the window were gone.

CHAPTER SIX

Present Day

Petra felt as if Euric had slapped her when he'd turned his back on her, but when the window misted and then closed, she'd felt a little bit panicky. She hadn't wanted to end their night like that, especially when he had to fight the next day. He may be confident in his ability to keep himself from being killed, but the thought that he could be and she would never know terrified her.

Just hearing that he had to fight in the *munera* in less than twenty-four hours had caused a shiver of fear to run down her spine. It was that fear that had led to her to be more forceful than she should have been in trying to convince Euric to come to her time. She'd blown it big time. Thinking over what she had said, Petra knew she'd more than likely insulted him. He was a warrior, and in his society he didn't need to better himself. She had been grasping at straws at that point. Every time he refused to see things her way the more desperate she felt to get him to change his mind.

A little depressed and more than a little worried for Euric, Petra gathered up the plates of uneaten food and his wineglass. She put hers next to the bottle of red wine that sat on a tray on the dresser. After she took the plates to the kitchen, she cut a huge slab of cheesecake for herself and took it back up to the guestroom. She proceeded to drink the rest of the wine while she tried to drown her sorrows in the cheesecake. She wasn't much of a drinker so the alcohol had definitely gone to her head once she crawled into bed.

Before sleep claimed her, Petra sent up a silent prayer that Euric would survive the *munera*. She could handle having to lose him because the window no longer opened better than she could losing him to death. At least with the first one he had a chance to return home and have a life.

* * * *

Fourth Century Rome

Euric stared at the pile of armor one of the guards had brought him and who now stood waiting for him at the door to his cell. The armor laid spread out on his bed. There was not a sword included with it. He would not get that until just before he stepped out onto the sand of the *Amphitheatrum*. Focused and prepared on what lay ahead, he put on the armor piece by piece. He donned the helmet last. With a nod to show he was ready, he followed the guard out of his cell.

As they walked to the entrance of the underground tunnel that led from the *ludus* to the *Amphitheatrum*, Euric pushed all thoughts except for the upcoming fight out of his head, especially those that had to do with Petra. It had taken him a long while to fall sleep the night before. Every time he had closed his eyes, he saw the stricken look on her face when he had told her he thought it best she left him alone. She had been the last thing he had thought about before he had finally fallen into a deep sleep. And she had been the first thing he had thought of when he had woken up. Right now, she was a distraction he could not afford.

Entering the tunnel, Euric followed the guard through the semi-darkness. Calix would have already been taken to the *Amphitheatrum*. Euric would not come into contact with him until they met inside the arena. They would even enter from different entrances. Once he reached the *Amphitheatrum*, the guard led him through the hypogeum, the network of tunnels and cages beneath it.

Accepting his sword from another guard who met them at the entrance to the arena, Euric took a deep breath as he blocked out the sound of the mob. Once their cheers were nothing more than a slight noise, he stepped out onto the sand and walked to the center where Calix stood, waiting. The Roman was playing the mob, raising his arms, brandishing his sword to show how strong he was. Euric did not go for such displays. He turned to face the emperor's box. Constantine was not there, but one of the senators sat in his stead to preside over the *munera*.

After Calix had done the same, they both held their right arms over their chests and said in a loud voice, "Those about to die salute you."

This was something every gladiator had to say before they fought. The salute over with, Calix's and Euric's names were announced and then the fighting began.

They circled each other, looking for an opportunity to make the first strike. From watching Calix train, Euric knew he would be the one to hit first. Calix liked to overpower and beat down his opponents. He tried to make up for his lack of skill with brute strength. Euric had the skill and strength to not let that happen.

Once Calix finally made his first move, Euric easily blocked it with his small round shield, but did not make a strike of his own in return. It would only be a matter of time before Calix tired himself out. Then Euric would make his move to bring him down.

After a half a dozen hits that Euric had either blocked with his shield or sword, or had managed to sidestep, Calix showed signs of tiring. His hits were coming slower and he was starting to lose his temper, which would make him do something rash if Euric pushed him enough.

On Calix's last strike, Euric caught it on his sword. The other man kept their swords locked and pushed the blade of his down as he rammed into Euric.

With a snarl, Calix said, "What is the matter, Goth? Are you afraid to fight me? What kind of warrior stands there and does nothing to defeat his opponent?"

Euric shoved Calix away. "I am a warrior who waits for his weaker opponent to tire before he goes in for the kill."

In a maneuver Euric did not think Calix was capable of, he swung his sword under Euric's shield and sliced his blade across Euric's right biceps. Euric sucked a breath between his teeth at the sharp sting, but he ignored it and the blood that dripped from the wound.

Euric blocked Calix's next strike on his shield, but raised his sword to make a strike of his own. It slammed against Calix's shield, forcing the other man to take a step back. Euric landed a punishing blow across the Roman's armored chest, which had Calix scrambling backward. The mob either cheered or booed, depending on which one they rooted for. A few chanted Euric's name.

Wanting to end the fight, Euric hacked and slashed at Calix. Soon the Roman bled from a sword cut in his upper thigh and his forearm. Calix's hits grew weaker and he no longer took the offensive. Much to Euric's satisfaction the overconfidence had left the Roman's eyes. Uncertainty had replaced it.

Euric struck again and again. After his final hit, he managed to ram his elbow into Calix's face, which was not protected by his helmet. He heard the satisfying crunch as the Roman's nose broke and blood gushed out of it. He used the flat of his sword to knock Calix's legs out from under him.

With the other gladiator flat on his back in the sand, Euric came to stand over Calix. He placed the tip of his sword at the other man's throat as he stood panting. Euric turned and looked at the mob. Out of the corner of his eye he saw Calix raise his left hand, asking for mercy. In response, the mob shouted *missum*, asking for Calix to be released from a death sentence.

The senator, who presided over the *munera*, stood in the emperor's box and moved to the edge so all saw him. He stuck out his fist with his thumb out to the side. While the mob continued to chant *missum*, the senator turned his fist to give the thumbs-up. Then in a loud voice, he declared Euric the winner.

Euric backed away from Calix and saluted the senator and mob, which now chanted his name. The *summa rudis*, the referee who had watched over the fight on the arena floor, signaled for the guards to take Calix's — who stood wiping the blood from his nose — and Euric's swords. Once they had been disarmed, the senator left the emperor's box and came down to the floor to present Euric with a palm branch for winning his match. Not only was he the winner, he was now *primus palus* in his *ludus*.

Once the senator returned to the box, the guards led Euric and Calix away. Inside the hypogeum, Calix rammed into the back of him. The guards quickly pulled them apart before the Roman could do more than hurl taunts at Euric.

"You had better watch your back, Goth," Calix shouted. "If we fight again, I will take back my *primus palus* status and make you regret ever taking it from me."

At that moment, their *Lanistae* came up behind them. "Calix, keep your threats behind your teeth or I will be forced to have you put in the punishment cell." He motioned to the guard who held the Roman back. "Take him to the *ludus* and have the physician tend to his wounds."

On the way to the underground tunnel, Calix spit in Euric's face, spraying him with spit and blood. Euric used his palm to wipe it off, then fisted his hands at his sides, knowing he could not show any reaction while in the presence of his *Lanistae*. Inside, he wanted nothing more than to plow his fist into the Roman's face and see if he could shatter his nose even more.

His *Lanistae* grabbed Euric's right arm and looked at the wound there. "You will need patching up as well." He squeezed the sword cut, not caring whether it hurt Euric or not. Euric gritted his teeth against the pain. "After that, you can clean up in the bath and rest for the remainder of the day." His *Lanistae* released him and nodded to the guard at Euric's side. "You can take him back now."

As he walked beside the guard, Euric did not feel tired—adrenaline was still pumping through him—but once he started to unwind he would be more than ready to relax. Before he found his rest, he needed to see Petra, to show her he was all right. And despite their earlier argument, he wanted to lose himself in her arms.

* * * *

Present Day

Petra found herself unable to concentrate on anything. Knowing Euric could be fighting for his life at that very moment made her feel sick to her stomach with worry. She'd purposely woken up early—even though her head pounded from the wine she'd drunk the night before—with the hope of seeing Euric before he had to go to the *munera*. She'd wanted to apologize for what she'd said and to tell him she'd no longer push him to come to her time. The window hadn't appeared, even when she'd become desperate enough to yell at it to open.

After she'd checked her work email and didn't find anything from Mr. Dunn, Petra had left a note for Sally to tell her that she'd gone and would return in the late afternoon. She needed to get out of the mansion and wasn't in the mood to be around other people.

Now she sat on the couch in her apartment with the TV on, not paying any attention to it, while she thought about Euric. She was so stressed out her stomach burned. She hadn't eaten yet and doubted she'd be able to keep anything down even if she managed to get any food past the tightness in her throat.

The not knowing of what had been Euric's fate was killing her. Pictures of him lying in a pool of his own blood on the sand-covered floor of the Colosseum while his eyes stared sightlessly up at the sky refused to leave her mind. If only the window would open and show her that her fears were unfounded, but it still wasn't cooperating.

Petra wrapped her arms around her burning gut and took some deep breaths as she tried to get herself to calm down. She told herself that Euric could be perfectly fine, that there was no point crying before she got hit, but she was beyond thinking logically.

Once the sound of the television grated on her frayed nerves, Petra switched it off. She looked at the clock on the digital cable box. It was already three in the afternoon. After six hours of being in a perpetual state of worry, she figured she had to be well on her way to an ulcer. She had no idea how the wives of men in the military stood it when their husbands were deployed. They didn't just have a day of worry, they had months of it.

Petra stood and walked into her bedroom. She needed something to distract her. She'd been intending to go through her overstuffed dresser drawers for months, but she'd been putting it off. It was the perfect mindless task she needed right now. As she pulled open a drawer, she caught the flicker of something out of the corner of her eye. Spinning around, she watched the window form close to the foot of her bed.

Her heart raced while she slowly walked toward it. Petra whispered, "Please let Euric be alive, please let Euric be alive."

The mist cleared, and Petra's tears of happiness burned behind her eyes as her gaze landed on Euric, standing tall and straight on the other side. That he appeared to be unharmed was enough to have her rushing toward the window and reaching through it as he hurried toward her. Their bodies came together hard. His much greater weight pushed her backward. She wrapped her arms around his neck and held on as his lips slammed down onto hers.

Euric kissed her like a man who was drowning and she was his only lifeline. With teeth and tongue, he devoured her mouth. Petra clung to him, kissing him back with the hunger that had replaced her fear. After a day of thinking he could have been killed, she needed to have him inside her, to connect with him in the most intimate of ways.

Petra reached for the rope belt tied around Euric's waist as he walked her backward. She'd just managed to untie it when the back of her knees hit the mattress of her bed. Falling back onto it, she grasped the front of his tunic and pulled him down with her. The feel of his solid weight on top her, pushing her down deeper into the mattress—and his hard cock coming to rest between her legs—made her moan. This was what she'd been longing for most of the day—the feel of him against her, touching and tasting her.

She rocked her hips against him and rubbed her pussy against his erection. Wetness pooled between her legs as her body prepared itself to have him take her. This time she wanted more than his fingers bringing her to release. She wanted all of him, to have the full length of his cock pumping in and out of her.

"I need to feel your skin against mine," Petra mumbled against Euric's lips. She bunched the back of his tunic in her hand and lifted it.

Euric released her mouth, slightly raised himself and pulled his tunic over his head. "You have too many clothes on." He pulled her t-shirt off and then nuzzled between her breasts.

As Euric struggled to free her breasts from her bra, Petra undid the front clasp and wiggled her way out of it. Not wanting to wait to be skin-to-skin, she undid her jean shorts, pushed them down past her hips and kicked them the rest of the way off.

Left only in her panties, she reached for the waistband to pull them off as well, but Euric placed his hand over hers to stop her. "Let me do it."

He rolled to his side next to her and propped himself up on his elbow. Using his fingers, he traced a path across the top of her breasts to one nipple. He took it between his thumb and index finger and rolled it between them. He bent his head and followed the same trail his fingers had taken. Once his lips reached her nipple, he circled it with his tongue. He blew on it gently, making it tighten even more.

Petra arched her back with a moan as Euric closed his lips over her nipple and sucked it inside his mouth. While he did, he took hold of the top of her panties and slowly inched them down past her hips and off. Switching to the other nipple, he caressed his fingers back up her leg to her inner thigh. She opened her legs, wanting him to touch her where she ached for him the most. She took her bottom lip between her teeth as he ran a finger along the opening to her body.

After releasing her nipple, Euric shifted so he straddled her legs. He took hold of her waist and pushed her up higher on the bed. Petra looked down to find his cock standing out from his body. She wrapped her hand around it and stroked him. His eyes closed for a second as he moaned deep in his throat, but soon pulled her hand away.

"First I get to claim my prize for being the winner of my match in the *munera*."

Euric moved to kneel between her spread legs and pressed light kisses to the underside of her breasts before he lowered to her stomach. He shifted off his knees to lie on the bed between her thighs while he made his even way lower her body. With his large shoulders spreading her wider, he pushed a finger and then a second inside her pussy. Feeling her own wetness against her skin, Petra lifted her hips in offering.

Euric pumped his fingers in and out of her a few times before he removed them only to replace them with his tongue. Petra dug her heels into the mattress and moaned loudly while she rocked her hips against his mouth. He licked and sucked her pussy, arousing her to the point where she was almost mindless with need.

Petra reached down and pulled Euric's hair. Panting, she said, "I want you inside me. Now. That feels too good."

Rising between her legs, Euric settled his hips between them. He took her hand and put it on his fully erect cock. "Put me where you want me." His voice sounded gruff with need.

Not hesitating, Petra wrapped her fingers around his shaft and led it to her core. She released him when the tip of his cock pushed inside her. Euric drew back and then with one thrust buried himself to the hilt inside her. She let her eyes drift shut at the pleasurable sensation of his thick length stretching her, filling her to capacity. He moved and she could only focus on the pleasure building inside her with each thrust of his hips.

Euric rested his weight on his bent arms while he

pumped between her legs. Petra wrapped them around his waist, arching her back to take him deeper. Their heavy breathing filled the room as they moved together. She wouldn't last too much longer. Wanting him to come when she did, she squeezed her inner muscles around his shaft. He groaned and pumped faster, harder.

Petra held on to Euric's biceps and he sucked in a breath as her fingers encountered a strip of cloth around his right arm. Before her brain registered what that meant, she fell over the edge into release. She moaned, her inner muscles rhythmically clutching his cock as he surged into her one last time before he too came.

Spent, Petra fought to catch her breath. Euric collapsed on top her with his head on her chest just under her chin. She wrapped one arm around his shoulders and used her other hand to push the hair off his sweaty brow. His semi-hard cock was still buried inside her.

Once she breathed normally, Petra opened her eyes. She stiffened when she realized exactly where she and Euric had ended up. "Oh, god, Euric. We're on my bed."

*

Lifting himself on his bent arms, Euric looked down at Petra. Her eyes were wide in shock. "Your bed?" She silently nodded.

He did a quick scan of the room only to realize Petra told the truth. They were lying in the middle of her mattress on her side of the window. Euric pulled out of her embrace and then jumped off the mattress. He looked to see if the window had closed behind him. His gut clenching with worry, he soon breathed a sigh of relief when he found it still open at the end of the bed. The sight of it had him sitting.

Petra came up behind him and put her arms around him. She kissed the side of his neck. "I didn't intentionally pull you through."

"I know. I pushed us through. I was not thinking when you reached for me." He turned his head to look at her. "All I could think about was being with you."

After bathing and having the physician take care of his wound, Euric had not been able to find any rest. The need to have Petra in his arms naked and willing, pressed against him, had ridden him hard. Whenever he fought in the *munera*, he craved a woman afterward. Joining his body to theirs, after facing life or death, helped reaffirm that he was still alive. Now that he had met Petra, none of the women who visited the gladiators for a stolen moment of pleasure would do for him. He only wanted one — Petra.

When the window had appeared, and he had seen her standing there with her eyes bright with unshed tears, Euric had only acted. As soon as she had pulled him toward her, his need for her had overpowered him. And once he'd had her on the bed, being inside her, claiming her as his, it had been something he could not control.

Euric reached up and cupped the back of Petra's head. He brought her lips down to his and gave her a lingering kiss. After he pulled away, he turned his head back toward the window. She kept her arms around him and rested her chin on top of his shoulder.

"You want to go back, don't you?" she asked softly.

"I need to go back, but not right now. As long as the window stays open, I can stay here with you. I want to spend the rest of the day with you."

Petra kissed his cheek. "I'll take whatever you'll give me." She ran her hand down his right arm. Her fingers brushed against his bandaged wound, and she shifted until she sat next to him. "You got hurt."

Euric looked down at his arm and back up at Petra. "It is only a flesh wound. The physician took care of it after my match."

Petra slid off the bed. "No offense to the physician, but I

want to take a look at it to make sure he did a good job. Let me get a couple things from the bathroom first."

His gaze followed Petra as she walked out of the room naked. She was beautiful, and Euric doubted he would ever get enough of her. Even now his cock stirred with interest. Once she returned, he could not stop his gaze from running over her full breasts and curved-in waist. He wanted her again. He wanted to take her over and over again, make her crave him as much as he craved her.

If Petra noticed his hardening cock, she did not show it when she sat on the bed next to his right arm. She held an opaque bottle in one hand, a couple small white puffy looking balls and a long, slim container of some kind that had a cap on the end of it. All business, she undid the knots on his bandage and carefully unwound it from around his biceps.

She seemed to grow pale when his wound was exposed. "Ah, that looks deeper than a flesh wound."

Euric looked down. "It is nothing. I have had worse."

"I'll have to take your word for that." Petra opened the opaque bottle and placed one of the small white puffy balls on the end of it. She tipped it so some of the liquid inside wet the ball. Putting the bottle down on the floor, she said, "This may hurt, but it will clean out any germs. This," she pointed to the other capped, slim container that still sat on the bed between them, "is an antibiotic ointment that will help the wound heal faster and keep out an infection."

He had no idea what germs were, but asking Petra to explain them left his mind once she pressed the puffy ball to his arm. He sucked in a sharp breath. It felt as if a hundred bees stung him at the same time.

"This is supposed to make my wound better?" Euric asked through gritted teeth.

Petra cringed. "I know it doesn't feel like it now, but rubbing alcohol does a much better job of cleaning out a wound than just plain water."

"Alcohol? You mean you can drink this as well?" Wherever Petra touched the puffy ball to his wound it left a trail of fire behind.

"No," she said with a chuckle. "If you were to drink this stuff, you'd either go blind or end up dead. This is strictly for disinfection purposes only."

"It is poison then?"

"Only if you drink it." Now finished wiping the puffy ball along the length of his wound, Petra put it down on the floor next to the opaque bottle and picked up the slim container. She took off the cap and squeezed a thick, almost clear substance out of it. Gently, she smeared it on his arm. "So you won your match?"

Euric nodded. "Yes. I'm now *primus palus*, first sword, in my *ludus*."

"Does that mean you'll get extra privileges?"

"Not really, but it does mean if I can keep that status I could receive my rudis sooner."

"That's good. What about the guy you beat and took his first sword status from? Is he still alive?"

Euric lifted his gaze to find Petra staring at him. "Yes, Calix is still alive. There would be too much cost to train a new gladiator to replace him, especially one of Calix's caliber. There is also the fact that Calix is a Roman and voluntarily chose to become a gladiator. He took a gladiator's oath, swearing to fight for a set amount time before he will once again be free."

Petra put the ointment container on the bed and then wrapped his bandage back over his wound. "I still don't know why someone would want to choose to live that kind of life."

"Some who do make that decision do not really have much of a choice. They are the ones who can only pay off their debts with the money they earn fighting."

"Do you get paid?"

"No. I was taken in battle. I do not have the option of being compensated with money for fighting in the *muneras*. Only the Romans who volunteer do. Eventual freedom is all I have to look forward to."

Finished with the bandage, Petra cupped Euric's face in her hands. "I owe you an apology. I'm sorry I pushed you so hard last night. I was being selfish."

Euric pulled her onto his lap. She turned in his arms to sit facing him while she straddled his thighs. He ran his thumb along her bottom lip. "It does not matter now. I am here and the window has not shut. Let us not waste the time we have with regrets." He locked gazes with her. "I want you again, Petra," he said with hunger making his voice thick.

A small smiled played on her mouth when she looked down to where his cock, already hard, stood erect between them. "I can see that." She licked her lips, which made his cock jerk in response. "I guess I should do something about it."

"I will not complain if you do." He cupped her breast and flicked his tongue against her taut nipple.

Petra made a throaty moan. "I'd better get busy then."

She shifted her hands higher and threaded her fingers through the sides of his hair. Bending her head, she claimed his lips in a kiss that made his heart beat faster. Her mouth slanted over his while she pushed her tongue inside to twine with his. The taste of her pushed his arousal even higher.

She dropped a hand between them and gently touched the head of his cock. He groaned into Petra's mouth as she circled it with her finger, wiping the bead of pre-cum she found there into his skin. She trailed down the thick length of his shaft. At the base, she wrapped her fingers around him.

Euric increased the pressure of his kiss when Petra pumped her hand up and down his cock. He ground his hips against her, pressing himself harder in her grip. The feel of her pleasuring him had all the blood in his body surging to his sex. He grew even harder as she continued to work him up and down. He stroked down her body and delved between Petra's legs. He moaned at how wet her pussy was.

Breaking their kiss, Petra rose to her knees. With one hand on his shoulder, she positioned his cock with her other, and with her gaze on his, she slowly impaled herself on his shaft.

Once he was seated to the hilt, she said low and husky, "God, you feel so good inside me, Euric."

"Take me, Petra. Ride me until we both find our pleasure."

Petra put her other hand on his shoulder while she slowly slid up his length and then back down again. They moaned at the pleasurable friction her movements caused. In this position, she took more of him. He was in so deep the head of his cock butted up against her womb with each stroke in. As she set a slow and steady pace, she wrung another moan out of him.

Taking the twin globes of her ass in his hands, Euric got Petra to ride him faster. Her inner muscles gripped him as his cock slid in and out of her pussy. Looking down, he watched her body take his. The sight had him fighting to hold back his release. He did not want to come until he heard Petra's cries of pleasure. He reached between them and stroked his finger between her legs, rubbing her clit.

Petra's fingers dug into his shoulders as she threw back her head, her long hair falling down her back. With her body clutching his cock, squeezing him in a tight fist while she came, she called out his name. Unable to hold back any longer, Euric rammed up into her one final time as his shaft pulsed deep inside her.

Still feeling the little aftershocks of Petra's orgasm along the length of him, he wrapped his arms around her and let himself fall back onto the bed. She cuddled against him, holding him tight. Euric kissed the top of her head while he stroked her back. Each time they made love, a stronger bond formed between them. It would never be just sex with her. She made him crave something he had not for a very long time. He wanted to have what every man wanted—a woman he loved always at his side. He hadn't reached the stage where he could say he was in love with her, but if he continued to see her, make love to her, it would only be a matter of time before his feelings grew that strong.

Not yet ready to face how he felt for her, Euric decided he would take one day at a time and enjoy what time they could find together.

CHAPTER SEVEN

After they'd caught their breath, Petra and Euric had curled up on her bed. As his eyes had started to flutter shut, she told him to go to sleep and that she'd watch the window to make sure it didn't close on him. Before he fell asleep, he'd made her promise that she'd awaken him if it looked as if it was starting to so he could get back to his own time. Of course she'd given him that promise. It would have to be his decision to stay, not hers.

Now, while Euric slept beside her sprawled out on his back, Petra watched him and the window. She still found it hard to believe he was in her bed. And making love to him had been an experience she soon wanted to repeat. He knew how to touch her to send her body flying. Having him join his to hers felt as if they'd been made for each other. The pleasure was unlike anything she'd experienced with another man.

Petra gently stroked her hand across Euric's well-muscled chest. She saw the faint outline of a scar that cut across one of his pecs. She had a feeling if she looked more closely at his body there would be more scars to be found.

Carefully, so as not to awaken him, she brushed a lock of hair off Euric's forehead. She wished they could lie in her bed together for the rest of the day. Make love and forget about the rest of the world. Now that she'd taken him as a lover, Petra didn't want to give him up. Never one to believe in love at first sight, she couldn't help feeling as if she'd started falling for him when she'd first caught sight of him in the window. He was slowly taking up residence in her heart. He was the type of guy she'd been looking for. Petra had always wanted a man who was no nonsense, sure of himself and comfortable in his own skin. A man who made her feel loved and protected. He fit the bill for all those things. Why couldn't he have been born in her time? It would have made things so much easier.

With a soft sigh, Petra turned to look at the window. It still stood open, showing a clear view of Euric's cell. It'd been over an hour since he'd come through it. She just wished she knew how to control it. The not knowing of what it'd do next added an element of risk to the time she spent with him. Never much of a risk taker, it made her a tad uncomfortable. She liked predictable, something the window was not.

Euric stirred beside her. Petra brought her gaze down to find his eyes open. She smiled. "Did you have a good sleep?"

He returned her smile. "Very. I have never slept on a bed this comfortable before."

"I'm glad you like my cheap mattress. There are better ones, but they're way out of my price range." She looked down the length of the bed where Euric's feet hung over the edge of her queen-sized mattress. "I can see if you're going to be spending a lot of time in my bed I'd better look into investing in a king-size. This one is too short for you."

Euric's face grew serious. "What if this is the only time I can share your bed?"

Petra swallowed the lump that suddenly formed in her throat. "What are you saying, Euric?"

"The window has stayed open now, but what if it does not the next time I try to come through it?"

She picked up his hand and held it to her cheek. "It'll stay open. It has to. When something different happens to it, it seems to stay that way."

Euric rolled her to her back so he lay on top her and gently kissed her lips. "I hope so, because I am not ready to let you go."

Even though she'd promised herself she wouldn't beg, Petra couldn't stop herself from saying, "Then stay. Please, Euric. Don't go back. I don't want to lose you, and with you returning to your time, I can't help feeling I'm going to."

He silenced her with another kiss, then rested his forehead against hers. "I cannot."

"At least let me show you my world. Give me the chance to change your mind. The next time you come through the window, give me an hour to let you see what it's like in my time. That's all I ask. Please."

Euric sighed. "Fine. I will give you your hour, if it looks as if the window will stay open for as long as it has now. It will have to be once I am locked in my cell for the night. I do not want the guards to know I am missing. If my *Lanistae* thought I was trying to escape, my punishment would be much worse than a night in the punishment cell."

Petra gave him a hard kiss. "You have my word. If the window opens again during the day, we'll wait until it's the right time. I promise you won't regret this, Euric."

"As long as I get to spend time with you, I will never regret it." Euric suddenly stiffened.

"What is it?" Petra asked worriedly.

"I all of a sudden have this intense need to go back to my cell. If almost feels as if something is pulling me back."

As Euric slipped off the bed and picked up his tunic off the floor, Petra looked over at the window. "Hurry, Euric. The window is starting to fill with mist." A thin layer was slowly creeping up the sides and inward to the middle.

Petra jumped out of bed and followed Euric to the window. He'd just finished tying his rope belt when he pulled her roughly into his arms and gave her a quick toe-curling kiss. He released her and stepped through the window.

Petra turned to face it and tried to put her hand through to touch Euric one last time before it closed, but the window didn't allow it. The mist grew thicker. "Euric. I miss you already."

He held his hand up to her palm on his side of the window. "It will be all right, Petra. The window will open again for us."

The window closed shut. Petra wanted to yell and scream that it wasn't fair. She wanted to curse at whatever, or whoever, controlled it. The short amount of time she and Euric had been together hadn't been enough. She did neither of those things. Instead she gathered up her clothes and then dressed.

While making the bed, Petra pressed her face to the pillow Euric had used. She closed her eyes and took a deep breath, pulling his scent that still lingered on the pillowcase into her lungs. Wishing more than anything that he was still there with her, she sat heavily on the bed and held the pillow clutched against her chest.

Feeling sorry for herself, Petra sighed deeply. Things had to work out for her and Euric. Fate couldn't be that cruel. There had to be a reason they'd found each other, even though over a thousand years separated them. On the brighter side of things, at least he'd promised to let her show him what the future was like.

That thought perked Petra up a little, and it gave her something to do to keep her mind off missing Euric. If she was to take him out into the outside world he couldn't do it wearing his tunic. He'd need clothes from her time to fit in. With a renewed sense of purpose, she grabbed her purse and headed out of the apartment. A trip to the closest mall was in order.

* * * *

Petra returned to Mr. Dunn's mansion loaded down with the clothes she'd bought for Euric. She had to admit that she'd gone a bit overboard. Not sure of what he'd like, or what exact size he was, she'd bought him a couple t-shirts, two pairs of athletic shorts, two tank tops and a couple pairs of underwear — one pair boxers and the other boxer-briefs. She'd never bought underwear for a man before, and considering he didn't exactly wear any, she thought it better to play it safe with two types. She'd also bought him a pair of athletic pants in case he didn't like the shorts. As for footwear, she chose a pair of sandals that had adjustable Velcro straps. She'd had to guess at the size, not really knowing how big his feet were.

Managing to open the mansion's front door without dropping any of the plastic bags she carried, Petra stepped inside and then closed it with her hip. She'd hoped to make it upstairs to the guest bedroom before Sally or the maid spotted her, but Sally came out of the kitchen and met her at the bottom of the staircase.

Sally eyed the bags Petra carried. "You're back early. And I see you were busy."

"Yeah. I managed to get my errands done quicker than expected."

"Do you have any money left or did you max out your credit card?" Sally asked jokingly.

"My credit card took a bit of a beating, but it was well worth it." Petra stepped around Sally. "Just let me put these upstairs and I'll come down in a bit."

Sally stopped her before she got very far. "Oh, your friend Lia called while you were out. I told her you weren't here and to try you on your cell phone, but she said you had it turned off. After I asked her if she enjoyed the girls' night you two had here last night, she said for me to tell you to call her. And I quote, 'If you don't, she'll stalk you to the ends of the earth until you talk to her.'"

Petra rolled her eyes and laughed. "That sounds like Lia. I'll give her a call while I'm upstairs."

Once she reached the top of the stairs, Petra headed straight for the guest bedroom and shut the door behind her. She put the bags on the bed before she pulled her cell phone out of her purse. Sure enough, she'd forgotten to turn it on when she'd left that morning. Now she had some explaining to do to Lia. Of course her friend would want to know about the girls' night they supposedly had last night.

Bringing Lia's number up on her cell, Petra hit send. Lia picked up after the second ring. "Hey, Lia. I hear you called while I was out."

"Yeah, I did. My schedule got switched again and I have tonight off. I thought we could get together, but supposedly we already did that last night while I was at work. I never knew I could be at two places at the same time."

"I can explain. Sort of. It's kind of complicated."

Lia was silent for a few seconds before she said, "You have a new guy, don't you? And you don't want anyone to know about him. That's who you had over for that roast beef dinner. Come on, spill. I want to hear all the details."

Petra piled the shopping bags on the floor next to the bed. "Yes, I've met someone. And no, I'm not trying to keep him a secret. It's just a little awkward right now."

"Awkward how?"

"As in if I told you everything you'd think I've totally lost it. It would also require a fair amount of alcohol and you believing me, even though you think there would be no way in hell it could be possible."

"All right, girl, you have me curious. I'll supply the wine and you can supply the juicy details. And I promise to keep an open mind."

Petra figured Lia would be the best person to talk to about Euric. She'd known her long enough to know that Lia would be the only one she'd have half a chance of convincing that what she'd tell her wasn't so farfetched as to be out in woo-woo land. And Petra really needed someone to talk to about Euric. She'd gone to Lia in the past with her man troubles and always felt better for it afterward.

"Fine. Come over at seven."

"I'll be there," Lia said, then hung up.

Not sure how she was going to convince Lia that the window she saw through time and Euric were real, Petra decided she'd deal with that when the time came.

* * * *

Fourth Century Rome

Standing in the chamber where his *Lanistae* handled the business end of the *ludus*, Euric faced the man himself. A guard had come to his cell to get him shortly after he had come back from Petra's time. It was almost as if the window had known he was going to be summoned before his *Lanistae*. The pull to return had been so great, Euric had not been able to ignore it. He could only think it had been the window's way of forcing him to return to his own time. He had already seen and experienced firsthand what it was capable of. What was one more aspect of it he could readily accept?

A little surprised his *Lanistae* would have summoned him so soon after his match in the *munera*, Euric waited for the other man to speak. He sat behind a wooden table, reading a parchment scroll. Once he finished with it, he released the ends and let it roll up on itself before he looked at Euric.

Euric met his gaze. "You summoned me, *Lanistae*?"

"Yes. The senator who presided over today's *munera* has written me a letter." His *Lanistae* nodded toward the rolled-up scroll that sat on the table. "It would seem he was impressed with your fighting skills. He also has enjoyed watching you fight a number of other times in the *muneras*. Since you defeated Calix and have now become *primus palus*, the senator would like to see you fight one last time. He has planned to have another *munera* next week in honor of the emperor soon returning to Rome. He also wishes, whether you win or lose your match, that you be given your rudis and set free."

Euric had to force himself to keep his face from showing the roiling emotions that raged inside him. From the disgusted expression his *Lanistae* wore, he knew the senator's request to set him free had not been highly looked upon. That being the case, Euric thought it best not to show how much his freedom meant to him. He did not need his *Lanistae* to think of some reason to punish him for his windfall.

Clearing his throat, Euric nodded once. "Who shall I fight in the next *munera*?"

His *Lanistae* gave him a sneering smile. "Why Calix, of course. Defeating you in your last match as a gladiator and reclaiming his *primus palus* status will more than make up for the defeat he suffered today. Since it will not be a death match, you do not have a problem with allowing Calix to reclaim what should be his?"

"No, *Lanistae*."

If his *Lanistae* wanted him to take the fall and allow the Roman to once more be the first sword, Euric had no problem with that. After this next fight, he would not be a part of this world anymore. What did he care? If his *Lanistae* expected him to allow Calix to beat him into a bloody pulp while doing it, that Euric would not allow.

"Good. I am glad we understand each other. You can return to your cell now."

Euric waited until he was once more locked inside his cell before he allowed himself to feel any kind of excitement over the prospect of finding his freedom. Being presented with his rudis at the end of his match at the *Amphitheatrum* while the mob cheered in the stands was all the reward he wanted for the years he'd had to serve as a gladiator. His freedom was so close, he could almost taste it.

He thought of Petra and how she would react once she learned he would be a free man come this time next week. She would be as pleased with the news as he was. He would able to go home, go back to his tribe and see his family. His mother and father had still been alive when he had been captured by the Romans. Since they had only been able to have Euric, his parents would be overjoyed at the return of their only offspring.

The smile he wore slowly left Euric's face when he thought of something else. If he had the chance to return to Germania, he could not see himself making the choice to stay and be with Petra in her time. As his parents' only son and child, he needed to stay by them, to be there when they had need of him. He could not abandon them. He had already been gone for too many years as it was.

He did not want to lose Petra. Making love to her earlier had proven how much he wanted her for himself. Just the thought of her ever being with another man made him want to commit mayhem. If he returned to his tribe, giving her up was precisely what he would have to do. He could not expect her to remain celibate for the rest of her life just because he was no longer with her.

He pushed the thought of Petra being in another man's

arms away. There was no point feeling jealous over something that had not happened. Euric still had time to make his decision. He had a choice to make. Either he returned to his parents—who probably had already accepted his no longer being with them—or leave Petra and yearn for what could have been. It was one decision he did not relish.

* * * *

Present Day

Petra answered the door to find Lia standing outside the mansion, holding out a magnum of wine a half hour before she was expected to arrive.

Petra arched a brow. "You're early." She took the wine from Lia. "Do you intend to get me drunk and take advantage of me?"

Lia stepped inside. "What can I say, the curiosity was killing me. I figured you wouldn't mind if I showed up a little early. And sorry, I'm not that hard up…Yet. I still like my lovers to be built like brick shithouses and have a dick between their legs, thank you very much."

Petra laughed. "You do have a way with words, Lia."

Crossing the foyer, Petra brought Lia to the kitchen. She took two wineglasses out of one of the cupboards and then found a corkscrew in one of the drawers. Lia's gaze watched her every move. It wasn't hard to tell that Lia was anxiously waiting for Petra to start talking about why she'd wanted her to come over.

Once Petra had poured each of them a glass of wine and given one to Lia, her friend didn't remain silent any longer. "Okay, we have our wine. Now talk."

"How about we take the wine upstairs first, then I'll talk about him."

"Come on, Petra, this has been driving me nuts all

afternoon. You know how I hate being left out."

After she picked up the wine bottle, Petra headed out of the kitchen to the stairs. Lia fell into step beside her. "Tell me about it. Any little secret I had when we were in school you'd practically go insane until I told you. I thought you would have grown out of that by now."

"Well, you thought wrong."

Once they reached the guest bedroom, Petra put the bottle of wine on the nightstand next to the side of the bed she sat on. She patted the mattress next to her. "I won't make you wait any longer. You just have to promise me you won't laugh or phone one of your doctor friends at the hospital to come and lock me away in the psycho ward."

Lia sat down. "You have my word. Now spill your guts already."

"What would you say if I told you I've seen the past?"

"I've seen the past too, and it was just yesterday," Lia said with a snort.

Petra shook her head. "I don't mean the immediate past. I mean the past as in ancient times past."

Lia's brows drew together. "How far back are you talking about?"

"Ancient Rome. The fourth century to be exact."

"Fourth century Rome? You want me to believe you've somehow seen fourth century Rome?"

"I said you'd have to keep an open mind."

Lia took a big sip of her wine before she said anything else. "Jesus, Petra, I didn't think I'd have to have *that* open of a mind. Being able to see the past is impossible. There is no such thing as time machines."

"I never said it was a time machine that let me see the past. The best way to describe it is to call it a window. It's one that's letting me see fourth century Rome." Deciding to just jump in with both feet, Petra took a big sip from her wineglass and then said, "I met a man from that time, Lia. A gorgeous, mouthwatering man who I want so much I can't think of anything else but him."

Her friend stared at her as if she tried to see if Petra was all there or not. "Let me get this straight. You met a Roman from the fourth century that you want to screw your brains out with?"

"Euric isn't a Roman. He's a Visigoth warrior who was captured in battle and was forced to become a gladiator."

The mouthful of wine Lia had just taken sprayed out of her mouth. She coughed and wiped her chin with her palm. Petra wiped what hit her off her arm.

"You're kidding, right? You want to knock boots with an ancient gladiator? Are you sure you haven't watched that movie *Gladiator* one too many times and can't separate reality from fantasy?"

"Of course I know what's real and what isn't. Euric is real."

"And how would you know that?" Lia eyed her. "Unless you already had sex with him."

"Well…" Petra gave Lia a sheepish look, but soon regretted it when she got hit with another spray of wine. "Would you cut that out? The wine is for drinking, not spraying me with."

Lia downed what remained in her wineglass and then got off the bed to pour herself another one. "Hearing your best friend has been having sex with a hunky gladiator from ancient Rome tends to make a girl do that. I have to tell you, Petra, that I'm having a really hard time believing any of what you said is true."

"I'd prove it to you if I could. The window, whatever it is, tends to be a bit temperamental. It seems to open when it wants. At least I think it does. I don't think Euric and I have any control over when it appears. Even if I could get it to open, I have a feeling you wouldn't be able to see it, anyway. I know when someone in his time came into his cell when I was talking to him through the window that person couldn't see it."

Sitting on the edge of the bed next to Petra, Lia said, "So I may or may not be able to see this window if it decided to appear when you wanted it to. And you not only can see this Euric but you slept with him as well. How did you manage that? Unless you went to his time or he came through to ours."

"He came to ours."

Lia blew out a breath and shook her head while she chuckled. "You got laid and then he just up and went back to his own time? How romantic."

"It wasn't like that. He felt as if he were being pulled back into the window, as if he were compelled to step through it." Petra couldn't keep the irritation she felt out of her voice. Lia had to know she wasn't the type of woman to sleep with a man and then let him just run out on her once the act was completed.

Lia shook her head. "Okay, relax. Don't get your panties in a bunch. I didn't mean anything by it. I was just trying to lighten things up. How about you start from the beginning? Tell me when you first saw the window. Maybe it'll help me to believe what you're saying."

Petra took a deep breath. "All right. I noticed something strange when I first held Mr. Dunn's rudis."

"The one you manhandled the other night while I was over?"

"Yes. When I touched it, I felt some kind of energy jolt through me. It wasn't until I picked it up did the window first appear. Then it was only the size of a large beach ball, but it was large enough for me to get my first glimpse of Euric."

"Did he see you?"

Petra couldn't stop the blush that heated her cheeks. "Let's say he was otherwise occupied at the time and didn't see me at first, but he did in the end. Shocked that he could, I dropped the rudis and the window closed."

Lia looked at Petra closely. "By otherwise occupied, you

mean he was with another woman?"

"He's a gladiator. They had groupies just like movie stars of today. The only difference is Euric was chained to the wall while the woman was with him."

"A hunky gladiator naked and chained to a wall while a woman gets to have her way with him. Sounds like the stuff of my best sexual fantasies."

Petra rolled her eyes. "Can you keep on topic? And stop thinking dirty thoughts about my man."

"All right, all right. I'll try to keep my mind out of the gutter. So when you touch the rudis, it opens the window for you?"

"Not now. It only did that the first or second time. I no longer need to hold the rudis for it to appear. It just does."

"Weird," Lia said. "Hold up a second. You said Euric is in ancient Rome. How are you able to understand him? I know for a fact you don't know how to speak Latin, or whatever language the Visigoths spoke."

"That's the funny thing. I couldn't understand him until we touched our hands together on either side of the window. We got another jolt and then we understood what we said to each other."

"It sounds as if this time window of yours is more than just a window into the past if it did that," Lia said slowly. "So you don't need the rudis anymore to see Euric. Has there been a time when you wanted the window to open and it just did?"

"Yeah, but not every time. At least I don't think so. I know I wanted to see Euric this morning, but it didn't cooperate. Maybe that could have been because he wouldn't have been there. He fought in a *munera* in the early afternoon. Plus, we had a bit of a disagreement the night before."

"If you guys had a bit of a tiff, maybe Euric didn't want to see you until the fight had ended."

"Maybe." Petra frowned. "What are you getting at, Lia?

You have that look on your face that says you're thinking about something deep."

"I'm wondering if this window only opens when either you or Euric want it to. Maybe the two of you are able to influence it a tiny bit. I bet you were thinking you wished you could understand Euric before you and he touched the window."

"I did." Petra sat up straighter. "Now that I think about it, the window became the size of a large doorway when I told Euric I wished he could touch me."

"I think we're on to something here." Lia took Petra's wineglass from her and put it on the nightstand. "Let's test our theory. How about you stand in the middle of the room and tell the window you want to see Euric?"

Petra shook her head. "That won't work. I tried demanding it to open once and got nowhere."

"Then ask it politely, for Christ's sake. Just do it."

Petra walked to the center of the room after she slipped off the bed. "Here goes nothing. Can I please see Euric?"

Just like that, the window formed and when the mist cleared Petra saw Euric sitting on his bed, smiling.

"Petra, I did not think I would see you again today," Euric said while his gaze looked past her to Lia. "You are not alone."

"It's okay, Euric. This is my best friend, Lia. I told her about you and the window. Why don't you come meet her?" Petra tried to put her hand through the window, but she hit some kind of barrier. "Damn, I guess it doesn't want you to come through it again."

Lia cleared her throat. "I take it the window opened and you're talking to Euric?"

Petra turned to look at her friend. "Yes, I was going to bring Euric through so you could see him, but the window isn't letting me. It usually lets me reach over to his time. Euric has never been able to."

She turned back and saw frustration etched on Euric's

face. Petra really wanted Lia to be able to meet him. With her hand still held against the window, she wished she could get the window to let Lia see that it was actually real.

The sound of Lia spraying another mouthful of wine behind her had Petra looking over her shoulder at her again. "If you don't stop doing that I'm going to have to steam clean the rug in here."

Lia got to her feet and stood next to her. "Ah, Petra, did you happen to ask the window to let me see Euric?"

"Not out loud. I thought it." She followed Lia's gaze and noticed she stared right at him. "You can see him now?"

"Yes." Out of the side of her mouth, she said quietly, "You weren't kidding when you said Euric was mouthwatering."

Petra elbowed her. "Stop it or he'll hear you."

"Hear what?" Euric asked. "I can't understand your friend."

She looked to Lia. "Can you understand Euric?"

Her friend shook her head. "No. He's speaking in Latin, dude. I don't know it anymore than you do."

"Let's see if I can get the window to work so you can."

Lia squeezed Petra's arm before she said anything more. "Hold up. Why don't we really give this thing a test? Instead of just asking it to allow me to understand Euric, and he me, why don't you ask it to make him able to understand and speak English."

Petra nodded and turned back to meet Euric's gaze. She knew he'd only understood half the conversation between her and Lia. "Lia has a theory about the window. So far, it has done what we thought it'd do. We're going to give it a bigger test and see if it will allow you to be able to understand and speak the language Lia and I speak."

"It may not work, Petra," Euric said.

"I know, but at least it's worth a shot." Petra cleared her

throat. "Okay, here I go. I wish Euric was fluent in English."

A big jolt of energy shot through her hand where she still held it against the window. She and Euric jumped back at the same time. Petra shook her hand. "Dammit, that hurt."

"It hurt worse than the first time it did it," Euric said as he rubbed his hand against his thigh.

Lia let out a whoop. "I totally understand him now. He's speaking English."

Petra looked at Euric to find him looking at her with longing in his eyes. There was also something else lurking in them as well. He looked at her as if he wanted to hold her and never let her go.

Her brows drew together. "Is something wrong, Euric?"

He quickly shook his head. "No."

"Your wound doesn't feel as if it's getting infected, does it?"

Euric put his hand on the white bandage that still encircled his right biceps. "I told you it is nothing. It is just a sword slice and it is not very deep."

Lia practically elbowed Petra out of the way as she walked over to stand in front of Euric. "You were wounded during your fight? Take off that bandage and let me have a look at it," she said in her best nurse's voice.

Eruic grinned and looked at Petra. "Is she always this bossy?"

"Sorry to say, yes," she said with a laugh. "In this instance, you should listen to her. Even though I treated it with some antibiotic ointment, I'd feel better if she looked at it as well. Lia is a nurse."

With a nod, Euric undid the knot on the bandage and unwound it from around his arm. While Lia got him to move closer to give her a better look at it, Petra watched Euric. There had been something in his eyes, almost a sadness lurking just under the surface. She hadn't imagined it. He held something back. Lia being there, she couldn't exactly press the issue, but once she had him through the window and all to herself, Petra would get it out of him.

CHAPTER EIGHT

The next evening Petra sat on the bed in the guest bedroom with some of the clothes she'd bought Euric spread out on it. Tonight she planned to show him a little bit of her world. Knowing she'd have to ease him into it, she decided to let him walk around outside in the backyard of the mansion, and if he was game for it, she'd take him for a drive in her car around the block. After cutting the tags off a pair of black shorts and a gray t-shirt, she put them aside and added a pair of boxer-brief underwear to the pile.

She was anxious to see Euric again. She hadn't seen him all day. After he'd spent a few hours talking with her and Lia through the window, he'd eventually told them he had to get some sleep. He'd said he'd have a full, hard day of training, and that if Petra decided to open the window during that time, he wouldn't be in his cell. She had no idea if it would allow her to see him anywhere else, so she hadn't even bothered trying to get it to open.

Now that they'd figured out that in some small way they each were controlling it, Petra had decided she'd have it stay open for as long as she wanted it to. It'd closed the night before only because Euric had wanted to go to bed. Keeping in mind wording was also the key, she'd had all day to figure out what she'd say to get the window to cooperate.

Satisfied with the clothes she'd picked out for Euric, Petra went to the center of the room. "All right, window. I wish for Euric to cross over to my time, spend the night with me while you stay open so he can return to his time before the guards open his cell in the morning." If this worked, she'd decided she'd ask the window to do this every night for as long as it'd let her.

The window appeared a few seconds after Petra had finished speaking. She found Euric standing in the middle of his cell, waiting for her. With a smile, she reached through it and took his hand. "Will you come over to my time again, Euric?"

He hesitated. "I want to, but I don't want the window to shut."

"It won't. When I asked for it to let me see you, I also said I wished for it to stay open so you could spend the night with me and return to your time in the morning." The heated look Euric gave her made Petra's breath catch.

"In that case, how can I say no?"

Euric walked through the window and took Petra into his arms. The length of his erection pressed against her stomach as he pulled her close. Her nipples tightened and an ache throbbed between her legs in response. Just like that, thoughts of taking him outside fled her mind. The idea of getting him out of his tunic so she could explore every inch of his body replaced them.

Euric bent and nuzzled the side of her neck, and Petra moaned softly at the feel of his lips against her skin. He ground his hard cock against her, making her pussy grow wetter by the second. She decided to make one valiant attempt to get back on track before she lost the ability to think completely.

"Ah, Euric. I thought... God, that feels good." While Petra had spoken, Euric had brought his hands down to her bottom and lifted her slightly so his erection came in contact with where she ached the most. "Ah...ah, I thought I'd take you outside so you can see a bit of my time."

Euric kissed the corner of her mouth. "Later. Right now I need to be inside you. All day I did nothing but think about you. I almost embarrassed myself a few times on the training ground with my wayward thoughts. All the sword practice I did today did nothing to make me want you less."

Petra shivered. Her arousal pounded through her. She wrapped her arms around Euric's neck and rubbed her pussy against his cock, causing them both to moan. "I can always take you outside later."

"Later sounds good." Euric covered her mouth with his.

Getting lost in his kiss, Petra dropped her arms from around his neck and down his front to his rope belt. With nimble fingers, she undid it and let it fall to the floor. She took hold of the bottom of his tunic and pulled it up his body. Euric lifted his head only long enough for her to tug it over it before he returned to feast on her mouth once again.

Having Euric's hard, naked body against hers had Petra pulling at her clothes. With his help, they had her t-shirt and shorts gone and soon they were skin-to-skin. While he licked and sucked at her mouth, she ran her hands down his wide chest and washboard abs to his fully erect cock. The feel of him, hard and heavy, caused wetness to leak between her thighs. She wanted him buried deep inside her, knowing how good it would feel.

Petra pulled away from Euirc's mouth as she pumped her hand up and down his shaft. She kissed her way down his chin and throat to his chest. In between placing kisses across his hard pecs, she said, "There has been something

I've been dying to do since I first saw you."

"And what would that be?" Euric asked gruffly.

She smiled against his skin. "Something I'm sure both of us will enjoy."

Deciding action was better than words, Petra slowly kissed her way lower on his body. Euric's cock jerked in her hand when she went on her knees and dragged her tongue across his well-defined abs. She looked up and found him watching her, his blue eyes dilated with arousal. His chest rapidly rose and fell with each breath he took. Knowing she had this kind of effect over him pushed her own arousal even higher.

With their gazes locked, Petra kept a firm grip on his cock and licked the single bead of pre-cum that sat on the very tip. Euric moaned loudly. She circled the head with her tongue. His hips jerked forward, pressing himself closer to her mouth.

She dropped her gaze and focused her attention on what she held. With no other preliminaries, she opened her mouth and took him inside. Euric half groaned, half moaned as she sucked. While she moved up and down on him, he rocked his hips in time. His cock grew even harder, making more wetness pool between her legs.

Petra continued to pleasure Euric in this way until he pulled at her arm. Releasing him, she stood once again. He wrapped an arm around her waist as he dipped his head and sucked one of her nipples into his mouth. He picked her up and carried her to the bed. He roughly pushed the clothes on it onto the floor before he placed her in the center and came down on top her.

More than ready to have him inside her, Petra spread her legs and pushed down when the head of his cock brushed against her wet core. With one thrust of his hips, Euric joined their bodies. He pulled back only to sink back inside her to the hilt. She put her legs around his waist and held on while he pumped in and out of her. Her orgasm built. It wouldn't take much to send her soaring over the edge into bliss.

Euric rode her faster. While he rested his weight on one bent arm, his other hand moved to where they were joined and stroked her clit. "Come for me, Petra," he said huskily against her lips. "I want to hear your cries of desire when your body takes mine."

His words and the extra caressing were enough to send Petra into an intense climax. She cried out with a whimpered moan as wave after wave of pleasure hit her. Once it started to recede, Euric pulled his still-hard cock out of her and urged her onto her stomach. With his hands on her hips, he got her up onto her hands and knees. After moving between her spread thighs, he positioned his cock and pushed himself home.

Petra gasped when he moved. In this position, she took him even deeper. As he stroked in and out, another orgasm built. She squeezed down on his cock with her inner walls, which wrung moans out of them. She pushed back to meet each of his thrusts and his shaft grew even harder.

Euric worked his cock faster inside her welcoming body. Their harsh breathing filled the room, along with their moans of pleasure. Just as Petra reached another peak, he surged into her one last time and stiffened. With his hands on her hips, he held her still while his erection pulsed deep inside her, filling her with his cum.

Out of breath and satiated, Petra shifted to lie on her side once Euric pulled out of her. He spooned around her, placing an arm along her waist and a leg between her own. She caressed his arm. The sex seemed to get better and better every time they came together. It also made how she felt about him stronger.

As Euric relaxed, she turned her head to look at him over her shoulder. "Hey, no sleeping. At least not yet, anyway."

The arm around her waist shifted and Euric reached up to cover her breast. "Are you sure you would not like to continue what I am trying to start?"

Petra took his hand off her breast and linked their fingers together. "Enough of that. And no, not right now. Later, after we've had our time outside."

She lifted his arm and slipped off the bed. Deciding she'd clean up a bit first before she got dressed again, Petra crossed the room to the en suite. She turned to shut the door and jumped when she found Euric right behind her.

He pushed past her and walked into the en suite. "What is this chamber used for?"

"It's a bathroom. It's where you can take a bath or shower, and the, um, toilet is used for taking care of other personal business."

Euric turned to face her. "Show me how everything works."

"I'll show you how the shower and bath work, but you aren't going to watch me use the toilet."

Petra stepped around him and headed to the bathtub. She slid the glass shower door open before she leaned in and turned on the water. Euric walked over to stand beside her. Once she had the water the right temperature, she turned on the shower.

Euric held his hand under the spray. "It's like a warm waterfall," he said with some awe.

"We call it a shower. It's a lot easier to wash your hair in than a bath, at least if you have long hair like I do." Euric shifted to step into the tub, but Petra stopped him before he could. "You don't usually get into the shower from this side. We don't want to get water all over the floor."

She closed that side of the glass door and then opened the other for him. After Euric got inside, she closed it again and went back out into the bedroom to get him a clean towel from the closet. Once she returned to the en suite,

119

she saw Euric standing with his head under the spray. She grabbed her bottle of shampoo and conditioner along with her bar of soap from the counter and brought them over.

Petra opened the shower door at the end of the tub. "Do you want to wash your hair?" Before she knew what Euric intended, he swung around and lifted her into the tub with him. "I only brought one towel."

Pulling her under the spray with him, Euric said, "That is okay. We can share. Will you wash my hair for me, Petra?"

With Euric standing there, his muscular body slick-looking from the water, Petra knew she wouldn't be able to tell him no. She nodded, then put the bottles she carried onto the side of the tub and the bar of soap in the soap dish. Knowing full well where this would eventually lead, she picked up the shampoo bottle and squeezed some into her hand. He bent his head slightly when she asked him to so she could reach and worked it into the length of his hair. The expression of pleasure he wore while she massaged his scalp told her he was more than enjoying this. As did the fact that his cock had hardened once more.

Petra managed to keep her hands to herself while she finished washing Euric's hair. Once she'd used the conditioner and had him rinse it out, she picked up the bar of soap. That was when she got sidetracked again. By the time she turned off the shower, she'd shown her ancient gladiator how good it could be to make love inside it.

* * * *

Euric eyed the piece of clothing Petra held up for him to take. "You want me to wear that under those short leggings?"

The boxer-brief underwear, as Petra had called them, looked far from being comfortable. She had said all the men of her time wore them, but he had to wonder why they would. The underwear could not possibly have enough room in them for their manhoods.

"Yes, and they aren't call short leggings. They're just called shorts. I bought you some boxers as well, but I don't think you'd like wearing them with shorts. Just try them. You may like them."

He highly doubted it, but he took them anyway and pulled them on the way Petra had shown him. He did not want to disappoint her after she had gone to the trouble of getting him clothes from her time. Much to Euric's surprise they were not as binding as he had first thought.

He held his arms out at his sides. "How do I look?"

Petra gazed up and down his body with feminine interest clearly showing in her eyes. "Good. Really, really good. You look like an underwear model. If other women saw you just in your underwear, you'd have to beat them off with a stick. Or I would have to do something extremely nasty to them."

Euric smiled. He liked the possessive way Petra had spoken. "You do not have to worry. I will not be walking around in front of other women dressed like this."

"I should hope not unless you want me to do something extremely nasty to *you*. Here," Petra held out the shorts, "put these on."

He pulled them on over the underwear. The shorts he found to be very comfortable. And when he pulled on the short-sleeved, very short tunic that Petra called a t-shirt, Euric liked the fit of it as well.

Now dressed, he looked at Petra. "Do I look like a man from your time?"

She nodded. "Very much so. And I have to say you look extremely hot in those shorts and t-shirt, if I do say so myself. I must have guessed right on the sizes, after all."

Euric frowned. "I do not feel hot. It feels cool in here."

Petra laughed. "I guess you being fluent in English doesn't include you being able to understand slang. When

I called you hot, I meant you look sexy, as in I'd jump your bones, take you to bed."

He gave her a grin that said he was more than willing to go to bed with her. "Well, it is just over there."

Petra held up her hands. "Oh no. You're not going to distract me again." She took his arm and led him to a large piece of furniture that had several drawers in it. "Let's go to the dresser so you can take a look at yourself in the mirror."

Euric looked into the large mirror that was attached to the dresser. He had not really looked at it before. He had been more interested in seeing Petra than the furnishings. Reaching out, he touched the mirror in front of him. It was so clear it almost looked like a sheet of thin ice, and it reflected back a perfect image of him. He stared, taking in the clothes he wore and his appearance. Since becoming a gladiator he had bulked up a bit. His muscles looked more defined. The almost constant training had obviously made him stronger.

Euric met Petra's gaze in the mirror. "I have never seen a mirror before. Only the very rich can afford one, but even they do not have one of this quality."

She smiled and put an arm around his waist. "Mirrors are pretty cheap now, and they're made out of glass instead of polished metal."

He touched the mirror again. "I never would have guessed that it was made out of glass. It looks like a sheet of ice."

Petra led him back to the bed. "Take a seat. I didn't know what size your feet were so I guessed when I bought the sandals." She picked up two black pieces of footwear that sort of resembled the leather sandals he wore in his time.

Euric took them from her and tried to put them on his feet, but he could not quite figure out how they would go on. Petra took them from him and knelt to show him how to loosen the straps enough that he could slip his foot inside. They turned out to be a perfect fit.

He stood and took a few steps in them. They were heavier than he was used to his sandals being. "You guessed right again."

Petra got up on her feet. "Good. Now let's get out of here for a bit."

Linking their fingers together, Petra led Euric out of the bedroom and then down the long set of stairs to an entranceway that he was sure would far outrival one found in the emperor's palace. He stared at the large light that hung suspended from the ceiling. Colors of the rainbow reflected off the pieces of glass where the light hit it.

He looked at her when Petra tugged on his hand. "The man you work for must be very rich indeed if he can afford a home such as this."

She walked him toward a door at the end of the entranceway. "You could say that. Mr. Dunn has done well for himself over the years. I know I could never in a million years be able to afford a place like this. Sorry to say, but in a couple nights, you'll have to put up with being in my small apartment."

Euric pulled Petra to a stop and caressed her cheek with the back of his fingers. "Where you live is a palace compared to my cell. As long as you are with me, I do not care where we are."

She stood on tiptoe and placed a soft kiss on his lips. "As long as you're with me I'm happy as well."

Petra pulled him forward before she opened the door and motioned for him to step outside ahead of her. She shut it behind her and then walked him a short distance away once she got him to turn around. The building they had exited was like nothing he had ever seen before. Instead of being made out of stone, it was made out of bricks unlike any he had come across. Glass windows dotted the front of the building. The roof was made out of some material he had no name for. Large and sprawling, the building took up a lot of land.

"Let's go to the backyard," Petra said as she got him moving once again.

They walked around the building to the back of it. Lights shining from inside and ones on the outside chased away the darkness enough for Euric to see the large gardens and stretch of green grass. Given how exact and neat they were, and the shortness of the grass, he had a feeling this was done by man and not by nature.

He looked at the night sky. The stars did not seem as bright as when he looked at them a while back in his village at home. A blinking red light that moved across the stars caught his attention. It was very high up and seemed to be moving quite fast.

He pointed to it. "What is that light? It can't be a star."

Petra lifted her head to look where he pointed. "It isn't. It's an airplane. Remember I showed you a picture of one on my laptop?"

"Yes, but it looked so much larger than that dot in the sky. It cannot possibly be the same thing."

"Well, it is. The plane is just so high up it appears small to us. There are probably over a hundred people in it, flying to some faraway place."

Euric was sure the horror he felt had to be showing on his face when he looked at Petra. "You mean people are in it right now?"

"Yes. It's the fastest way to travel very long distances. They say it's safer to travel by airplane than a car."

"How can that be safe? Do they not ever fall out of the sky?"

"There are airplane crashes, some bad enough that all the passengers and crew die, but that doesn't happen very often when compared to the number that take to the sky every day."

He looked back up at the fast moving red light. "I do not think I would like to go on an airplane. I would much rather face down a hundred enemy warriors on my own than go up in the sky in one of your airplanes."

"There are people who are afraid to fly. Me, I'm not one of them. I've flown on an airplane a few times and there was nothing scary about it. Once you've done it, you'll see it isn't all that bad."

There may not be a chance of him ever having to face flying on an airplane if he chose to stay in his time. He had not told Petra yet about his being set free in a week's time, or the fact that he would have to fight one last match in the *munera* to get it. Given how badly she had reacted to the idea of his fighting in the last one, he did not think it would be a good idea to bring the subject up just yet. He did not want to put a dark shadow on the time they were spending together now. If he did decide to return to his tribe, he wanted only good memories of Petra to take home with him.

As Petra tugged on his hand to get him to walk back to the front of the building, Euric thought again of how much he would be giving up if he turned his back on her. Just being with her made him feel as if everything in his world had become right and good. She lightened his soul, made him feel like a whole man. If he walked away now, he had a feeling he would be leaving a piece of his heart behind.

*

Petra led Euric to the opposite side of the mansion to where she had her Camry parked outside the large four-car garage. She turned expectantly toward him. "How would you like to go for a ride in my car?"

Euric let go of her hand and walked closer to the Camry. He ran his hand along its hood. "This is one of the horseless chariots you showed me."

"Yes. I think you'll like riding in a car. It stays on the ground so it shouldn't bother you as much as the thought of riding in an airplane did."

"People ride around in cars all the time?"

"Yes. We'll just go on a short ride."

"All right. I would like to see how it works."

Petra fished her car keys out of the front pocket of her jean shorts. She walked around the back end of her Camry and then unlocked the passenger door. Once Euric stood at her side, she opened it and motioned for him to get inside. He cautiously sat on the seat. After he was settled, she put the seatbelt around him before she shut the door. She quickly went to the driver's side and got in. Belted in, she put the key in the ignition and started it.

Euric jumped at the sound of the engine turning over. "It sounds as if there is some kind of animal inside it."

She chuckled. "That's the engine, the thing that makes the car run. Believe me, my old Camry is far from being the most powerful car out there, but as long as it gets me from point A to point B I can't complain."

Petra put the car into reverse, backed it up and then steered down the long driveway. At the end of it, she put on her indicator to turn right and pulled out onto the street. Able now to drive faster, she took a quick look at Euric. He had his gaze pinned to the front windshield.

"How are you doing over there?" she asked.

"It is much faster than a chariot."

"This is relatively slow compared to the speed I can drive on the expressway."

Hoping there weren't any cops around, Petra decided to give Euric a little demonstration on how much faster a car could go. She hit the accelerator and shot down the street well over the speed limit. She came to a stop sign and slowed to a stop. She glanced at him and found him bracing one hand on the dashboard while he held on to the armrest in a death grip.

Petra slowly turned onto one of the streets that would take her around the block and back to the mansion. "Are you okay, Euric?"

He didn't move or as much as turn his head toward her. "I did not expect it to go so fast so quickly," Euric said tightly.

"Sorry about that. I guess I should have warned you first. That wasn't even the fastest I can drive. You'll get used to driving in a car. It's more convenient than having to walk everywhere." Euric's grip didn't loosen. She added, "Maybe it'd be better if you look out the side window instead of the front."

Once he did as she had suggested, Euric seemed to relax by slow degrees. He dropped his hand from the dashboard, but kept his grip on the armrest. After a few seconds, he said, "The buildings here seem very large."

"This is a rich part of the city. All of Los Angeles doesn't look like this. There are some rather poor parts of it that I wouldn't want to set foot in, but all in all, it's a great city."

After arriving back at the mansion, Petra spotted Lia's car in front of the garage. She parked her Camry next to Lia's blue Ford Escort. Lia wasn't in the car, but Petra spotted her walking toward them from where she'd been standing near the front of the mansion.

She showed Euric how to undo his seatbelt and open the car door before she climbed out and met Lia halfway. "What are you doing here? I thought you'd be at home, catching up on your sleep."

Ignoring Petra's question, Lia looked around her at Euric. "Holy shit, he looks even better out of the window. And dressed like that, oh Mama."

Petra waved in front of Lia's face. "Hello? I'm standing right here. You're ogling my man like you would a big piece of chocolate."

Lia tore her gaze off Euric and looked at Petra. "Come

on, Petra. The man is hot. I'm only looking and I promise not to touch — much."

Euric came to stand at Petra's side and wrapped his arm around her waist. "Nice to see you again, Lia. Petra did not say anything about you coming for a visit."

"That's because she didn't know. I just decided to drop by on the off chance Petra had managed to get you through the window again." She nodded toward his bandaged right arm. "I thought I'd take a better look at that arm of yours." Lia held up the small plastic bag she carried. "I even brought some supplies if you need something for infection."

"The physician looked at my wound this morning and changed the dressing. He said I was healing nicely."

Petra put her arm around Euric's waist and started them walking toward the front door of the mansion. Lia fell into step on his other side. "Lia is using your wound as an excuse to come over uninvited."

Lia snorted. "I am not. You know the medical standards in Euirc's time aren't anywhere near ours. I'd hate for him to get an infection or gangrene and have to lose his arm when I could have fixed it before it got that bad."

"His wound is not *that* bad, Lia. You're being a bit extreme," Petra said with a laugh.

"Who's the nurse around here, huh?" Lia asked. "The last time I looked you hadn't been to nursing school. I'll be the judge of how bad his wound his."

Petra let go of Euric's waist and took out the other set of keys she'd stuffed into her pocket before leaving and unlocked the front door. Once they were all inside the foyer, she turned to Euric. "You don't mind if Lia does take a look at it? She's here now, and I know from past experience that she won't back down until she's done what she thinks needs doing."

"No, I don't mind," Euric said.

Lia took Euric by the arm and led him toward the

kitchen. Petra had to smile. Even though Lia was half his size, she'd already taken control and had him answering the rapid-fire questions she asked about what the physician in his time had said about his wound. Following, Petra couldn't really complain about Lia's unexpected visit. After all, if he did come to live in the present with her, Petra wanted her best friend and her boyfriend to get along. This would just be one more step in introducing him to what he'd be missing out on if he decided to stay in ancient Rome.

CHAPTER NINE

L ia had thoroughly examined Euric's wound and applied some more antibiotic ointment to it before she bandaged it with tape and gauze. The original cloth bandage, which had gotten wet while he had taken a shower, had been set aside to dry for when he had to return to his time.

Euric had been intrigued by how the tape stuck to his skin and had kept pulling at the edges while Lia had bandaged him up. Petra had had to bite her lip to stop herself from laughing when Lia kept slapping his hand away while threatening to duct tape his other arm to his side if he didn't leave it alone. It wasn't so much the threat she'd found funny, but the sheepish look he'd given Lia when she'd given him her best reprimanding stare.

Once Lia had finished with Euric, they'd all moved upstairs to the guest bedroom to watch some TV. Since the king-sized bed was large enough for all three of them to sit on, Petra sat in the middle between Lia and him. Lia and she took turns explaining all the different shows Petra flipped through to him. They had the hard job of trying to explain how the pictures got onto the television. Since neither one of them knew the technical aspects of it or cable, for that matter, they'd done their best to answer the million and one questions he had asked.

After finding an older romantic comedy movie, they'd settled back to watch it. Euric had seemed to enjoy it, but about halfway through he'd slouched down on the bed. With his head on her stomach and his arm around her waist, he'd fallen asleep.

Looking down at Euric, Petra stroked a lock of hair off his forehead. He didn't stir. She looked up to find Lia watching her. "He's zonked out."

Lia smiled. "You love him." She said it as a statement rather than a question.

"I think so," Petra replied slowly.

"Have you told him yet?"

"No."

"Why not?"

"I'm afraid to."

"Why?"

"Because I'm not sure Euric feels the same way about me. Plus, I don't want him to think I'm only saying it to convince him to stay in our time. I want the decision to be his."

Lia shook her head. "Stop being so blind, Petra. The man loves you. I've seen the way he looks at you. I'd be very much surprised if his feelings weren't as strong as yours. He seems like a great guy, even though he is way, way too old for you being from the past and all. And who says you have to play fair? If you want to keep him, don't hold anything back."

"And if later on down the road he regrets his decision and blames me for pushing him into doing something he really hadn't wanted to do?"

"It won't come to that. I think you two were meant to be together. If not, then why would that thing be here, giving you the chance to fall in love with a man who was born well over a thousand years ago?" Lia had nodded toward the window that still stood open on one side of the room while she'd spoken.

Petra turned her head to look at it. A candle still flickered inside Euric's cell, casting enough light for her to see the small bed, the stone floor and walls. She hated the thought that he had to exist in such conditions. The sight of the empty chains hanging from one of the walls was just a stark reminder of his being a slave. No one should have to live like that.

She looked back at Lia. "I keep asking myself that very question — would the window have appeared if Euric and I weren't meant to be together? I'd like to think it's here for that very reason. I don't know what I'll do if he decides he can't be with me here in our time."

"Stop thinking that way. You have to think positive thoughts and it'll work out in the end, Petra. You can be your biggest enemy if you let yourself believe you can't do something."

Petra chuckled. "Are you going to take up motivational speaking now?"

Lia rolled her eyes. "No, but I know what I'm talking about. I've seen it lots of times when we get some really serious cases in the ER. You can tell when someone has given up the fight to overcome what has happened to them. The ones who haven't tend to make a startling turnaround in their recoveries."

"So you think I should trick Euric into staying?"

"I never said that. What I meant was tell him exactly how you feel. Lay it all out on the table. Convince him that you aren't going anywhere, and that you two are better together than apart. At least that's what I'd do if I were in your situation. And screwing his brains out every night should help as well."

Petra laughed. "And here I thought you were all deep and insightful, then you had to go and say something like that."

Lia shrugged. "Hon, with a man like yours, sex would never be far from my mind. We'd be lucky if we ever came up for air."

"Don't you ever stop thinking about sex?"

"Sometimes," Lia said with a grin.

"I think you had to have been born a man in your other life."

"I'm not that bad." Lia shifted to the edge of the bed. "I'm going to leave you two lovebirds alone." When Petra shifted to try to get free of Euric, Lia stopped her. "You can stay there. I'll make sure to lock the door on my way out. He looks nice and comfortable where he is. I wouldn't want to disturb him. Just remember, sex is your friend."

Petra shook her head and laughed. "Yes, Nurse Feel Good. Oh, and Mr. Dunn will be home in a day or two. He said in his last email he didn't know if he'd need an extra day or not. So the next time you want to get together we'll have to either meet at my apartment or your place."

"I guess your week of being spoiled while you live in the lap of luxury is almost over. How will you ever adjust to living in your lowly apartment?"

She glanced down at Euric. "As long as I have a certain someone with me, I doubt I'll care."

Lia crossed to the door. Before she left, she said, "I'd better get out of here before you start making me wish for something I haven't found yet. Tell Euric I said bye."

Once Petra heard the front door close behind Lia, she flipped through the channels, content just to sit there with Euric snuggled against her side.

* * * *

Euric knew he was dreaming, but he could not get himself to wake up. It started off pleasant enough. He was with Petra and she looked at him with love showing in her

133

eyes. Seeing it made him feel as if he could take on the world. With her at his side, his life would be better for it.

He was about to tell Petra he loved her when the smile she wore disappeared and her eyes went flat as she looked at something behind him. Turning, he found his parents standing a short distance away. They looked as they had when he had gone to fight the Romans in the battle that had ultimately led to his being made a gladiator. His mother had tears in her eyes as she reached for him. His father, once one of the best warriors in their tribe, blinked as if he tried to hold back his emotions. Euric had taken a step toward his parents when he remembered Petra.

With the thought of introducing Petra to his parents, Euric turned back only to find she was no longer in front of him. She stood a few feet away in the arms of a faceless man. She had her head thrown back while the man appeared to be kissing the side of her neck. She moaned as the faceless man intimately ran his hands over her body.

A jealous rage built inside him, and Euric stalked toward Petra and the man, but with each step he took, he could not close the distance between them.

Hurt that she would let another man touch her while he was so near, Euric shouted, "Petra! You are mine."

She slowly turned her head in his direction while the faceless man continued to touch her. "You turned your back on me, Euric. What else would you have me do? You chose your parents over me. I gave you my love, and you threw it back in my face. I'm no longer yours."

A mist suddenly surrounded Petra and the faceless man until Euric no longer saw them. With a roar of anger, he ran toward where they had been and into what felt like a wall of glass. Using his fists, he pounded on it, but it remained solid and strong. He bellowed her name over and over, desperate to have her back.

Euric jolted awake at the feel of someone shaking him. His heart thundered and his throat felt raw as if he had been actually yelling. Blinking, he looked around the room, not seeing the familiar surroundings of his cell. A gentle hand stroked his cheek.

"It was only a bad dream, Euric."

He looked up to find Petra sitting next to him on the bed. The sight of her looking at him with gentle concern had him pulling her down onto the mattress next to him. He rolled her onto her back and came down on top her. He kissed her until she clutched at him and moaned into his mouth. He lifted his head and then buried his face in the crook of her neck, squeezing her to him.

Petra stroked the back of his head. "It's okay now. You had a nightmare. You were screaming my name as if you'd lost me or something. I'm right here and I'm not going to leave you."

Euric took a deep, shuddering breath. Petra's familiar scent filled his lungs. His heart slowly stopped racing. Finally, no longer feeling as if he had lost a part of himself, he said, "I love you, Petra."

She yanked on his hair until he lifted his head and looked at her. "I love you too, Euric." The love she felt for him shone in her eyes just as it had in his dream. "I don't want to lose you, but you have to be the one to decide whether we can be together or not."

Euric did not want to think about that right now. All that mattered was that Petra loved him. With the memory of his nightmare still fresh in his mind, he took her lips before she said anything more. He needed to be inside her, to claim her once again as his.

With hands that shook, he stripped them of their clothes. He stretched back on top Petra and took her mouth in a hungry kiss. He pushed his tongue past her lips and thoroughly tasted her. She twined hers with his and moaned into his mouth. The sound made his cock grow harder.

He rocked his hips against Petra, but did not enter her.

He left her mouth and cupped her breast while he swirled his tongue around her taut nipple. The bud tightened even more when he gently blew on it. She burrowed her hands into his hair and held him to her chest. Euric rubbed his cock along her slick pussy, wetting the length of him. He opened his mouth and sucked her nipple deep inside.

Petra arched her hips, trying to take him inside her body as he suckled at her breast. When he did not enter her, she pulled on his hair. "Now, Euric. I want you inside me now."

He released her nipple. He took hold of his cock and rubbed the head of it against Petra's clit. He looked deeply into her eyes. "Tell me you love me again."

She reached up and cupped his jaw. "I love you, Euric."

To hear Petra say those words sent an intense wave of pleasure through him. He brought the tip of his shaft to the opening of her body, and said, "I will always love you, Petra."

He slowly entered her, loving the feel of her body stretching to take his. Once she had taken him to the hilt, he slowly pulled back and then pushed back inside. Even though his body demanded he take her hard and fast, Euric slowly made love to Petra. He wanted to last as long as he could, to show her with his body how much she meant to him.

Hooking one of Petra's legs over his arm, he opened her wider. He angled his hips higher on her body so he stroked her in the right place to have her moaning. Her inner walls clamped around his shaft, increasing the pleasure he felt.

Euric pumped his hips faster and felt the first flutters of Petra's orgasm just before it crashed over her. As she let out a whimpered moan, he too found his release. He held her to him while his cock pulsed deep inside her and her pussy held him in a tight fist.

He collapsed onto Petra and kissed the side of her neck.

He shifted to move off her, knowing he had to be too heavy, but she wrapped her arms around his back.

Once he could breathe without puffing, he said, "I am too heavy."

"I don't mind.

"Well, I do."

Taking Petra with him, he rolled onto his back. She lay sprawled across him with her head pillowed on his chest. Euric managed to grab the covers without dislodging her and pulled them over them. As her body grew heavy and her eyes drifted shut, he closed his. Still feeling the effects of his bad dream, he held her close, needing the skin-to-skin contact. Before he fell asleep, he knew deep down inside he had already made the decision that would change his life forever.

* * * *

Just as dawn broke over the horizon, Euric came suddenly awake. Feeling the window pulling at him, he knew it was time to return to his cell. He gently shook Petra where she lay snuggled against him.

As she blinked open her eyes, he said, "I have to return to my time."

She quickly sat up. "Already? It can't be."

Euric gave her a hard kiss before he got out of bed. He crossed to the dresser where his folded tunica sat on top it. He pulled it on and then tied the belt around his waist. His gaze landed on the clothes Petra had bought for him, which lay discarded on the floor. They were not the clothes of a slave.

"Wait," Petra said as she jumped out of bed. "We have to take that bandage off before you go through the window."

He looked down at his arm and at the bandage Lia had replaced with his cloth one. Petra ran to the bathroom where they had left it to dry overnight. After she returned with it, he lifted a corner of the tape that held the other bandage to his skin and pulled it off. She quickly wrapped the cloth one around his arm and then tied it.

Ready to leave, Euric glanced at the window that stood open in the middle of the room. He looked at Petra and opened his arms. He closed them around her as she stepped into his embrace.

"I do not want to leave you, but I will come to you again tonight if the window allows it."

Petra snuggled closer. "I'll ask it to open the same way I did last night. I wish you'd stay, but I'm not going to beg."

Euric tipped her head up and gave her a thorough kiss before he stepped back. "I can feel the window pulling on me harder. Remember, I love you."

Petra wrapped her arms around herself. "I love you too. The night can't get here fast enough."

With one last look, he turned and walked through the window. Back in his cell, Euric watched it slowly close. Once it disappeared, he had to fight the almost overwhelming urge to call it back so he could return to Petra's time, but he was not ready yet to let go of his. He still had to fight once more in the *munera* before he started a new life with her. If he was going to leave everything he knew behind, he at least wanted his rudis as a symbol of what he had once been.

* * * *

With Euric in his time, Petra went back to bed, hoping to catch up on a few hours of sleep. Since it was a Saturday, and Mr. Dunn didn't expect her to work on the weekend, she really had no reason to be up early. She also needed the sleep after spending most of the night being thoroughly loved by Euric.

They'd fallen asleep after they'd made love right after

she'd awakened Euric from his bad dream. Petra had woken up a few hours later with the feel of his mouth and hands doing delicious things to her. He'd awoken her in that way twice more during the night.

Petra slept for a couple more hours before she rolled over and looked at the digital clock on the bedside table. It was just after ten. Stretching, she rolled out of bed and then headed for the en suite. She grimaced a bit when she felt aches in certain muscles she obviously hadn't been using much lately. A small smile played across her lips as she thought of how she'd ended up with those sore spots. She also knew those muscles would be getting a nightly workout. At least she hoped it'd be every night.

After turning on the shower, she stepped inside the tub and shut the glass shower door. While she washed her hair, Petra let her mind wander over the events of the night. She thought Euric's first introduction to the modern world had gone pretty well. He really hadn't balked at any of her suggestions, and had seemed genuinely interested in her time. If that interest meant there was a good chance he'd leave his old life to be with her in hers, she couldn't honestly say. Even though he'd told her he loved her, there was still no guarantee he'd want to give up everything he knew for her. She was asking a lot of him, and to be honest, if it was her, she didn't think she'd be able to take that final step and decide to live in a time that wasn't her own. The only way she could ever see herself doing that would be if his time was even further into the future than hers and offered a better life, which his right now decidedly did not.

Petra smiled, gushing inside as she replayed the memory of Euric telling her he loved her for the very first time. It'd be one moment she wouldn't soon forget. She'd only had one other man tell her he loved her, but she'd known it really hadn't been true love. He'd only said it because she'd put him on the spot. Thinking that was how she'd felt about him, she'd blurted it out over a meal inside a crowded restaurant. She'd known she'd made a mistake when the guy had looked as if she'd thrown a live rattlesnake in his face. He'd quickly looked around the restaurant and mumbled that he loved her too. Of course after that night, their relationship had gone steadily downhill.

Having Euric say those three little words first and then make love to her so passionately afterward, Petra knew without a doubt he'd meant them. Just as she meant them when she'd told him she loved him.

Finished in the shower, Petra turned it off and then stepped out to dry herself. She thought about the nightmare Euric had had. Her skin broke out in gooseflesh just thinking about the way he'd called out her name. His voice had been filled with hurt, longing and loss. He'd shouted to her as if he'd lost everything that had mattered to him. She shivered. She never wanted to hear that much pain in his voice again.

Petra returned to the bedroom and dressed in her usual weekend attire of shorts and a tank top. Feeling lazy, she combed out her damp hair and decided to let it dry on its own. She left the guest bedroom to go downstairs to rustle up some breakfast.

She'd just reached the bottom of the stairs when the front door opened and Mr. Dunn walked into the foyer. Petra hurried over to him. "I wasn't expecting you home until tomorrow or Monday."

Mr. Dunn shut the door after he wheeled his suitcase inside. He smiled. "Good morning, Petra. I decided to fly home late last night. Since the Italian villa I bought closed the other day, and I was able to finish my other business ahead of schedule, I thought it best I come home and relieve you of your house sitting duties."

"I'm glad everything went so well, but you didn't have to feel as if you had to rush home on my account. To be truthful, house sitting for you is like me spending a week in a four-star hotel."

Mr. Dunn chuckled. "I take it you and Sally had no problems?"

"None whatsoever. You know I consider her one of my friends."

"Yes, I know you two get along famously."

As Mr. Dunn wheeled his suitcase toward the stairs, Petra asked, "Have you had any breakfast yet? I was just on my way to make some for myself and I'd be happy to make you some as well."

He paused at the bottom step. "I already ate on the plane, but I could use a cup of coffee."

"That I can do."

Once Mr. Dunn started up the stairs, Petra headed for the kitchen. She went straight to the coffeemaker on the counter. It didn't take her long to find the ground coffee in the cupboard. Soon she had it going.

Petra had just taken a single-serve container of yogurt out of the fridge as Mr. Dunn walked into the kitchen. She had to do a double take after she saw what he wore. He chuckled when he caught sight of her looking at him with a shocked expression on her face.

"You're staring, Petra," he said jovially.

"Sorry," she quickly replied. "I don't mean to stare, but I don't think I've ever seen you without a suit jacket or a tie on before."

Mr. Dunn had taken those items off while he'd been upstairs and now only wore his short-sleeved white dress shirt and the pants from his suit. He'd even opened the two top buttons on his shirt. She'd never seen him so underdressed.

He chuckled. "The weekends I tend to let my dress code slide a bit. I usually wear a golf shirt and dress slacks instead of a suit. I guess you've never seen me on a weekend if you find the way I'm dressed so out of character."

Petra smiled. "No, I don't think I've ever been here to see you on a weekend. I have to say you look a little less…constricted without the tie."

"Old habits are hard to break. I had to wear a suit and tie for too many years when I worked in the corporate world. I just never broke the habit."

"Well, it's good you can cut back and let loose at times."

Mr. Dunn laughed. "I doubt I'd go that far."

At that moment, the coffeemaker made its last gurgle and hiss as it finished brewing. Petra took a mug out of the cupboard and then poured Mr. Dunn a cup. Knowing he liked his coffee black, she didn't offer to get him any milk or cream.

She placed it on the center island in front of him. "There you go, Mr. Dunn." Petra ate her yogurt.

Mr. Dunn took a sip of his coffee, then cleared his throat. "I think it's about time we held off on the formalities, Petra. I won't be offended if you called me by my first name."

"All right, Greg, but if I slip back into the old routine of calling you Mr. Dunn, you'll have to remind me."

"You have a deal."

Silence stretched between them, but neither one of them seemed to mind. Petra finished her yogurt and then got rid of the container. She turned back, took Greg's empty mug and poured him some more coffee.

After another few minutes had gone by, Petra said, "So, Greg, Sally was telling me that Italian villa you bought you'd had your eye on for quite some time."

He really seemed to perk up at the mention of his newly purchased home away from home. "Yes, indeed I did. I like that it's in close proximity to Rome and the fact that it's in a smaller village. I've been to Italy a few times in the past and I love the climate and culture. To be honest, Rome's ancient history is the biggest draw for me."

Petra went and sat on one of the stools next to Greg. "Let me guess, you're mostly interested in the Colosseum and the gladiators who used to fight in it?"

"You guessed correctly. The first time my wife and I toured the Colosseum, I found myself wanting to learn more about it's fascinating past. And to set the record straight, that movie that came out a while ago about a Roman gladiator wasn't all that historically accurate."

She nodded. "I know that now. The gladiators weren't killed every time they fought in the *muneras* like the movie depicted."

Greg gave her a surprised looked. "I thought you didn't know much about Roman history or about the gladiators?"

Petra gave a short laugh. "Let's just say that since you bought your rudis, I've done some research on my own and found someone who is an expert on the subject."

Greg sat up straighter on his stool. "Really? This person is that educated about the gladiators?"

"Very. Euric knows so much about them you'd swear he had firsthand experience."

"Could I meet with this Euric? I'd love to have a discussion with him about that subject, and I'd be willing to pay him for his time."

Petra had to think that one over for a bit. If she introduced Euric to Greg, she'd have to make sure Euric didn't in any way let on that he wasn't from this time. Could he handle being around Greg and keep their secret? She had a feeling he could pull it off as long as she gave him tips on what not to say. This could also be a good thing. If Greg was willing to pay Euric for his knowledge about ancient Rome, it'd show Euric he had something he could do if he lived in her time. Christ, with everything he knew, he could write a book about his experiences. She'd even help him do it if that was what he wanted to do.

She nodded. "I think that can be arranged. It just so happens that Euric is my boyfriend."

Greg smiled. "Now I see where your sudden interest in gladiators has come from. Why don't you give him a call now and see if he is free this evening. You and he can come over."

"Ah, I can't call him right now. He won't be near a phone for most of the day." More like Euric would be thousands of years away from a phone and was more than likely spending his day in sword practice. "How about we tentatively set it up for this evening and I'll call you later if he can't make it."

"That's fine with me." Greg finished the rest of his coffee and then slid off the stool. "Thanks for making the coffee, but if you don't mind, I think I'll head upstairs for a shower and a change of clothes."

Petra stood as well. "I'll just pack my things and then head out to my apartment then."

After following Greg up the stairs, Petra went into the guest bedroom. Once she packed what she'd brought for her stay, she let herself out of the mansion. She had a feeling having Euric meeting Greg would prove to be an interesting evening.

CHAPTER TEN

Fourth Century Rome

uric lowered his wooden sword and wiped the sweat that dripped down his face with his other hand. His sparring partner bent down and picked up his wooden sword from the ground where it lay after Euric had disarmed him. Once he had straightened, he looked past Euric just as some of the other gladiators stopped their practice to stare at something at the edge of the training ground.

Curious to see what had drawn everyone's attention, Euric turned to take a look himself. Seeing the guards lead four new slaves onto the grounds, he now understood the preoccupation. Their *Lanistae* had not bought any new slaves to train to be gladiators in quite some time. Right about now, the others would be taking the measure of each new man.

Knowing he would never have to face any of them in the *munera*, Euric only gave them a cursory glance, but when he reached the last man in line, every muscle in his body clenched. This man he recognized. His name was Gerrit, and he was one of the warriors from Euric's village.

The four men were divided and given wooden swords of their own to train with. They were matched up with one of the more experienced gladiators of the *familia*. A guard took one of the newer gladiators to Calix. Euric had to pity the poor bastard. Being pitted against the Roman on your first training session would not be a pleasant experience.

Much to Euric's surprise, a guard led Gerrit to him. The guard said, "*Lanistae* wants you to work with this one since you are both Visigoth and speak the same language. Tell him he has to learn Latin." With that said, he walked away.

Left to themselves, Gerrit opened his mouth to speak, but Euric gave him a quick shake of his head before he lead him to the far opposite edge of the training ground. Once they were relatively by themselves, Euric spoke.

"We can talk while we practice," he said in his native language. Euric had not spoken it for so long it felt a bit strange on his tongue.

Gerrit nodded and took up a fighting stance. "So this is what happened to you, Euric. You have survived these last few years as a gladiator?"

Eruic crossed his wooden sword with Gerrit's. "Yes. I was chosen to be trained as a gladiator shortly after I was brought to Rome. How were you taken?"

"During battle, the same as you were. I guess the Roman bastards figured I was worth something more alive than dead. Obviously, they did not realize I can be more trouble than I am worth."

Euric could not hold back a chuckle. Gerrit was five years older than he. Gerrit was also one of the warriors Euric had admired when he had started his training to become a warrior. In their village, the other man had a reputation for doing nothing in half measures, be it fighting, drinking or chasing women. The latter had caused him to be in more than a few fights with some of the other warriors of their village, especially when the woman happened to already be married.

"Well, my friend," Euric said with a shake of his head, "you will just have to show them, will you not? Just a word to the wise, our *Lanistae* is not a very tolerant man. As long as you do not do anything to anger him, he will leave you be. And the more popular you become with the mob, the more women will come to visit you in your cell at night. And they are not there for conversation, either."

That bit of news seemed to perk Gerrit up. He smiled widely. "Hmm, now that sounds as if it will be one aspect of this life I will not mind at all. Anything else I should know?"

"Start learning how to speak Latin. Refusing to do so will get you nowhere. If anything, it will only annoy the *Lanistae* and earn you a night in the punishment cell."

They circled each other before they crossed wooden swords again. "And what exactly is this punishment cell?"

"A small dark room where you cannot stand up or stretch out. I have had firsthand experience of being inside it a few times and I did not find it enjoyable." Except for his last stay and Petra had been there to get him through it.

"I guess I have no choice but to learn their cursed language." Gerrit spat on the dirt. "Is there any chance of getting out of this life, except by meeting your death that is."

Euric nodded and took another swipe at Gerrit, which the other man blocked. "Yes. Becoming the mob favorite not only garners you women it also helps you to gain your freedom."

"And how often does that happen? I cannot see the Romans being willing to free any of their slaves."

"It so happens that after I fight in the next *munera* I will be given my rudis." At Gerrit's look of confusion, he added, "I will be a free man. I will be able to return to our village." Seeing the way Gerrit suddenly stiffened and his face grow emotionless, Euric lowered his sword. "What is it?"

Gerrit met his gaze. "You may soon be a free man, Euric, but there will be no village to return to. The Romans attacked and burned it to the ground. They killed almost everyone who came in their path and only took a few of us warriors they figured they could make a profit off by selling us into slavery."

Euric felt the blood drain away from his face. "What of my parents? Did they manage to flee?"

A look of sadness settled on Gerrit's face. "I am sorry, Euric. Neither one of them survived the attack. I saw them fall before I was taken."

It took everything Euric had not to throw back his head and howl with rage and anguish. The thought of returning to his village had been the only thing that let him get through each day of his slavery, until Petra had come into his life and then he'd had both. Now his parents were dead and he would never see them again.

He gripped the pommel of his wooden sword so hard he was surprised he had not cracked it in two. Euric somehow managed to get himself back under control enough for him to speak in a quiet tone. "Did…did they suffer?"

Gerrit shook his head. "No. I saw how it happened. They were cut down as they fled their burning hut. Your father tried to defend your mother, but there were just too many of them. And I think once your mother was gone he gave up."

Euric briefly closed his eyes as a wave of grief surged through him, almost stealing his breath. He did not want to think about what had happened to his parents' bodies if there was no one around to give them a proper burial.

"I thank you, Gerrit, for telling me."

"I just wish I had better news to give you, but do know

this—your parents never gave up hope that you would one day return. They never wavered from their belief that you yet lived."

Euric nodded. He could not push any more words past the thickness in his throat. He signaled for Gerrit to come at him again. As he crossed wooden swords with what could be the only other person from his village still alive, Euric knew now was not the time to mourn the loss of his parents. There he would be given no pity or any special treatment. His life not being his own, he was not afforded the luxury of being able to mourn the passing of a loved one. There he was not considered a person, just a slave.

Sparring with Gerrit, Euric's fury built inside him. If he had been back in his village, there would have been a good chance he could have saved his parents and gotten them away to safety. Instead, he was being used by the countrymen who had murdered them for their entertainment. It just made him hate the Romans even more.

As he hacked and slashed, the decision he had come to grips with, to stay with Petra in her time, no longer was one he wavered about. The choice to return to his village had been taken from him. The only person he had left in this world who loved him was her. He realized that if he had not had her he would have become a rudderless ship, letting the waves take him where they wanted. He also thanked the gods that he had her to turn to when he needed her the most.

* * * *

Present Day

After basically spending the day watching the hours pass, Petra stood ready to open the window to Euric. He had been on her mind almost constantly. Even when she had called Lia to let her know that Mr. Dunn, Greg, had come home early and that she was now back at her apartment, Petra couldn't stop talking about him. She was pretty sure she had bored her best friend to death, but if she had, Lia never once tried to change the subject. Lia had been more than happy to hear that Petra and Euric had confessed how they felt about each other.

Finally time, Petra asked the window to open with the same stipulations she had used the night before. And just the same, it appeared a few seconds after the last words left her mouth.

Unlike the night before, Euric wasn't standing in the middle of his cell with a smile. This time he sat on his small bed with his elbows on his knees and his face in his hands. If he noticed her presence, he didn't look up.

"Euric?" Petra asked tentatively. He lifted his head, He appeared haggard-looking. Lines of strain bracketed his mouth and eyes. And his eyes, there was such sadness in them she wanted to wrap him in her arms and hold him until it went away. "Euric, are you all right?"

He didn't say a word as he stood and came to the window. Petra reached through it and took his hand before she pulled him to her side. Once he stood in front of her, Euric let out a choked sound and crushed her to his chest. He bent his head over hers while he took deep, shuddering breaths. She held him and rubbed her hands comfortingly up and down his back.

After a while, Euric muttered something she couldn't understand. He hadn't spoken in Latin or English. "In English, babe. Say it in English so I understand."

His chest expanded as he took a deep breath. "I am so glad you are mine."

"You're scaring the hell out of me here, Euric. You have to tell me what's wrong." He released her enough for her to lean back in his arms and look up at him. Sorrow was etched on his face.

"My *Lanistae* bought four new slaves to train to become gladiators. One of them was a man I know from my village. He had some bad news for me." Euric stopped and took another deep breath. He swallowed before he continued to speak. "The Romans burned our village to the ground. My parents were killed during the attack."

Petra cupped his face and rose on tiptoe to kiss him. "Oh, babe, I'm so, so sorry."

The news must have devastated Euric. In one fell swoop he'd lost the village he had dreamed of one day returning to and his parents. She only wished she could have been with him when he'd found out.

"I am alone now," he said gruffly. "My parents were my only remaining kin."

She brushed a lock of Euric's hair off his forehead. "You're not alone. You have me."

He bent and took her lips in a lingering kiss. After he lifted his head, he said, "I know. If not for you, I do not think I would be able to cope."

"I told you last night, I'm not going anywhere." Petra remembered about their having been invited over to Greg's place for the evening. "I guess I should change our plans for tonight. My employer returned ahead of schedule this morning, and he is very interested in meeting you. I'll call him and let him know we can't make it."

Euric frowned. "You told him about me? I thought you were only going to tell Lia."

That first night Euric had spent with her and Lia, Lia and Petra had agreed it'd be best to keep where Euric was from a secret. "I did, but not everything. Greg—as Mr. Dunn wants me to call him now—has a fascination with anything to do with ancient Rome and gladiators. I sort of mentioned that I knew somebody who is an expert in that field. He really wants to meet with you so the two of you can talk about all things gladiator. Greg is even willing to pay you to sit down and talk with him."

"He would pay me?"

Petra nodded. "Yes. The knowledge you have in your head about your time could turn into a career here in mine. You know things I'm sure even our historians don't know about that age." She stopped talking when she realized she was already presuming now that Euric's parents had died that he'd decide to stay in her time. "Sorry. That was a bit presumptuous of me. You just found out you lost your parents and here I am going on about you staying with me."

Euric brushed his lips across hers. "It is all right, Petra. We will go see your employer this evening. If I am to live in this time, I need to find something to do in it. Plus, I should get used to being around other people who do not know anything about my past."

Petra blinked. "What did you say?" She couldn't have heard Euric right. He hadn't just said if he was to live in her time, had he? She sucked in a breath and held it while she waited for him to answer.

He gave her a small smile. "You heard me. I have decided I want to live with you, if you will have me."

She let her breath out in a whoosh and then hugged Euric tight. "Of course I want you to live with me. I hate the thought of you having to spend the day as a slave. I just wish I hadn't asked the window to allow you to go back in the morning."

Euric took Petra by the arms and held her slightly away from him. "I have to go back, Petra."

Her brows drew together. "I don't understand. I thought when you said you wanted to live with me, you wouldn't want to go back."

"I will not go back, eventually. I still have something I have to do there before I say goodbye to my time."

"What is there to do? The only thing you do there is fight." Euric remained silent, and Petra shook her head.

She stepped out of his hold. "You can't be serious? Why would you want to risk getting seriously hurt, or even killed, fighting in another *munera* when there is no reason for you?"

"There is a reason for me to fight again. It will be my last one. My *Lanistae* said I would be given my rudis after it."

"You have no need of your rudis if you're a free man every time you cross over to this time. It's crazy to fight just so you can get a wooden sword."

"The rudis is not just any wooden sword. It represents my freedom after all I have had to put up with these last years. I have lost everything — my village, my parents. And because the Roman's took me as a slave I was not there to help defend them during the attack. I at least want something to take away from this. It will be a reminder of all that I lost so I will never forget."

Seeing the stubborn set of Euric's jaw, Petra had a feeling no matter what she said he wouldn't change his mind about fighting. She sighed. "When are you to fight again? Please tell me it's at least a few months away."

"In four days' time, I will face Calix again in the *Amphitheatrum*."

"Why so soon? You said you only fought at the most four times a year."

"The senator who presided over the last *munera* wishes to hold another in honor of the emperor soon returning to Rome. He specifically requested to see me fight and that I be given my rudis at the end of the match, win or lose."

Petra looked at Euric's right arm. The cloth bandage had been removed. The sword slash he'd taken was well on its way to healing, but he'd have a bit of a scar once it finished. She didn't want to think about what new wounds he'd take away from his final fight in the *munera*. He may not be killed outright, but there was always the chance of him being wounded badly enough that he could die from it, or even end up damaged permanently. The thought made her stomach queasy.

Deciding there was no point in pushing the matter right now, Petra said, "I don't think I can talk about this anymore. If you still feel up to seeing Greg, we should leave soon before it gets too late. You'll have to change before we go."

As Petra started to walk toward the bedroom, Euric reached out and took her hand. "You are mad at me now."

"No, I'm not. It's just the idea of you taking that risk when it isn't a life or death situation makes me feel a bit panicky. If anything happened to you..." She let her words fall away.

"I will say what you said to me—I am not going anywhere."

Petra nodded, then went to her bedroom to get Euric some clothes. Until she had him safely and permanently in her time, she wouldn't stop worrying about what he'd have to face in his last *munera*.

* * * *

The drive to Greg's mansion Euric seemed to handle a bit better than his first ride in a car. He sat silently staring out the passenger window. Petra had a feeling he was lost in thought over the loss of his parents, which was understandable. Even though he really didn't show it on the outside he still had to be grieving on the inside.

Petra took a quick glance in his direction. Tonight she'd picked out the athletic pants and another t-shirt for Euric to wear. Since he planned to stay in her time, she figured another trip to the mall was going to be in order to buy him some more clothes. She'd be taking him with her so he could try everything on. She snuck another quick look at him and found him watching her.

"What are you thinking about, Petra?" he asked. "You

look a little preoccupied."

She smiled. "I was just thinking we're going to have to buy you some new clothes soon." She glanced down at his sandaled feet. "And some shoes as well. You can't wear sandals all the time."

"Why not? It is what most people wear in my time. And did you not tell me Los Angeles does not get any snow in the winter like Rome?"

"Yes, but sandals are considered really casual. You need at least one pair of running shoes. Maybe some boots as well. I think you'd look good in a pair of shit kickers and black jeans."

"A pair of what?" Euric asked incredulously. "I do not think I will be kicking shit around if I can help it."

Petra laughed. "Shit-kicker boots aren't used for that. They're combat boots that are basically designed so you can kick the shit out of someone."

"Ah. I like that purpose for them better than what I thought they were meant for. If I could, I would wear a pair of those boots while fighting in the *munera*. We have to fight barefoot."

"You fight in your bare feet? That has to hurt."

Euric chuckled. "Not really. My feet are used to it now. In the beginning, it was a bit of an adjustment since I was used to fighting in my leather boots."

Making the gladiators fight in their bare feet had Petra thinking it was just another instance of how primitively the Romans treated their slaves. She quickly pulled her thoughts from the whole subject of the Romans before she thought about things that would only upset her.

A short while later, Petra pulled her Camry onto the long driveway of the mansion. As she drove up it, she quickly reminded Euric of a few things that he'd have to watch out for when he spoke with Greg. The main one being that he in no way could let it slip that he was from the actual time the two of them were going to be discussing.

Parking in front of the large garage, she quickly added, "And don't refer to yourself as a Visigoth. Germania is now called Germany, and the people are no longer separated into tribes. So you would be considered German." Actually, when Euric spoke English, he did have quite a distinct German-sounding accent so there really would be no question as to where other people would think he was from.

"I will remember, Petra. Stop worrying. Nothing will go wrong."

"All right, I'll try to stop worrying so much. Let's go."

They climbed out of the car and then walked side by side up to the mansion's front door. Petra rang the doorbell. They didn't have long to wait before Greg opened it. He smiled and waved them inside.

He closed the door behind them, and said, "Petra, I'm glad you both could make it." Greg turned to Euric and held out his hand. "You must be Euric. I hear we have a lot in common when it comes to historical interest. I'm Greg Dunn."

Euric shook Greg's hand. "Nice to meet you."

"How about we go to my study to talk. Would you two like anything to drink?" Greg asked as he led them to his study.

"Water is fine for me," Petra said.

When Greg looked at Euric, he quickly added, "I will have the same."

"All right. I'll be back in a minute with your water. Feel free to take a look around while I'm gone."

Once Greg left the room, Euric walked over to the rudis that sat on the shelf on the wall. He ran his finger down the length of the wooden blade. Petra, who stood beside him, saw the longing on his face. If only he'd accept an antique replica like Greg's, she'd gladly pay any amount of money to give it to him, but she had a feeling receiving his own would only do.

Greg returned carrying two bottles of water, which he handed to Petra and Euric. He motioned them over to the black leather couch at the other end of the study while he sat in the matching black leather chair kitty-corner to it.

After they were all comfortably seated, Greg said, "I saw you were admiring my rudis, Euric. Did Petra tell you it's one of my latest finds?"

Euric nodded. "Yes, she did."

"Of course it isn't an original," Greg continued. "I doubt any of the real ones have survived the ages."

"I hope to own a rudis myself sometime soon."

"I should give you the card of the antiques dealer I bought mine from. Paul has a knack for finding hard-to-find items. It may cost you a bit, but if you really want one, he'd be the man to call."

"Actually, I still have one of Paul's cards," Petra said before Euric said anything. "We'll be sure to contact him about it."

"Good." Greg nodded. He focused his attention on Euric. "So you're an expert when it comes to ancient Rome and gladiators. Do you have your degree, or is your interest more of a hobby as mine is?"

Euric looked at Petra. She saw his confusion plain as day on his face. She quickly jumped into the conversation. "Ah, Euric's English isn't quite perfect yet. Sometimes he has trouble translating some words." She said for Euric's benefit so he'd know what a degree meant, "Greg wants to know if you went to school to learn about ancient Rome."

"Oh," Euric said. "No, I did not go to school. And Petra is right. I sometimes have trouble understanding some of the things people say in English."

"You're German, correct?"

"Yes. I recently learned how to speak English. I also know how to speak Latin."

Greg smiled. "As do I." He said, "*Du ju metior iris iri*

mensus sum Rome?"

"*Interdum*," Euric replied.

Petra shook her head. "As someone who doesn't speak Latin, the two of you have lost me."

Euric smiled. "Greg asked if I traveled through Rome, and I told him sometimes."

"Okay. How about we stick to English? That way I can participate at least a little in the conversation."

Greg chuckled. "I think Euric and I can manage to keep the conversation in English from here on out."

The conversation turned back to the ancient histories of Rome. When Euric confessed that he mostly knew more about fourth century Rome—she'd told him that was the time period he lived in—and mostly about gladiators from that era, Greg was happy to hear anything Euric had to tell him about that time.

Petra sat back and listened to the two men talk. Euric was doing surprisingly well for his first time at pretending to be a modern man. Not once did he slip. He spoke about his time as if it were indeed the ancient past for him. If she was to meet him on the street right now, she wouldn't be able to tell he didn't belong.

Greg became more animated the longer he and Euric spoke about the gladiators. Some of what Euric had to say Petra had a hard time hearing, especially about what had obviously been his experience in the slave market before he'd been bought by his *Lanistae*.

The other thing that sent a chill down her spine was when he talked about what happened to a gladiator who'd lost his match and hadn't been shown any mercy. Apparently, the loser had to hold on to the thigh of the winner while the winner held on to the loser's head. The winner then would thrust his sword into the loser's neck. What was even worse was what happened after the loser died. An attendant wearing the costume of Dis Pater, the Roman god of the underworld, would hit the dead body in the head with a mallet. Another attendant dressed as Mercury would take a heated "wand" to the body. Both those things were done to make sure the poor loser was indeed dead. It wasn't bad enough that he'd had a sword stabbed into his throat.

Petra didn't want to think about Euric ever having to face something like that. It was so barbaric. While he spoke of what happened to the dead gladiators, she hadn't been able to stop herself from taking hold of his hand. He gave her a smile and continued with his conversation. He would once in a while give a tight squeeze, as if he knew what he said bothered her.

By the time the conversation wore down and it became late, Petra was more than ready to get Euric to herself. Before they left, Greg made Euric promise he'd come to see him again sometime soon. He'd also given Euric fifty dollars in cash. Petra tried to get Greg to take some of it back, but he said he wouldn't hear of it and that Euric had more than earned the money.

After they were in the car driving to her apartment, Petra asked Euric, "So what do you think of Greg?"

"He is very nice. He knows quite a bit about Rome and seems to really like the history of it."

"Yes, he does. He just recently bought a villa not too far from Rome." Jokingly she said, "If you're really nice to him, maybe he'll invite you to visit him at the villa sometime."

Out of the corner of her eye, Petra saw Euric turn his head to look at her. "Really? To be honest, I would not mind experiencing Rome and seeing the *Amphitheatrum* in this time."

"We don't need to stay in Greg's villa to do all that. It'll take me a little while to save up the money for us to make the trip, but I promise you, I'll get you there."

"Will this help?" Euric held out the fifty dollar bill Greg had given him.

Having reached her apartment building, Petra pulled into her parking spot in the underground parking garage. She turned off the car and then pushed the money back toward Euric. "It would, but you keep it. You earned it."

Euric unfolded the bill and closely looked at it. "How many more of these would we need to go to Rome?"

"Quite a few. Flights to Italy aren't cheap and then there is the price of staying in a hotel, plus any spending money you want to take with you."

He looked at her. "Flights? We would have to take an airplane?"

Petra laughed at the look of horror on Euric's face. "Yes, we'd have to fly there. It's the fastest way."

He swallowed. "I guess if it is what will be necessary to get me to Rome I will somehow manage, even though I will not look forward to it."

"I promise you, it won't be that bad. And it's not as if you'd be alone on the plane. I'll be there with you to help you through your very first flight."

They climbed out of the car and then headed up to her apartment. After Petra had let them in, closed and locked the door behind them, Euric stepped to stand at her back. His arms came around her front and pulled her against him while his hands came up to cover her breasts. He nudged her hair out of the way with his chin before he kissed the side of her neck. The hard length of his cock nestled against the small of her back.

Euric pinched her nipples through her shirt and bra as he said, "I have been dying to touch you like this all evening."

Petra leaned her head back against his shoulder. "Well, we have the rest of the night to make up for lost time."

"I intend to do just that. Starting right now."

Leaving her neck, Euric cupped her chin in his hand and turned her head to the side for him to take her lips in a heated kiss. He slid his other down her body until it came to rest on her pubic bone. While he rocked his hips against her, he dropped it lower and stroked her pussy through her yoga pants.

Petra sucked Euric's tongue into her mouth and moaned. She pushed back against his erection while he continued to caress her. Wetness leaked between her legs and into her panties. Wanting to touch him as he touched her, she tried to turn in his arms, but he didn't let her.

At her moaned of frustration, he released her lips. "I want you this way."

Euric took hold of the bottom of her t-shirt and pulled it up and over her head. He made quick work of removing her bra. He kneaded her breasts before he plucked her already taut nipples. He shifted his hands lower and skimmed down her stomach to the top of her pants. With no button or zipper to worry about, he pushed on the elastic waistband until he worked her pants past her hips and legs. Once they fell, pooling at her ankles, Petra kicked off her sandals and then stepped out of her pants. She shoved them and her sandals aside with her foot.

Now standing in only her panties, Euric lifted the hair from the back of her neck and placed a kiss there. He let her hair fall back into place and ran his hands down her sides to the waistband of her panties. He hooked his fingers into it and slowly inched them down her hips. Once they fell to her ankles, Petra stepped out of them and kicked them over to the pile of the rest of her clothes.

Euric kissed the top of her shoulder as he ran his hands caressingly up and down her thighs. Petra breathed heavier when with each caress he came closer and closer to where she wanted him to touch her the most. As he stroked his hands along her inner thighs, exerting enough pressure so she opened them wider, he still avoided the place where her body grew wet for him.

With a frustrated moan, Petra said in a breathy voice, "Euric. Stop being a tease."

The back of his hand gently came up against her pussy before he pulled it away, which caused Petra to moan again. "You have a gorgeous body, Petra. I could caress and kiss it all day."

"I don't think I could handle that." She sucked in a quick breath as he grazed her with his knuckles her once again. "Touch me, Euric. You're driving me crazy."

"Put your hands on the wall first."

Petra did as Euric said and placed her hands flat on the wall in front of her. Once she'd done that, he took hold of her hips and pulled them back so she stood a little away from it while she braced her upper body. He kept his hold on her as he dragged his tongue up her spine.

He shifted behind her and then went on his knees. Running his hands down her bottom to the back of her legs, Euric spread them apart even more. In this position she was totally open and exposed. He caressed up her inner thigh. Petra whimpered with need when he delved between the folds of her pussy and pushed inside her core with a finger.

A second joined the first while Euric pumped them in and out. "You are so wet for me, Petra."

She could no longer keep still. Petra pushed back on his fingers as he worked them inside her. "I need you inside me, Euric."

"I thought I could make this last longer," he panted, "but I am just too hungry for you. Do not move."

His fingers left her body and Euric stood. She heard the rustle of clothing as he undressed himself. Out of the corner of her eye, she saw his clothes join the pile of hers. His hands came down on her hips. He pulled them even closer, causing her to be practically bent over with hers still supporting her on the wall in front of her. Petra moaned at the feel of his hard cock sliding against her pussy, coating the length of him in her wetness.

As he continued to tease her by bringing the head of his

cock to her slick opening, then quickly pulling away, Petra arched her back the next time and rubbed herself against him. With a loud groan, Euric's grip on her hips tightened while he held her in position and surged forward.

Once she'd taken all of him, Euric pulled back and plunged inside her again. He stroked into her hard and fast over and over again. Petra clenched her inner muscles around his thick length as her orgasm built. Panting and moaning, she pushed back to meet each of his strokes. His cock grew even harder inside her.

Then she was there. With a keening moan, her core clutched his shaft while wave after wave of intense pleasure shot through her. Euric surged into her once more, then deeply moaning, he came. His cock pulsed deep inside her, filling her with his cum.

Her legs shaking, Petra pushed herself away from the wall and leaned back against Euric. His softening shaft slipped from her body as he wrapped his arms around her, supporting her weight. He turned her and kissed her until he'd made her breathless once more.

Lifting his head, Euric said, "How about we continue this in your bed?"

"The bed sounds good, but I don't know if my legs will hold me up long enough to get to the bedroom."

"I think I can manage to get us both there."

Euric scooped her up and carried her to the bedroom. After he had her on the bed, he once more sent her body soaring.

CHAPTER ELEVEN

Tired but not yet ready to sleep, Petra lay beside Euric with her head resting on his pillow next to his, facing him. She idly ran a caressing hand over his wide, muscular chest. His eyes were closed, but she knew he hadn't fallen asleep yet.

"Euric?"

"Yes." He blinked his eyes open and turned his head so his blue-eyed gaze met hers.

"I've been thinking."

"About what?"

"About you wanting to stay in your time until you've fought your last match in the *munera*."

"And?"

"I know you want your rudis, but I don't know if I like the idea of you staying in your time until then when it really isn't necessary."

"It is. If I was to stay here and I was not in my cell come morning, my *Lanistae* would think I had somehow escaped. I would not be able to just show up on the day of the *munera* and not expect some repercussions."

"How about this then? The window has so far

cooperated and let me put some stipulations on it when I've asked it to open. What if instead of asking it to only stay open overnight I ask it to stay open for say a week. Or ask it to close and then open again after the week has gone by."

"That would not fix the problem of me being considered missing in my time."

"I'm not done yet. What if I not only ask it to open again in a week, but on the day you return it will be the exact day and minute you left." Seeing Euric didn't quite understand what she meant, Petra added, "For example, we wait until the night before you're to fight and when I ask the window to open I also ask it to allow you to go back at the exact same time you crossed through to my time, but only a week has gone by on this side. That way it'll give you that length of time to stay with me here, to live better and get stronger before you have to fight."

Euric's gaze took on a faraway look as he thought it over. "I now see what you mean. That way I can stay with you and then return to fight as if I had never left."

"Exactly." Not sure if Euric would be game for this next part, Petra took a deep breath. "I would also give the window one more stipulation to go along with the rest. I would ask that when the day arrives that you'd have to return to fight, you'd be given the choice of returning or staying here without ever having to go back again."

Euric frowned. "I will go back, Petra."

"Just wait a second. Hear me out. I'm not saying you don't have to return, but I want to give you the choice. Say you stay here for a week, and during that time, you decide you'd rather not go back. And that getting the rudis ends up not being as important as you once thought. Not that I'm saying that could happen, but there is a possibility. If I don't give you this choice and you decide you don't want to fight, the window will force you to go back, anyway. You haven't been able to ignore its pull on you so far."

"My not wanting the rudis will never happen."

Petra fought the urge to growl in frustration. "And there could be a chance you won't want it, especially if you start settling into life in this time. Wouldn't you want to keep all your options open even if you don't use them?"

Euric turned on his side to lie facing her. He put an arm around her waist and pulled her closer until their bodies touched. "It would make you feel better if I had that choice?"

"Of course it would."

"And if I agree to it, you will probably try everything you can to get me to change my mind about going back to fight, will you not?" He kissed the tip of her nose.

Petra shrugged. "Can you blame me? The thought of the man I love doing something that dangerous makes me feel overprotective."

Euric smiled. "All right. If it will make you feel better, you can add that stipulation."

"So you'll do it? You'll stay with me for a full week to see exactly what you'll be giving up your old life for?"

"Yes to both. If anything, staying in this time will give me a bit of an advantage over Calix. I will be eating better meals than him."

Petra chuckled. "Oh, babe, I'll feed you all the meat you can eat. Even though I'm not big on working out at a gym, I'll get you a membership."

"A gym?"

"It's a place where people go to work out, to train. You won't be able to train with a sword. We'll have to figure something out for you, but lifting weights will help keep your muscles in condition."

"I like the sound of this gym. Will you teach me how to use these weights you speak of?"

"I'm not really into weight lifting, but I know enough to get you started."

"I think I am going to like this time of yours, especially

since you are in it. All right, three nights from this one, open the window with all the stipulations you mentioned and I will stay for a week." Euric cupped her cheek. "I just want you to promise that when I go back to fight you will not try to stop me. It is only one fight and then you will have me here always."

Petra nodded. "I promise on the night you have to leave I won't do anything to stop you from going back, but that doesn't mean I won't try the rest of the time you're here."

Euric smiled. "You have a deal." He tucked her head under his chin. "Now let us get some sleep. The window will awaken me early to leave."

Snuggled close to Euric, Petra let herself relax. She only had to get through three more days, then he would be with hers for seven days. They could finally be like a real couple.

* * * *

With Euric back in his time, and it being a Sunday and she didn't have to work, Petra had a lot of free time on her hands. She decided to put it to good use by making a list of things to do with him once their week together started.

First would be clothes shopping. She couldn't wait to take him to the mall and see the look on his face when he saw all the stores and people who shopped there. She already knew from which gym she'd get memberships for each of them. There was one close to her apartment that was part of a big chain.

Thinking about gym memberships also got Petra thinking about something else Euric would need once he came to live in the present—identification. Being a man of the past, he didn't exactly have a birth certificate or a social security number. As far as Petra knew, he didn't even have a last name. She didn't think people in his time had them. If he was to have a life in her world, somehow she had to find a way for him to get some fake ID. Having never had a reason to acquire some, she really had no idea how to go about it, or who to go to.

She was already reaching for her cell phone before she'd decided to take a chance and give Lia a call. If she was sleeping, the phone wouldn't bother her friend since Lia turned off the ringer before going to bed. Petra could just leave her a message. Hitting Lia's number in her contacts list, she hoped her friend would be awake.

"Hi, Petra," Lia said after she picked up after the fourth ring. "What's up? How's that hunky gladiator of yours?"

"Euric is good and back in his time, which I hate. I'm calling to see if you can help me out with a little problem."

"And that would be?"

"To make a long story short, Euric has to fight one last time so he can be presented with his rudis. Once he has it, he's decided to live in our time. I've also convinced him to give me a full week where he's going to stay with me all day and night before he has to fight. If he's going to stay in this time permanently, he's going to need some fake ID. Since you've met some pretty colorful people in the ER, I was wondering if you knew of anyone who does them."

"Sure, think of me when you want something done that's illegal."

"Well, do you or don't you know somebody?"

Lia let out a long drawn-out sigh. "Of course I do. And it isn't someone I met at the hospital. It's a friend of my brother. At one time, he was a wizard of the fake IDs. He's not into doing that shit anymore, but the guy owes me one."

"Oh yeah? How did you get him indebted to you?"

"When I was still in nursing school, my brother and he decided to do some binge drinking. Both of them ended up at my apartment rip-roaring drunk. I spent the rest of the night helping them when they started puking their guts up. It was like looking after two sick kids with all the whining they did. The next morning I told them they owed me big time. I haven't collected yet, but I don't mind calling this one in to get your Euric what he needs."

"Thanks, Lia. I'll owe you one."

"No, you won't. Unlike other people, I haven't had to clean up your barf. And besides, even though my guy will do it as a favor to me, you'll still have to pay him for it. And I doubt it will be cheap."

"I didn't think it'd be. It's fine. I have a little money stashed away. Euric is worth it."

"I'll make the call after I hang up here and get things rolling. I have a feeling I'll be the go-between for the two of you. I'll call you back when I get the list of things my guy will need to do the IDs."

"Sounds good."

"Oh, I just thought of something," Lia said. "Now that you and Euric are basically a for-sure thing, are you going to introduce him to your parents and brother during the week while he stays with you, or will you wait and do it after he fights?"

Petra really hadn't thought about that. She'd been more preoccupied with thinking of ways to get Euric to stay, and what she needed to do to make things easier for him to adjust to her time. Obviously, she had to introduce him to her family at some point, especially since they'd be living together. She had no problem introducing him to her parents. It was her brother who could cause trouble. Chad would want to know everything about Euric. He'd give him the third degree and dissect everything he said under a microscope, looking for some kind of failing in Euric. And there would be no escaping Chad. Once he found out about Euric, he'd make a point of coming over to her apartment to meet him.

"I think it'd probably be best if I introduce Euric to them next week. It's Chad's birthday a week from tomorrow. My mom invited him and his wife over for a birthday dinner and I was also invited. I might as well jump in with both feet and get it over with then. Hopefully with my parents around, Chad won't give Euric too much of a bad time."

Lia snorted. "That brother of yours is a jerk off. I don't know how you put up with him. If he were my brother, I'd have socked him a good one by now."

"Believe me, I've been more than tempted over the years. If I ever did something like that, I'd have to suffer through a long lecture from my mom about why I should be more tolerant of my brother."

Her mother had a definite soft spot when it came to Chad. In her eyes, she thought his overbearing way of treating Petra was how he looked out for his little sister. Her mom just couldn't see past what she believed to see he just liked bossing Petra around, and generally was a know-it-all. Her father knew exactly what Chad truly was like and had usually stepped in when things got too bad. He also knew how her mother felt about Chad and tried to make it up to Petra by being there for her whenever she needed him.

"More tolerant. Gotta love that. I think you'd be very tolerant if you just kicked Chad in the head rather than in the balls."

"I'll leave the ball kicking to you," Petra said with a laugh.

"Maybe I'll tag along with you and Euric when you go to your parents' place. I have a feeling Chad is going to meet his match in Euric. I doubt your gladiator will take any shit from him. Now wouldn't that be a sight to see if Chad pushed Euric too far and he popped your brother one."

"That would so not go over well. I want my mom to like Euric."

"Forget your mom, Petra. She can be blind as a bat when it comes to your brother."

"I know. Enough talk about my mom and brother. Call me like you said you would once you talk to your guy. Euric will be here only at night for the next three nights and then his week here will start. So the three of us can get together any time in the evening to get the information you need for the IDs."

"That sounds fine with me. And just for the record, you're one lucky girl. I wish I could find a gladiator of my own."

"Maybe I should ask Euric to see if he could set you up on a blind date with one of the gladiators in his *familia*."

"Now wouldn't that be the making of a great blind date. Not only would we have to get to know each other while out on said date, but he'd have to accept the fact that he'd have to travel through time to meet me. I can see it crapping out even before the date started."

Petra chuckled. "You're such a pessimist."

"No, I just happen to see how weird life can get and I don't expect much from it."

"Do you know how depressing that sounds?"

"I'm just in one of those moods. I think the ER is starting to get to me. Maybe it's time I thought of finding another nursing job outside the hospital."

"You've been saying that for the last year. Why don't you just bite the bullet and do it already?"

"Yeah, yeah. I'm going to go before you start lecturing me. I'll call you later."

After she hung up with Lia, Petra returned to her list making. If Lia could get the fake IDs it'd be one less thing Petra had to worry about. As for Euric meeting her family, she fully expected her brother to be his usual grating self. Sometimes she wished she could pop Chad one just like Lia said to do. And hopefully Euric wouldn't do it for her.

* * * *

Fourth Century Rome

"Do you not look like a man who spent the night in enjoyable pursuits," Gerrit said as he sat next to Euric. He put his bowl of food on the table in front of him. "Did you get paid a visit last night?"

Euric smiled. "You could say that." He and Gerrit were speaking in Goth, so he did not have to worry about anyone listening in on their conversation. Even though Euric trusted Gerrit with his life, and had a couple times on the battlefield, he doubted his friend would be able to accept where Euric spent his nights.

"I cannot wait for the night when I get some female Roman company."

"Once you make a name for yourself, you will get your fair share."

Euric did not have the heart to tell Gerrit that it could take months for him to reach the stage where their *Lanistae* would deem him ready to fight. Being as how Gerrit had not been sentenced to die in the *munera*, his training would be more intense and would take longer than those who were.

They started to eat. After a few mouthfuls, Gerrit said, "We seem to have an observer. The bastard over there has not stopped staring at you since I came in. If he thinks he is intimidating you, he will have to try a lot harder than that."

Euric glanced over to where Gerrit looked and met Calix's glare. "That would be my opponent in the next *munera*, Calix."

"I have been watching him on the training ground. He has a mean streak to him."

"That he does. He is Roman and volunteered to take the gladiator's oath. He figures that gives him the right to lord it over all of us who were taken in battle. He is also not happy with me."

"Why would anyone want to volunteer to become a slave other than being forced into it? The way his eyes are shooting daggers at you, I can tell you are not one of his favorite people. What did you do to cause that?"

Euric pulled his gaze off Calix and looked at Gerrit. "I defeated him in the last *munera* and took his first sword status."

Gerrit let out a bark of laughter. Euric glanced back at Calix to see the scowl he wore become even more pronounced. Euric quickly looked away before the Roman thought to cause some trouble.

"I take it the Roman thinks to take his first sword status back from you when he fights you again?"

"Of course. He will not want to reclaim it by default when I have been given my freedom."

"I do not know, Euric. I would watch my back around that one," Gerrit said as he stared down Calix. "He looks like a bully and bullies do not like to lose. I would not put it past him to try to do something to ensure your defeat."

"He can try, but I doubt he would be able to accomplish much. Our *Lanistae* may consider Calix one of his best gladiators, but that does not mean he would relax the rules that much for the Roman. Calix is locked up in his cell every night the same as we are, and the guards watch us closely during training to make sure no real fights break out between rivals."

"I would still keep on my guard around that one."

"Do not worry, I will. I will just be happy when I can put this life behind me."

Gerrit left off his staring match with Calix and turned to look at Euric. "I wish I could leave with you. This is no life for warriors such as us."

"You know if I could, I would take you with me."

"I know. Since the village is no more and your parents are gone, where will you go?"

The reminder of his parents' death sent a wave of

sadness through Euric. He had not let himself properly mourn their passing, and would not until he was completely free of his servitude. It would only cause him to become weak when he needed to stay strong.

"I will not go to Germania."

"You do not think to stay in Rome?"

"No. I want to get far away from this place. I am going to travel somewhere far away where I have never lived before. Start off fresh where no one knows what I have been." Going to live over a thousand years in the future would grant Euric both those things.

"I cannot blame you for not wishing to return to Germania. There is not anything left there for you. Same with me. Maybe when I am given my freedom we can meet again."

"Maybe."

That would never happen, not where he would be going. If only he could take Gerrit with him when he went to the future, he would save his friend from the life he'd had to live. Euric doubted the window would allow it. He could not even step through it on his own without Petra touching him in some way. There was always a chance Gerrit could if Petra asked the window to let him.

He gave himself a mental shake and concentrated on the food in front of him. Gerrit was a seasoned warrior who would have an even harder time than Euric giving up the sword. Even if Gerrit believed Euric about being able to travel to the future, there was Petra to think about. She would not only have him to watch out for until he adjusted to her time, she would also have the added burden of Gerrit to clothe and feed. It would be hard to leave his friend behind, but he would have no choice. He could not change everyone's life for the better, no matter how much he wanted to.

* * * *

Present Day

Two evenings later, Petra buzzed Lia up to her apartment. Lia had called her that afternoon to let her know she'd finally gotten in touch with her guy and that he'd agreed to make Euric fake IDs. All he needed Lia to get him were a picture of Euric, his full name, birth date and where he was born. They were going to have to fudge most of that information.

After Lia knocked on her apartment door, Petra let her in. As she closed it behind her friend, she saw the digital camera Lia carried. "You didn't have to bring your camera. I do have one of my own and it even has fresh batteries in it."

Lia headed for the living room and then put the camera along with her purse on the coffee table. "I figured it'd be easier if I just brought mine. That way I don't have to take your card, bring it to my guy and then have to return it to you. This way it eliminates one step." She looked around the apartment. "So, where is your gladiator, anyway?"

Petra joined Lia in the living room. "I haven't opened the window yet. I was waiting until you arrived."

Moving to the side of the living room, Petra asked the window to open as she had every night for the last few nights. The window appeared, showing a view of Euric, standing in his cell.

"That will never grow old," Lia said when she walked toward Petra.

Euric held out his hand, and Petra reached through the window for it. Their fingers linked, he stepped to her side. He gave her a hug and a quick kiss. "I missed you."

"I missed you as well," Petra said as she hugged him back.

Lia cleared her throat. "No getting carried away, you two. I may be the third wheel, but that doesn't mean I'm going stay here when you start sucking face."

Euric put his arm around Petra's shoulders and turned to face Lia. "Would you feel better if I gave you a hug too?"

"Maybe a little." As he held out his other arm, Lia stepped into it and gave Euric a hug. Before she let him go, she reached down and gave his ass a squeeze.

"Hey," Petra said. "No pawing my man. Get one of your own."

Lia shrugged. "I couldn't help myself. And seeing him dressed in that short dress thingy, I just had to see if his butt felt as good as it looked."

Petra shook her head with a laugh. "It's a good thing we're best friends or I'd take exception to that. And for your information, Euric isn't wearing a dress. It's a tunic." She looked at Euric. "I washed your clothes today and put a t-shirt along with a pair of shorts on the bed for you. Lia needs to take your picture."

Euric nodded. "All right. I will go change."

Petra and Lia watched Euric walk to the bedroom. Once he went inside and didn't shut the door behind him, Petra hurried over to the bedroom and closed it. She went back to the living room.

Lia rolled her eyes. "It wasn't as if I was going to sneak a look at Euric naked."

"I know," Petra said as they went to sit on the couch to wait for Euric to return. "Let's just say Euric can have no shame at times. Being naked is nothing to him."

"In that case, maybe you should see about getting him in *Playgirl*. He'd sell a ton of magazines."

"Not in this lifetime. The only woman who gets to see him naked is me."

"I was only joking, Petra. I've never even looked inside that magazine. Do you seriously think I'd suggest Euric do something like that?"

"Do what?" Euric asked as he joined them on the couch.

"Nothing," Petra quickly said.

Euric looked at Lia. "You want to take my picture? How are you going to do that?"

Lia picked up her digital camera. "With this. I guess since this is going to be for identification purposes, we should probably get you to stand in front of a neutral-looking wall." She stood and walked to the wall closest to the apartment door that didn't have anything on it. "This should do." Once Euric stood where Lia wanted him, she took the picture and looked at it when it appeared on the camera's screen. "Damn, you're tall. This one looks as if I took the shot while I'm looking up at you."

Petra came up beside Lia and looked over her shoulder at the picture. "That's because you're short."

"Ha ha. You're not that much taller than I am." Lifting the camera again, Lia backed up. "I'll use the telephoto this time and see if it helps." She pressed the button to take the picture and the flash went off.

Euric blinked. "I see spots before my eyes. Are you sure that thing will not make me blind?"

Petra chuckled. "You'll be fine. The spots don't last." She said to Lia, "How did you do this time?"

Lia turned the back of the camera toward her. "I think this one will work."

Euric joined them and looked at his picture over Petra's shoulder. "I still do not understand how that small object can create an exact likeness of me."

"It's a bit complicated," Petra said.

"What will you use the picture of me for again?"

"To get you some fake identification. Everyone in my time has some form of it, starting with a birth certificate when we are born. Without ID, you wouldn't be able to fly, join a gym or work."

Lia switched off the camera. "Don't worry, Euric, the guy I know who is going to do the IDs will have you all set up with a birth certificate, a passport and a social security number. Now that we have the picture, I need a last name, date of birth and where you were born. We're going to have to make it look as if you became an American citizen with that accent of yours."

They went to sit on the couch. Euric wore a confused expression. "I do not have a last name, and I have no idea what the exact day was when I was born. And Petra says Germania is no longer called that."

Petra squeezed Euric's leg where he sat next to her. "Don't worry, Lia and I will help you with this. We'll have to pick a last name that will be something easy for you to remember. What was your father's name?"

"Berhard." The way Euric said it, it sounded like bayr hard.

"That sounds like a good Germanic last name. So your full name will now be Euric Berhard. You told me you had seen twenty-seven summers. Were you born in the summer or the winter?"

"In the early winter, just before the snow falls is when I mark my birth."

"So if we take this year, 2015, and count backward twenty-seven years," Lia said, "it would make the year of your birth 1988. And if you were born just before the snow came it would probably be around November. Now we just have to pick the day. Any suggestions?" she asked Petra.

"Let's go with the nineteenth of November. Is that okay with you, Euric?"

He nodded. "All right."

"Now we just have to pick a city in Germany that he immigrated from," Lia said. "We can say that was where he was born as well."

"I only know the names of the major cities in Germany," Petra replied back. "We should stick with something easy. Make it say he emigrated from Munich. It's large enough that if Euric ever does come in contact with someone else from that city they wouldn't find it strange that they don't know each other."

"Smart thinking." Lia took a small pad of paper out of her purse along with a pen and wrote down all the information they'd decided upon. "All right, I have all the info I need so I'm outta here." She gathered up her things and stuck them into her purse before she stood.

"You don't have to leave, Lia," Petra said as she and Euric followed Lia to the apartment door.

"Actually, I do. My guy wanted Euric's info ASAP or he wasn't going to do the IDs for us. I guess he now has a fiancé and she doesn't know anything about his shady past. She's away for a couple days, and he wants to get the IDs done before she gets back. Apparently, if she ever found out he could do them she'd be far from impressed."

Before Lia opened the door, Petra said, "Oh, the money. Did he tell you how much it'd be, and does he want it up front?"

Lia waved her questions away. "No hurry on the money. He said he didn't expect payment until he finished the work and you were happy with them. He knows I'll get the money to him."

"Okay, good. Thanks for doing this, Lia. I know it has to be putting you out."

"Yes," Euric said. "I have to thank you as well."

"You're both welcome. And don't worry about it. That's what friends are for. We help each other out." Lia opened the apartment door. "Catch you both later."

After she closed the door behind Lia, Petra took Euric to the kitchen to make the popcorn she'd promised him the night before. They were going to watch a DVD she'd rented and pig out on popcorn.

While Euric watched the popcorn pop in the hot air popper with fascination, Petra watched him. They were another step closer to making him a part of her world, and tomorrow night would mark the start of his week with her.

Petra couldn't wait.

CHAPTER TWELVE

Petra arrived the following morning at Greg's mansion, feeling a sense of excitement, knowing what was to come that night caused it. She'd sent Euric back to his time with the hopes that it'd be the last time she'd have to watch him step through the window. As she'd told him earlier, she intended to do everything in her power to change his mind about going back to fight after the week was up. She hoped his spending twenty-four hours with her for the next seven days would show him he could start a new life without having the rudis as a reminder of what he'd been. She couldn't stop thinking about the risks he'd be taking to get it.

Arriving in Greg's study, she found him sitting behind his desk, typing something on his desktop computer. He wore his usual suit and tie. Petra gave her skirt a twitch before she walked across the room. She'd taken a little extra care with what she wore this morning since she wanted to ask him if she could have a few days off.

He looked up when she approached. "Good morning, Petra. How are you today?"

"Good, thanks. Before we get started for the day, I was

wondering if I could ask you something."

"Of course. Sit down." Greg motioned her to sit in one of the chairs in front of his desk.

Once she sat, Petra took a few minutes to gather her thoughts before she spoke. "I noticed for the next couple days your schedule is going to be pretty light. I was hoping I could take those days off. You see, Euric has decided he wants to immigrate to the States. We're going to be living together, and need to get things organized for his move. I figured we could get them done a lot faster if I was home during the day for the first few days at least."

As she opened her mouth to say more, Greg held up his hand and smiled. "You don't have to give me any more reasons as to why you want some time off. I have no problem with it. If anything, I'd like to help you and Euric in any way I can. I enjoyed our visit the other day, and I found him to be a good man. Is there anything you can think of that would help facilitate his being able to get his green card?"

Petra started to scramble. With the fake IDs, Euric wouldn't need a green card, but she needed to think of something. "Well, um, let me see."

"What about a job? Does he have one yet? He won't be able to get his green card until he has one."

"Ah, no he doesn't. That was one of the things we were going to start working on when I'm off."

"Well, consider that one less thing you have to worry about. If Euric is willing to take it on, I have a job for him. Tony—who takes care of the upkeep of my grounds as well as the pool and hot tub—handed in his notice the other day. If Euric could start sometime next week, it'd give him a few days to learn what needs to be done before he has to take over the job himself. It's a labor-intensive job, but from the look of him, he has the build for it.

Actually, it'd work out perfectly. It'd be something for Euric to do, and she'd be close by if he needed her for some reason. He'd basically be working on his own, so he wouldn't have to worry about a cover story to tell the people he had to work with.

Petra nodded. "I have to ask Euric first, but I have a feeling he'll take the job. Though I'm pretty sure he doesn't know a thing about pools and hot tubs, and as for looking after the grass and gardens, it may be something new for him as well."

"That doesn't bother me. I'm sure he'll pick it up in no time. And since I'll probably be picking his brain from time to time about ancient Rome, I'll even pay him a little above the going rate."

Greg rattled off what would be Euric's salary. Petra had to blink at the amount. It was a lot more than what he was now paying Tony, and she knew since she did the payroll for the maid and Sally as well. It was along the same line as what she made.

"I think Euric will be more than pleased with that amount, Greg. When I see him this evening, I'll tell him."

"Good. Why don't you bring Euric by tomorrow and I can show him around and introduce him to Tony. He won't have to start right away. Tony has given me two-weeks' notice. Since today is Wednesday, both of you can have the rest of the week off and start back on Monday. Will that work with your plans?"

"It will more than work."

Euric would have a few days to settle into her time before he had to start working. And the job would be perfect for when she had to go back to work. Petra had wondered how he'd cope being cooped up in her apartment alone all day.

"Now that we have that all taken care of, here's what I have for you to work on today."

Greg pushed a stack of papers across the desk toward Petra. She picked them up and thumbed through them as he went over some points he wanted her to pay close attention to.

Once they reached the last page, he said, "And before I forget, you can leave early today if you wish. I'm having a dinner party tonight. Sally has come in early to get things ready. She could use a little help, and as you've noticed, I don't have that much work for you today. You wouldn't mind helping her, would you? She said not to worry about it when I suggested I get her an extra pair of hands, but you know Sally."

Petra laughed. "Yes. She hates to ask for help. I don't mind."

"Just don't tell her I sent you. Pretend it was your idea or she'll ban you from the kitchen."

"I will. She'll never know."

"Thanks, Petra." Greg pushed the laptop sitting on top his desk toward her. "I guess we should get down to business."

* * * *

A few hours later, Petra stepped into the mansion's kitchen to find Sally trying to do two things at once. Pots bubbled away on top the stove while she kneaded some kind of dough on the center island. The other woman's face was flushed and she had a streak of flour on her nose.

Crossing to where Sally worked, Petra said, "All right, what do you need me to do?"

Sally left off her kneading and looked at Petra. "You don't need to do anything. I'm perfectly fine handling this myself."

"Really now? And here I thought you looked a bit frazzled with the flour on your face."

The other woman rubbed her face and only managed to put more flour on her cheeks. "I told Greg not to worry. Though I do have to say, I wish he'd given me a bit more notice about this dinner party. I love the man, but his last-minute decisions will one day be the death of me."

Petra let out a laugh and grabbed a clean tea towel out of one of the kitchen drawers. She went back to Sally and wiped the flour from her face. "I doubt he'll ever change. He's the type of man who likes to do things at the spur of the moment. I don't think he tries to put people out. He just doesn't think that far ahead."

"I know." Sally kneaded the dough again.

"Seriously now, what can I do to help? Greg didn't have much work for me to do, and when he told me about you being in early to get started on the food for the dinner party, I figured I could lend you a hand." When Sally didn't accept her offer right away, Petra added, "I have some news about me that you'd be interested in hearing. You know how you can't resist juicy gossip."

Sally cocked an eyebrow in her direction. "How juicy?"

"If you let me help, I'll spill my guts."

"How can I resist that?" Sally asked with a laugh. "All right, you can help. How good are you at peeling and slicing apples?"

"I'm pretty handy with a paring knife."

"Then you get the job. Greg asked me to bake some apple pies."

Petra understood why Greg had requested them. Sally's Dutch apple pies were to die for. After Sally gave Petra a bag of apples, a paring knife and a large mixing bowl, Petra pulled out a stool and sat on the opposite side of the center island where Sally worked. Petra grabbed an apple and then peeled it while Sally took out a rolling pin and rolled out the dough she'd been working on.

After a few seconds, Sally said, "Well? What's this juicy gossip you have about yourself?"

Petra focused her attention on the apple she worked on. "I'm shacking up."

"Why that is scandalous," Sally said dramatically. "However will you live it down? Who are you shacking up with?"

Looking up, Petra smiled. "A certain German man who, until recently, was living in Rome."

"I thought you said he couldn't come to the States."

"Things changed quite suddenly and he's already here."

"And now you're going to move in together. Congratulations. When am I going to get to meet this boyfriend of yours?"

"Tomorrow. Actually, starting very soon you'll be seeing Euric every day."

"I will?"

"Yes. Greg has given Euric a job. Apparently, Tony has given his notice and will be leaving by the end of next week. Euric is going to fill his position."

"Let me guess. Since Euric is obviously going to be living here permanently, Greg offered the job to him to help with his immigration."

"You're right. It really isn't official. I haven't talked to Euric about the job just yet, but I'm ninety-nine point nine percent sure he'll take it."

"Greg does know how to treat his employees. The man has a heart of gold. Euric will find the grounds work a pretty easy job."

"I'm hoping he won't mind it." Petra sliced the apple she'd peeled and cored into the large mixing bowl. "I'm just happy Euric and I can finally be together."

"Yeah, the long-distance relationship must have been tough on you two. I'm glad it's working out for you. You never did tell me what your Euric looks like."

Petra smiled. "He's six-foot-three, blond, blue eyes, very handsome, and as my friend, Lia, would say, he's built like a brick shithouse."

Sally let out a loud whoop of laughter. "Lia sounds like my kind of gal. Blond and blue eyes, huh? And all those other things? I definitely want to meet him now. Don't mind me if I end up ogling him."

"You wouldn't be my first friend to do it. Lia has already met Euric and she's done her fair share of ogling."

"Is Euric starting work tomorrow?"

Petra shook her head. "No. He's just coming here so Greg can show him the grounds and introduce him to Tony. He won't start until next week. Greg also let me take the rest of this week off so Euric and I can get ourselves organized."

Sally took out a pie plate and put the dough she'd rolled out into the bottom of it. "Does Euric have to fly back to Rome?"

"No." Which was the truth. He wouldn't be flying. "In Rome, he didn't own much of anything, except for his clothes." Another truth. "So we don't have to worry about getting furniture or anything like that shipped over here."

"That should make things easier. I'm really happy for you, Petra."

"Thanks."

They fell silent as they focused on their work. Petra glanced at the clock on the stove. She had another six hours before she opened the window for Euric. She was kind of glad Greg hadn't had a lot of work for her to do, and that she could help Sally out in the kitchen. She had a feeling if she'd had to concentrate too hard on anything, she wouldn't have been able to keep her thoughts from straying. As it was now, she'd probably start counting down the hours.

Petra ended up staying to help Sally almost until the time she normally would have left work. With the promise to make sure she brought Euric to see Sally the next day, Petra left the mansion and then drove to her apartment. Smiling like a silly teenager, she couldn't wipe the smile off her face while she drove. Sure that anyone who saw her would think she looked like a goof, she really didn't care. She was going home and soon she'd have her gladiator at her side where he belonged.

* * * *

Euric found himself unable to stop pacing the length of his cell. He was excited and a little worried at the same time. He was excited about the prospect of being able to stay with Petra for the week, and a little worried that something would go wrong and the window would not open. Contrary to what she thought, there was nothing she could do to stop him from wanting to return to participate in his last *munera*.

The sound of the lock being turned on his cell door brought his pacing to a standstill. Euric turned as one of the slaves who worked in the *ludus'* kitchens walk around the guard who had opened the door with a large tray of food in his hands. Without a word, he went and placed it on the small wooden table that sat against the wall. His task completed, the slave walked out of the cell, and the guard closed the door behind him. The sound of it being locked once more could be heard right after.

Euric crossed to the table and looked down at the food. He gave it a cursory glance. It was a veritable banquet with meats, greens and even some kind of sweetmeat to end off the meal. Since tomorrow was to be his last day to fight, he had been given a better meal than the rest of the gladiators would have eaten that evening. He had also been locked in his cell earlier than he normally would have been. Since he was to be given his freedom the next day as well, his *Lanistae* did not want to take any chances that some of the others in the *familia* would try to get back at him because of it.

Euric turned his back on the food. There was no point eating it. If everything worked out, he would be back at this exact moment in time a week from now. He would eat it then. If he did not, it would look strange.

His heart beat faster as the window formed in front of him. After the mist cleared, he found Petra standing on the other side. She smiled, practically glowing, as her gaze met his. By the gods, how he loved her. He roamed his gaze down her body. Her long, light brown hair hung around her shoulders. By now he had every curve of her body memorized by touch. The feel of her held against him felt more than right. He still found it hard to believe at times that she was actually his woman.

Euric lifted his gaze and looked into Petra's dark green eyes. "You had no problem getting the window to appear when you asked it to open again a week from now?"

She shook her head. "None. It opened just as easily as it's done every night. Are you ready to come over here?"

He was more than ready. He had done nothing but think about it all day. His thoughts had also included those of Petra. Even though he had come to her every night, and they had usually made love at least once, this one seemed different. He wanted her with a yearning he could not ignore. Maybe it was the thought of this being the first step for them to be together on a more permanent basis. Whatever it was, just standing on his side of the window, seeing her, caused his cock to grow hard. Euric was glad to see Lia wasn't with Petra this night, because it was a given that as soon as he crossed her time he would have her in her arms. He ached to have her under him, to have her long legs wrapped around his waist while he rode her.

Petra must have been able to see the stark need on his face, because he heard her take a quick breath. Her cheeks flushed as she breathed a little faster. The tip of her tongue come out and wet her lips, which made his cock harden even more. He knew what it felt like to have it, and her mouth, on his sex, bringing him closer to ecstasy.

As Petra reached through the window, Euric quickly took her hand and allowed her to pull him through. Once he was completely on the other side, he quickly looked behind him in time to see the window shut. It was too late to turn back now, not that he wanted to. Euric closed the distance between them before he wrapped her in his embrace.

Petra sighed as he brought his mouth down onto hers. He kissed her greedily, unable to get enough of her. He pushed his tongue past her lips. The taste of her went straight to his head. Lifting her off her feet, Euric urged her to put her legs around his waist while he carried her to the bedroom. He ached to be inside her, but he wanted to take her on the bed.

He placed her on the center of it and then stepped back to take his clothes off. Petra's gaze followed his every move. After he was naked, he said huskily, "Take your clothes off for me, Petra."

"My pleasure."

Euric stayed where he was as he had his turn to watch her strip out of her clothes. With every inch of bare flesh she revealed, his arousal beat at him a little harder. By the time the last of her clothing hit the floor, he was ready to dive on her, but he held back. He wanted this to be as good for Petra as it would be for him.

She held her arms out to him when he climbed onto the bed next to her. He took her mouth and moved into her embrace. He rolled them to their sides as he took hold of Petra's thigh and put it over his hip. The tips of her taut nipples brushed against his chest as he urged her even closer. The head of his cock came to rest along the inside of her thigh, but he made no move to enter her.

Euric took Petra's hand and led it to his erect cock. She wrapped her fingers around his shaft, stroking up and down his length. His blood pounded in his ears as he left her lips and bent his head to take a nipple into his mouth. Her grip tightened around him when he sucked. She gave a breathy moan. The sounds she made while he made love to her always pushed his arousal even higher.

He had wanted to wait a little bit longer before he took her, but Petra had other plans. Shifting her hips into position, she led his cock to the slick entrance of her pussy. "No more waiting. I want you inside me."

Unable to resist the warm wetness of Petra's body closing around the very tip of his shaft, Euric pulled her hand off him and slowly sheathed himself to the hilt. He groaned loudly at the sensation of her body stretching around his, holding him tight. He gripped her thigh, pulled back, then pushed his full length inside her.

Petra buried her fingers in his hair and brought his mouth back to hers while he continued to pump between her legs. She kissed him with her teeth and tongue, moaning into his mouth when he hit the right spot inside her. She slanted hers over his, deepening the kiss while her inner muscles squeezed around his shaft. Euric pumped his hips faster, feeling his orgasm edging ever nearer.

He let go of her leg, shifted his hand to where they were joined and found her clit. He stroked, wanting her to find her release before he found his. The combination of his surging inside her and stroking the small bundle of nerves between her legs was enough to send her tumbling over the edge into climax. She tightened her hands in his hair while her body rhythmically clutched his cock. Unable to hold back any longer, Euric surged into her one final time as he too found his release. He moaned while he emptied himself deep inside her pussy.

Once they were no longer breathing hard, Euric rolled onto his back, taking Petra with him. She lay sprawled along the length of his body with her head tucked under his chin. After a while she lifted her head and drew lazy circles on his chest with the tip of her finger.

Euric put his hand on top of hers to still her movements. "You are thinking about something."

She lifted her gaze and smiled. "Yes. Something that

concerns you."

"I like the sound of that. Does it have anything to do with you and me in your bed? Are you thinking about all the pleasurable things I want to do to your body?"

Petra's gaze fell to his lips. She swallowed. "Ah, no, but I don't think it'd take much to get me thinking along those lines."

"Then what is going on in that head of yours?"

She lifted her gaze back up to his. "I had a very productive day today with Greg."

"How so?"

"I managed to get you a job with him. How good are you working outside with plants?"

He was not all that surprised that Petra had found him a job already. She was nothing if not resourceful. "I have had some experience if you are talking about planting and tending fields. I may have been a warrior, but I still had to help my father till his plot of land."

"Well, the job Greg has for you wouldn't be as hard as looking after a field. His groundskeeper/pool maintenance guy is leaving at the end of next week, and Greg has offered you the job. If you want it."

"What exactly would I be doing?"

"You would have to tend the flowerbeds, cut the grass when it needs doing and do the general upkeep of the pool and hot tub."

"I guess I could do all those things. Cutting grass can be back-breaking work, though."

Petra chuckled. "Using a riding lawn mower is hardly going to break your back. You're thinking of how it would be done in your time. We now have a better way of doing things like that. Even looking after the pool will be relatively easy once you learn how to do it. The money will be good. You'll be making close to what I make. Plus, the added bonus is we'll be working together."

Euric had not said anything to Petra, but he had known

he would not have been able to sit around every day all day without something to do. He was used to hard work. While living in his village, he was either training or helping his parents with the farming. Even as a gladiator, he was always training. Being idle for any length of time would have gotten to him eventually.

"This job sounds like something I would want to do."

Petra kissed his chin. "Good. Greg will be happy. He thinks he's helping you get your green card. It's something anyone from another country who wishes to stay and work in the States needs. You won't need one since you'll be an American citizen when you get your fake IDs. Greg doesn't need to know about them, by the way. About them being fake that is."

"I will not say anything. So when would I start this job?"

"Tomorrow Greg wants you to meet with him so he can show you around and introduce you to Tony, the man whose job you're going to be taking over. Tony will start training you next week."

Euric had a feeling Petra would not like his next question, but he had to ask it anyway. "What will you tell Greg when I go back to fight in the *munera* and do not show up for my job that day?"

Petra put her hand over his mouth. "I don't want to hear anything about you having to fight. You just got here. As for that day, if — I'm not going to be able to think of it in any other way than a big if — it comes to that I'll think of something when I have to."

He pulled her hand away. "Fine. I won't speak of the *munera*." Euric held on to Petra and rolled her under him. "I would much rather use my mouth for other things."

And he did. He soon had Petra moaning with pleasure while she clutched his back. Neither one of them spoke about his having to fight for the rest of the night.

* * * *

The next afternoon Petra walked hand and hand with Euric to the front door of Greg's mansion. They'd slept in late. Not surprising, considering they hadn't done much sleeping during the night. He'd been almost insatiable. Not that she was complaining. It was as if they'd started their new life together with a bang.

Petra didn't ring the bell since she'd called ahead to let Greg know they were coming. Plus, during the day she was used to just walking into the mansion when she was working.

She took Euric to the kitchen first to meet Sally as she'd promised. Sally had her back to them when they first stepped into the room, but turned around when she heard them come up behind her. She took one look at Euric and then looked him up and down with appreciation showing in her eyes.

Sally turned to Petra and gave her a wink. "So are you going to introduce me or do I have to do it myself?"

Petra smiled. "Sally, this is Euric. Euric this is Sally. She cooks for Greg."

"It is a pleasure to meet you, Sally," Euric said.

"Oh, he's polite too," Sally said with a smile. "Nice to meet you as well. I've heard lots about you from Petra. I hear you two are shacking up."

When Euric turned to look questioningly at Petra, she added, "Sally means we're living together."

"I understand now. Yes, we are living together."

"I'm glad things worked out for you and Petra, and that you were able to come to the States. And it'll be nice having you work here as well. I have a feeling Petra will be thinking up lots of excuses to go outside to see you."

Petra pretended to be shocked. "I will do no such thing."

Sally laughed. "If you did, I wouldn't blame you.

You've got yourself a looker here."

"A looker?" Euric asked, obviously not understanding the slang word Sally had used.

Petra took pity on him. "Sally means you're good looking. I guess we should see Greg." She turned Euric toward the kitchen doorway. As they walked away, she turned her head in Sally's direction, and said, "When Greg is showing Euric around, I'll come back to keep you company."

They found Greg in his study. He walked around his desk and greeted them. "How are the moving plans going?"

"Good so far," Petra answered for them. She took a quick look at Euric. "Euric is settling into my apartment nicely."

"Did Petra tell you about my job offer?"

Euric nodded. "Yes, and if you are still willing, I would like to accept it."

"Excellent. Petra also said you don't have much experience doing grounds work or working with pools, but I'm sure you'll be able to handle it. I've already told Tony he'd have to train you, and he's willing to show you everything he knows."

"I look forward to getting started next week."

"Great." Greg looked at Petra. "I'm going to show Euric around now. I'm sure you'd like to go visit with Sally while we're gone."

Petra smiled. "I already promised her I'd come back for a talk after I introduced her to Euric."

Greg nodded, then led Euric out of his study. Petra followed them. Once they headed for the French doors that opened to the backyard, she went to the kitchen. Sally sat at the center island, waiting for her to return.

Petra went and sat on the stool next to her. "Greg has taken Euric outside. We should have enough time for a bit of a chat."

Sally looked out the kitchen window that gave a good view of the backyard. Petra followed her gaze. Greg and Euric were talking as they walked across the grass to where Tony worked on one of the flowerbeds.

Sally let out a low whistle. "Honey, you must have done something right to land a fine piece of ass like that."

"Sally!" Petra said, then burst out laughing when she gave her an "Oh, come on" look. "All right, I have to admit Euric has an amazing body."

"That's putting it mildly. Your friend is right. Euric *is* built like a brick shithouse. No ifs ands or buts about it. If I were about twenty years younger, I'd be giving you a run for your money for that one. That deep accented voice of his..." Sally shivered dramatically. "It just goes right through you."

"Tell me about it," Petra said dreamily.

Thinking Sally had to be right, that she had done something in her life to deserve Euric, Petra couldn't help thinking how perfect her life had become with him in it while they talked about other things. While she talked to Sally, her gaze strayed to the kitchen window now and again, falling unerringly on him. They really were a perfect match. Even though they hadn't ever discussed it, she already thought she'd found her happily ever after with him.

CHAPTER THIRTEEN

The following day, Lia came over to Petra's apartment with the finished fake IDs. Seeing them, Petra would never have known they were fakes, they had been done so well. Even when she took out her own passport to compare it to Euric's, she couldn't tell the difference. They were well worth the large amount of money she'd written a check for in Lia's name.

"So what do you two have planned for the rest of the day?" Lia asked as she stuck the check inside her purse.

"Petra is going to take me to buy some clothes," Euric replied.

Petra nodded. "I was going to take him to the mall. You want to tag along?"

"I would love to. I wouldn't want to miss out on Euric's first trip to the mall. If you don't mind, let's drive separately. I have to hit the bank while we're there to cash your check and then I have to run the money over to my guy."

"Sure, no problem."

After the three of them arrived at the mall, Petra watched Euric's face as they headed for the entrance.

There was a stream of people coming in and out the doors. This would be his first time having to be around such a large crowd. So far, he didn't seem bothered by them.

Once inside the mall, Euric's steps did falter a bit while he looked all around him. This wasn't a busy Saturday afternoon, but there were enough people milling around.

As he looked at her, she asked, "Are you all right?"

"Yes. I have never seen a market this large before. It must have just about everything I could possibly imagine for sale."

Lia laughed. "And probably then some. Come on. Let's get you some new duds."

Euric took Petra's hand, lacing their fingers together, as Lia took charge and brought them to one of the trendier clothing stores in the mall. His eyes widened when they went to the men's section and he saw all the racks of clothes.

"There are so many. I do not know where to start," he said.

Petra squeezed his hand. "Lia and I will help you."

They spent the next half hour picking out several pairs of jeans, long-sleeved t-shirts, some more t-shirts, shorts and a few button-down shirts. Euric tried everything on, coming out of the change room to show Petra and Lia how the clothes fit.

Near the end, Petra could tell he was getting a little fed up with it all, but they weren't done yet. Next they went to another store to buy him some underwear and socks. Eruic didn't find that as stressful since she was quick to reassure him he wouldn't have to try any of those on.

After that, they went to a shoe store. When Euric realized what type of store it was, he asked, "Is this where I can get the shit-kicker boots you told me about?"

Lia half-snorted, half-laughed. "I think we can get you a pair of those, but not at this store." She led them to another shoe place on the other side of the mall. This one seemed to have an eclectic range in styles of shoes and boots. "Now this is more like it."

They found the boots Euric wanted near the back of the store. Black with chains around the ankle and heel, Petra had to admit they'd look really good with the pair of black jeans they'd bought earlier for him. They also found him a pair of skateboard shoes before they left the store. Her credit card had taken a beating, but she figured it was well worth it.

Lia decided to help Petra and Euric carry their purchases out to Petra's car since they were loaded down with shopping bags.

As she put the bags into the trunk, she said, "Euric, make sure you wear those shit kickers when you go to Petra's parents' place. I'm sure her brother will love them," she said with a snort.

Euric turned to Petra. "You are going to take me to meet your parents?"

Petra nodded. She'd forgotten all about being invited to her parents' house until just now. "It's my brother's birthday in a couple days. I was invited over for supper. It's just a small family get-together with my parents, brother and his wife. Which reminds me, I'd better call my mom and tell her I'll be bringing you."

"Are you sure you want me to meet your family?"

"Of course I do. Why wouldn't I? You need to meet them sometime, and this is the best way to do it when we'll all be together. That way it'll stop a certain family member from dropping by when I least expect it."

Lia gave a half laugh. "What Petra means is her brother is a prick and likes to stick his nose in her life where it doesn't belong."

Petra grimaced. "Bluntly put, but Lia is right about that one. Chad, my brother, *is* a prick. He usually annoys the hell out of me."

"Would you like me to talk to your brother about his

behavior toward you?" Euric asked with a hint of displeasure in his voice.

"No!" Petra said quickly. "No. That would just piss my mom off and then I'd never hear the end of it. When it comes to Chad, it's best to let him shoot his mouth off while you basically ignore everything he says."

"I will try, but I cannot promise you I will be able to say nothing if he starts to insult you."

Lia laughed. "God, how I wish I could go with you two. I have a feeling it'll be an interesting evening."

Petra rolled her eyes. "Don't encourage Euric, Lia."

"That's me. I'm just a bad influence. Well, I'm going to run to the bank before it gets too lined up. I have to work tonight, so I'll give you a call in a couple days." Lia walked away, heading toward the mall's entrance.

Euric remained silent until they were in the car and on their way to her apartment. "Why would you not want me to say anything to your brother? You are my woman. That means it is my right to look out for you."

"Ordinarily, I would be thankful for you sticking up for me, but Chad is another story. If you, or even I, were to say something to him in front of my mother, it'd cause a rift between my family. My dad would stick up for me while my mom would side with my brother. To her, the sun rises and sets on Chad. He never does any wrong in my mom's eyes."

"I have a feeling I will dislike your brother when I meet him."

Petra laughed. "Most of the friends I've had over the years haven't been able to stand Chad. Lia despises him. When we were younger, he told her she'd better watch what she said around men or she'd end up alone, or with a man who'd hit her to shut her up. Let's just say I've never seen Lia that mad since. She was ready to commit murder."

"There was a warrior in my village who had that kind

of attitude. He felt as if he could do everything better than anyone else and that he knew everything. He soon learned to keep his mouth shut."

"What happened to him?"

"He had angered one of the other warriors one too many times. The other warrior he had offended ended up beating him with the flat of his sword until he could not get up anymore. After spending a week in bed recovering, he no longer thought so highly of himself."

Petra shot Euric a quick glance before she focused on the road once more. "Are you going to miss not living in your village?"

Euric reached across his seat and put his hand on her thigh. "I will miss what I had, but the life I had there is no more. The Romans made sure of that. My life is now with you, Petra. If I did not have you, I do not know where I would have gone. You have become a part of me."

"You know I'll always love you, Euric, but where do we go from here?"

"I do not understand."

"We've told each other how we feel, we're moving in together, and you're taking the biggest step of all by deciding to leave your time behind to live in mine. Lots of couples in this day and age live together. It's not as big a deal as it used to be at one time. I guess what I'm trying to say is, are you thinking about us becoming husband and wife one day?"

Eruic gave her leg a squeeze. "Petra, I already think of you as my wife. In my village, when a man and woman made the decision to live together they were considered as good as married. My village wasn't large enough to have our own priest so a lot of marriages were not made official until months or years later when one eventually came there."

They'd reached her apartment building, and Petra parked the car. She shut it off and then turned in her seat to face Euric. "Well, husband," she said with a smile. "Then we'll eventually have to make it official as well, but I'm afraid weddings in my time can be very elaborate affairs. And people tend to get engaged, that's like being betrothed, sometimes for years before they marry. So there isn't any need for us to rush."

Euric shifted in his seat, moving closer, and placed his hand on her belly. "And if my child already grows inside you?"

"You don't have to worry about that. I'm on the pill so I can't get pregnant."

"You cannot have children?" Euric wore a look of pity on his face.

Petra quickly reassured him. "I *can* have children. It's just while I'm taking the birth control pill I can't right now. It makes sure I won't get pregnant. When I stop taking it, I'll be able to."

"Ah." He brushed his lips across hers. "I guess that means I can make love to you as many times as I want and not have to worry about the repercussions."

"Exactly. We can decide to have a baby when we're ready for one. Until then you'll have me all to yourself."

"Mmm, I like the sound of that. It also means we get to have lots of practice so we get it right when we want to have a child. I am thinking I would like to do a little practicing right now."

Euric ran his thumb along Petra's bottom lip. She opened her mouth and sucked it inside. His eyes grew heavy and he let out a low moan. She pulled away before she did something stupid like crawl across her seat and sit on his lap. She didn't want to have one of her neighbors calling the cops on them for committing a lurid act out in public.

Petra opened the car door. Before she got out, she said, "Help me get these shopping bags upstairs and then I'm all yours."

Euric hurried out of the car and stood at the trunk before Petra could open it. They raced to the set of elevators that would take them up to her apartment. Once they reached it, the door had barely closed behind them before they tore at each other's clothes.

* * * *

The rest of the week, and the weekend, seemed to fly by for Petra. Now that Euric had his fake ID, she'd taken him to the gym close to her apartment and both of them had gotten memberships. He took to the gym like a fish to water. She'd showed him what little she knew of weightlifting, but he quickly picked up more by watching some of the other men. And the amount of weight he could lift had more than one head turning his way. He thought nothing of it when curling fifty pound dumbbells.

Going to the gym had also become part of their daily routine. Euric wanted to train every day to keep in condition. Petra knew he did it to keep in fighting shape when he had to return for the *munera*, even though he hadn't said as much. His having to fight was one subject they tended to stay away from. Having him there, settling into her life, she found she couldn't think about him going back even if it was only for one day without feeling as if she'd have a panic attack.

Once Sunday rolled around, the day they were to go to her parents' house for dinner, Petra dreaded having to take Euric. It wasn't that she didn't want him to meet her family. It was just the thought of what he'd have to endure there that bothered her.

She'd called her mom a few days before to let her know she'd be bringing someone with her. Of course that led to her mother asking her a ton of questions about Euric. Petra wisely decided not to tell her mother that he was living with her and that they were basically engaged. She figured she'd wait until the family was all together to spring it on them.

When it was finally time for her and Euric to leave, Petra gave him a quick once over. He wore a deep burgundy-colored button-down shirt, black jeans that were snug in all the right places and his new shit kickers. She'd chosen to wear a pair of blue jeans and a peach-colored silk blouse. Even though it was a family get-together, her mother would expect her to not come dressed too casually.

Petra nodded at Euric when he held out his arms for her to give him the final inspection. "You look great, Euric. And the boots are the perfect touch."

"I am glad you approve."

She grabbed her purse and keys. "We might as well get this over with."

During the time it took to drive to her parents' house, Petra's muscles in her shoulders tightened more with each minute that passed. She always got this way when she'd have to be around her brother for any length of time. Once she pulled into her parents' driveway, her muscles in her neck had knotted.

After getting out of the car, she waited for Euric to reach her side before she took a deep breath and walked toward the front door. Before they reached it, he pulled her to a halt and wrapped his arms around her. He kissed her until she loosened up a bit. Her mother probably saw the whole thing through the front window, but she pretty much didn't care.

"Thanks. I needed that," Petra said as they starting walking again.

"I could tell," Euric said as he smiled.

Just as they reached the front door, it swung open. Her mother stood in the open doorway and gave Petra a reproving look before she turned to Euric with a smile. "You must be Euric."

"I am. And you must be Petra's mother."

Her mother nodded, then stepped aside for Petra and Euric to enter the house. "You can call me May." She said to Petra, "You might as well take Euric to the living room. Your father is in there. Chad and Ashley haven't arrived yet."

Petra motioned for Euric to follow her when she headed for the living room. Her father sat in one of the armchairs, reading the newspaper. He put it down once they walked in and stood to greet them.

She took Euric's hand, and said, "Dad, this is Euric. Euric this is my father."

Her father stuck out his hand and shook Euric's. "Nice to meet you. I'm Derek. Why don't the two of you take the couch while we wait for the others to show up?"

Once they were all settled, her father said, "So, Euric, what do you think of Los Angeles so far? It's not quite the same as Rome, is it?"

When Petra had called her mom to tell her she'd be bringing Euric, she'd used the same story she'd told Sally about him being in Rome before he came to the States.

"It is very different, but I have started to become used to it." Euric looked at Petra. "Your daughter has helped me to settle in."

Her father cleared his throat until they looked at him. "Glad to hear it. Did you have any problems finding a place to live? I imagine it must have been hard finding an apartment in Los Angeles while you were living in Rome."

Petra decided there was no time like the present to start breaking the news to her family about how things stood between her and Euric. "Ah, Euric didn't have to find an apartment, Dad. He moved in with me."

Her father gave a nod. He said, "Have you told your mother yet?"

"No. I figured I'd wait until after we've had dinner."

"Smart thinking. Though I doubt your mother will have

too much to say about it."

"She may when I also tell her that Euric and I are pretty much engaged."

"Now that may cause a bit of an uproar, considering this is the first we've heard about Euric. I think I'd wait to break the news until after we've had the cake. It's that rich chocolate fudge your mother gets from that bakery. I'd hate not being able to get a piece of it."

Petra smiled. "I can do that."

Euric spoke up. "Maybe you should not say anything right now if it could cause some trouble."

Her dad let out a little chuckle. "From experience, I've learned it's always best to be up front right from the start with May. If she were to find out she was one of the last people to know, it'd just upset her even more."

Euric looked at Petra. "Are you sure?"

She nodded. "Yes. Dad's right. It's better to do this now rather than later."

Euric turned back to her father. "Just so you know, I love your daughter very much and I intend to take care of her."

Her dad smiled. "Don't worry. It isn't me you'll have to impress. Your relationship with Petra may seem to have progressed faster than some, but I can tell from the way she looks at you that she loves you as well. When it's right, it's right. I know. May doesn't like to talk about it too much, but when we first met, we knew we were meant for each other. We were even all set to get married two months after we started dating. The only reason we didn't was because May's parents insisted we stay engaged for a year or they wouldn't pay for the wedding." He smiled at Petra. "Of course you know your mother wouldn't have wanted that to happen, so we waited."

"I didn't know that," Petra said. "I knew you two were engaged for a year before you got married, but I didn't know you two basically fell in love at first sight."

Her dad's smile widened. "Well, just remember that when your mother starts complaining that you two are moving too fast. She'll only be doing it because she figures it's the right thing for her to do."

"I'll remember," Petra assured him.

At that point, her mother walked into the living room with her brother and his wife. Petra looked at Chad. He was four years her senior. He had the same light brown hair and dark green eyes she had, but that's where the similarities ended. Chad was taller at five-foot-eleven, and now one year away from thirty, he had a bit of a paunch going on. Not that Chad had ever really been athletic in the first place.

His wife, Ashley, stood at his side. Her nervous gaze kept flitting on Euric and away again. She was shorter than Petra and had fine dark brown hair that she cut to her chin. Ashley wore a baggy pair of jeans and a loose-fitting blouse over her thin frame. And as usual, she looked to be as timid as a mouse. She was so unsure of herself she usually let Chad make all the major decisions in their life, which was probably one of the reasons he'd married her. Being overbearing, he wouldn't have wanted a wife who knew how to stand up for herself.

Chad's gaze landed on Euric. "I'm Petra's brother, Chad. You must be the new boyfriend. Ernie is it?"

Petra knew damn well Chad knew Euric's name. Her brother had a talent for remembering names. If this was anything to go by, she figured it was going to be a fun night for Euric and her. Not.

Euric stood and held his hand out to Chad. Petra had to hide a smile behind hers when Chad had to look up to meet Euric's gaze. In his shit kickers, Euric towered over her brother, which of course Chad surely hated. He liked to be the one able to look down at people.

With his hand still held out, Euric said, "No, it's Euric."

Chad reluctantly took Euric's hand. He grimaced

slightly when Euric closed it around his and gave it a hard shake. Petra had to cough to cover up the laugh that threatened to bubble out of her, especially when Chad seemed to take in Euric's muscular size.

Her mother quickly said, "The food is ready. You all can go sit in the dining room while I bring it to the table."

Petra got off the couch and walked beside Euric to the dining room. Her father went and sat at one end of the table while Chad and Ashley sat on one side with Petra and Euric opposite.

Her mother brought out a large platter of roast chicken, a large bowl of mashed potatoes, another filled with green beans and a gravy boat with chicken gravy. After she sat, they passed the food around the table.

When the platter of chicken reached Euric, he reached for his knife and was about ready to stab a piece of meat with it. Petra quickly cleared her throat to get his attention and shook her head.

She whispered softly, "Use the serving fork on the platter."

Euric nodded before he put down his knife and did as she'd told him. Petra looked up from putting some mashed potatoes on her plate to find Chad watching her and Euric. He gave a snort and shook his head. She decided she'd let that one slide.

Once everyone started to eat, Petra looked at Euric to see how he managed. Since they didn't have forks in ancient Rome, and slaves were usually given wooden spoons only to eat with, she'd had to teach him how to eat with one. He still hadn't quite mastered it yet, especially using a knife and a fork at the same time to cut meat. He tended to fist the fork while he used the knife, as he was doing now. Sensing her watching him, he looked up from his plate and turned his head in her direction. She gave him an encouraging smile.

The sound of her brother snickering across the table

caused Petra to scowl at him. He snickered again. "What? I'm not allowed to find humor in your boyfriend's ham-fisted attempts to use a knife and fork? Don't they know how to use cutlery properly in Germany?"

Petra started to say something, knowing she couldn't just sit there and let Chad ridicule Euric, but her father beat her to it. "Chad, keep your opinions to yourself. Euric is a guest, as well as your sister's boyfriend. As I recall, I don't think Petra was ever rude to Ashley when you first brought her home to meet us."

Properly rebuked, her brother's face turned a light shade of red. "Sorry." He quickly changed the subject since it wasn't something he liked. Chad turned to look at their mother. "Mom, the food is delicious."

Her mother beamed at Chad. "I'm glad, dear. I know it's one of your favorites." She turned to Petra. "And speaking of rudeness, Petra, you never wished your brother a happy birthday."

Of course her mom would want to turn the tables on Petra. Once again having to bite her tongue to stop herself from saying something to her mother that she'd regret later, she said in a monotone voice, "Happy birthday."

Chad gave her a knowing smile. "Thanks."

The rest of the meal passed with no more caustic remarks from Chad, mostly because her mother had gotten him talking about his middle management job at a large insurance company.

After her mother cleared the table and then dished up Chad's birthday cake, Euric leaned into Petra and said in her ear, "I do not know how you can stand being around your brother and not want to strike him."

Petra chuckled softly and then whispered back, "I've had years of practice."

"What are you two whispering about over there?" her mother suddenly asked.

"Nothing," Petra quickly answered.

Everyone was just about finished eating their cake when Petra figured the time had come to break the news about her and Euric to the rest of her family. She put down her fork and loudly cleared her throat. Once she had everyone's attention, she put her hand on his where it sat on top the table. She smiled at him, then looked at her family.

"Euric and I have some good news to share with you all."

Her mother gave her a small smile. "And what would that be?"

At her father's encouraging nod, Petra took a deep breath. "Now that Euric has immigrated to the States, we've moved in together. We're also going to get married."

There was a shocked silence before her mother said haltingly, "Petra, you and Euric just met. How can you possibly know each other well enough to make that kind of decision?"

"Let's just say it was love at first sight."

"What bullshit," Chad said sneeringly. "There is no such thing. And if he was living in Rome up until a few days ago, how could you possibly fall in love with him that quickly."

Petra's jaw ached when she clenched it to stop herself from screaming at Chad. Instead, she said, "I've known Euric longer than a couple days. We met a couple weeks ago."

"Where? Over the Internet? I didn't realize you were so hard up, Petra. Only losers use online dating services."

"I didn't meet Euric that way," she said through gritted teeth.

"It may not have been a dating service, but you obviously had to have met on the Internet, considering he was living on the other side of the world. I thought you were smarter than that, Petra. This kind of behavior just shows how wrong I was. You're an idiot who obviously needs someone to tell her when she's being a brainless twit."

Euric's large fist smacked down on the table, causing the dessert plates to jump. "That will be enough," he said in a strained voice. "I will no longer sit here and listen to you talk to Petra that way."

"Oh yeah," Chad shot back. "You can't tell me what to do."

Euric glared across the table at her brother. "When you deliberately insult my woman, I have every right to make you stop."

Chad shot to his feet and walked around the table to stand at the back of Petra's and Euric's chairs. "Your woman? You sound like a throwback to the Dark Ages. So you think you can stop me from saying what's on my mind in my parents' house? Just try it, big man."

The muscles bunched in Euric's forearm as she put a hand on it. "Just let it go, Euric."

"Not this time." He shook her off and surged to his feet. He grabbed the front of Chad's shirt and pulled him closer. He bent down and put his face in front of Chad's. "Don't start something you will never be able to finish. And I have given you my last warning about insulting Petra." Euric shoved her brother away hard enough that he almost fell over.

Chad's face turned a bright shade of red and his upper lip snarled just before he threw a punch at Euric, which never connected. Euric easily blocked it with his left forearm while at the same time he pulled back his right arm and smashed his fist into Chad's face.

Having caught the punch squarely on the chin, Chad staggered backward before he fell to the floor. Her mother let out an ear-piercing shriek as she got up and rushed to his side.

"How dare you hit my son in my home," her mother

yelled at Euric. Turning to her husband, she said loudly, "Just don't sit there. Do something. Your son was just assaulted. Call the police."

Her father picked up his napkin and wiped his mouth. "Calm down, May. As far as I'm concerned, Chad got what he deserved. He threw the first punch. Euric was only defending himself."

Her mother's mouth opened and closed a few times like a fish gasping for air on dry land. One she brought herself back under control, she turned a furious stare on Petra. "Get him out of my house right this instant. That man is no longer welcome here. I also forbid you to marry him."

As her mother tapped Chad's face when he moaned, Petra got up and stood beside Euric. "We'll leave. And Mom, I'm a grown woman. You can't forbid me to do anything."

Her mother's head snapped up in her direction. "That man hit your brother. You can't possibly think to marry him now."

"That man is my fiancé, Mom. I love him and I *will* marry him whether you like it or not. Dad's right, Chad got what he deserved."

"He's your brother."

"And Euric is soon to be my husband."

"So you're going to take his side instead of your family's?"

"If you push me to it, yes, I will. Euric is now my family too."

Her mother's head shot back as if Petra had physically slapped her. "If you still intend to marry him, then I'm afraid I won't have anything to do with you anymore."

Feeling her temper soar with each word that came out of her mother's mouth, Petra decided she'd taken enough. She looked at her father.

He motioned for her to go and mouthed the words, *It's all right.*

Petra nodded. Before she left with Euric, she glanced at Ashley. She was still sitting at the table, nervously wringing her hands, making no move to come to her husband's aid.

More than disgusted with some of the members of her family, Petra gladly turned her back on them and left her parents' house with no idea if her mother would ever let her come back.

CHAPTER FOURTEEN

E uric followed Petra to her car as she stomped over to it. She kept muttering angrily under her breath. Unable to hear what she said, he had to wonder if she was mad with him or just angry at her mother and brother. If she was angry with him, he was not about to apologize for something that had needed doing. In his time, if a man insulted a woman as Chad had insulted his sister, he would have gotten a lot more than a punch in the face. He would have counted himself lucky not to end up with a knife between his ribs.

After Petra backed the car out onto the street and then drove away, Euric could not take her angry muttering any longer. "Are you angry at me for hitting your brother? If you are, I will not say I am sorry for hitting the bastard."

Petra smacked the steering wheel with the palm of her hand a couple times before she answered him. "I'm not really angry at you. I'm furious at my mom and brother. A part of me is happy that you hit Chad, but another part isn't thrilled that you had to do it in front of my mom. I told you she'd take it out on me."

"I held back for as long as I could, Petra. If we had been

in my time, I would have used my sword instead of my fist."

"This isn't your time, Euric. You have to stop thinking about how you did things in the fourth century. You now live in the twenty-first century. You're no longer a warrior, and you sure as hell can't go around hitting people just because they piss you off."

Feeling a bit irritated by Petra's remarks, Euric said flatly, "I will always be a warrior. It is not something I can just walk away from. It is a part of who I am."

"Then I suggest you work on getting rid of that part of yourself. If you don't, you'll have a hard time fitting into my time."

Euric told himself Petra was just angry, that she really did not mean what she said. That did not stop him from feeling a bit hurt that she'd actually say that. "So my being a warrior will make me less of a man in this time?"

"I never said that."

"No, but that is basically what you mean. If I do not stop thinking of myself as a warrior I will not be like the other men of your time."

Petra smacked the steering wheel again. "Stop putting words into my mouth. You don't understand what kind of repercussions I'm going to have to face with your one thoughtless act of violence. My mother has disowned me and she probably won't talk to me again. Now that will put a strain on my relationship with my father. He's going to be stuck between my mother and me."

Euric was now more than a little irritated. "I will apologize for that, but I will not for the rest. If you think I have to change to live in your world, maybe deciding to come to this time was a mistake. Fighting is all I know and I am damn good at it. Maybe when I return to fight in the *munera* I should just stay in my time."

Having just about reached a stop sign, Petra slammed on the brakes so hard he was thrown forward against the seatbelt. She turned to him and said in a half growl, "Don't even go there. Not now. I don't need you to say things like that when I'm already ready to rip someone's head off."

The sound of a horn behind them had Petra turning to look out the car's back window. She turned back around and started to drive again. Neither one of them said another word the rest of the drive to the apartment.

* * * *

Once Petra's alarm went off the next morning, she shut it off before she stretched her arm out to the other side of the bed. Not feeling Euric's large body beside her, she sat up. Seeing the closed bedroom door had her remembering the big fight they'd had after they'd gotten home from her parents' place. She also remembered at the end of it she'd shoved a pillow and some extra blankets into his arms after she'd told him he'd be sleeping on the couch that night.

Petra let out a groan and fell back on the bed. Everything she'd said to Euric came rushing back. What she'd said to him...he hadn't deserved it. God, she'd been a bitch. If he was still angry with her, she wouldn't blame him.

After throwing back the covers, she got out of bed and then opened the bedroom door. In the living room, she found Euric stretched out on the couch with his feet hanging over the end of it. The blankets were half across his body and half hanging on the floor. He slept in the clothes he'd been wearing last night. He'd taken off his shit kickers and had left them near the coffee table.

Feeling like an even greater bitch, Petra quietly walked over to the couch. She knelt on the floor beside Euric's head. Gently, so as not to startle him, she caressed his cheek.

He jerked awake and blinked up at her. "Petra?"

"I'm sorry. I didn't mean to say all those things I said last night. I was just angry. Can you forgive me?"

Euric pushed himself up into a sitting position. "We were both angry and said things we should not have."

"I wish we'd never gone to my parents' place."

"What is done is done."

"I didn't mean it when I said you had to change, Euric. There's nothing wrong with the way you are."

"It is all right, Petra."

He pulled her to him and gave her a kiss. When he drew away, Petra was able to see the hurt that still lingered in his eyes at the mention of her telling him she wanted him to change. He may have forgiven her, but that didn't mean the damage hadn't already been done. She'd have been just as hurt if Euric had been the one to tell her she'd never fit in if she didn't change a big aspect of herself.

Petra wanted nothing more than to fling herself into Euric's arms and make love to him until she'd erased the hurt from his eyes, but there wasn't time. They had to be at Greg's to start work in less than an hour. It'd have to wait until after they came home at the end of the day.

She pushed off her knees and stood. "We have to get ready for work. You can take the shower first while I whip us up a quick breakfast."

Euric pushed off the covers and nodded. "All right. I will not take too long."

He walked to the bathroom. She took a shaky breath. She'd done more damage than she'd thought. Before last night, Euric would have been offering to share the shower with her. She'd have to do some major back pedaling. She was supposed to be using this week to convince him not to return to fight, and in one night she'd insulted him and told him the way he was wasn't good enough. Her anger had almost driven him away. She was pretty damn sure if the window had opened last night, he would have gone

217

through it and would have thought twice about seeing her again.

Sick at heart, Petra went to the kitchen and to fry some eggs. The shower ran in the bathroom. She made a promise to herself that she'd cook a nice meal for Euric that evening and then would make love to him until he knew her love for him hadn't changed.

* * * *

With the thick envelope of papers Greg had sent her out to pick up from his real estate agent, Petra walked through the French doors and out onto the flagstone patio. He sat at the table, sipping coffee while he looked out across the back lawn. He turned to her when she placed the envelope on the table.

"Here are the papers you wanted, Greg. The agent said if you have any questions to give him a call."

"Thanks, Petra. I noticed you look a little down today. Is everything all right?"

"I'm okay. Euric and I had our first fight last night, thanks to my dumbass brother."

"That bad, huh?"

"You could say that. I said some things I shouldn't have to Euric. Forget it."

"When my wife and I used to fight, we'd give each other some space to let our anger cool until we were able to calmly discuss what was bothering us. It usually ended up being something very trivial. We also enjoyed the making up part of the argument as well." Greg winked.

She gave him a small smile. "We didn't exactly have time to talk things out yet. I intend to do that after we get home."

"I'm sure the two of you will work things out. Petra, did Euric used to be a part of a recreation group in Rome as a gladiator?"

"No. Why?"

Greg jerked his head in the direction he'd been staring when she'd first come outside. "Watching Euric swing that lead pipe over there, it looks as if he knows how to handle a sword. I just thought since he's really into gladiators that he must have taken part in some recreation games."

Petra turned her head and held her hand to her forehead to shade her eyes from the bright sunshine. Sure enough, Euric stood in the middle of the large open lawn a short distance away, swinging a long lead pipe as if it were a sword. He'd taken his t-shirt off and his muscles shone with a layer of sweat. Even from that distance, she saw his muscles bunching as he went through a series of moves.

She couldn't pull her gaze off Euric. Watching him was like watching someone go through choreographed dance steps. Instead of dancing with a human partner, his was his sword. He twisted and turned, jabbing the lead pipe out in front of him. Just seeing him going through the movements, Petra had to admit he made a beautiful sight. He was good. Really good. She could imagine what he'd look like swinging a real sword. And she'd stupidly told him last night he had to give up that part of himself.

Greg cleared his throat to gain her attention. "Why don't you go over and talk to Euric? He and Tony are taking a lunch break. You can take yours as well. See if you can't start to smooth things over between you and Euric. I have a feeling he'd like to talk to you as much as you want to talk with him. He's been swinging that pipe for the last half hour without a break."

Petra silently nodded and headed out onto the lawn. When she'd almost reached Euric, he stopped what he and slowly lowered the lead pipe. He panted as she stepped to stand in front of him.

"I guess you found something to take the place of a sword," Petra said.

Euric wiped the sweat off his forehead with the back of

his arm. "Tony found it. It was with the other things at the back of the shed that Greg wanted us to throw away. I asked Tony if I could have it. It is not as heavy as a sword, but it is close enough."

"Have you eaten lunch yet?" Euric shook his head. "Come eat with me then. Sally insisted on making us some sandwiches. We can sit out here in the shade and have an impromptu picnic."

"All right. I will use the hose to rinse the sweat off."

While Euric went to do that, Petra returned to the mansion and got the sandwiches Sally had made. Once Sally heard they were going to eat outside, she found an old blanket for Petra so she and Euric wouldn't have to sit on the grass. With the sandwiches, blanket and two water bottles in hand, she thanked Sally and then headed back outside.

Euric had returned from soaking himself with the hose. His hair was wet and slicked back off his forehead. He'd also put his t-shirt on. After she reached him, he took the blanket from her and spread it out on the grass a little way away in a spot that was more shaded.

Once they were both sitting and had a sandwich in front of them, Petra asked, "So how goes your first day?"

"Not bad. Looking after the gardens will be easy enough. Cutting the grass with the riding lawn mower, I am still not too sure about. And the pool and the hot tub, I have seen more machines today that I never would have guessed existed. Tony has had a lot of patience with me. I am sure he thinks I am a slow learner."

"You still have the rest of the week with Tony before he leaves. And I'll be here if something confuses you."

They fell silent as they ate their sandwiches. After she finished half of hers, Petra said, "I hope you've forgiven me for the stupid things I said last night. Seeing you swing that pipe...I had no right. I know I hurt you when I said you had to stop being a warrior. I saw the hurt in your eyes this morning. I'd take back everything I said if I could. I love you just the way you are."

Euric put his sandwich on the blanket and then pulled Petra onto his lap. "I forgive you. Yes, it hurt to hear you say the things you did, but deep down inside I knew you really did not mean them. As I did not mean it when I said that maybe I should stay in my own time. You are my life now. I would never leave you, even if you say things in anger."

Petra wrapped her arms around his shoulders and hugged him. "I missed waking up with you beside me this morning. The next time I do something that stupid like tell you to sleep out on the couch, tell me to screw off. All right?"

Euric rubbed her back and gave a short laugh. "I promise. The couch is not exactly a comfortable place to sleep. My bed in my cell is more comfortable than that."

She leaned back to look Euric in the face. "On the way home from work, I'm going to take you to the grocery store and you can pick out what you want me to make for dinner. Something special. And I'll get a bottle of wine to go with it. It'll be my way of making last night up to you. How does that sound?"

"It sounds as if I will have something to look forward to this evening." Euric cupped the back of her head and brought her mouth down to his. He kissed her thoroughly until she clutched his shoulders. After he pulled away, he said, "That is just a taste of what you can expect from me in my way of making things up to you."

Petra sucked in a shaky breath. "Now I'm not going to be able to think about anything else for the rest of the day."

Euric kissed the tip of her nose, then put her back down onto the blanket next to him. "We both have something to look forward to then."

She picked up the rest of her sandwich and started to

eat as Euric did the same. Feeling as if she'd done a good job of working things out with him, Petra no longer felt as if she were going to lose him. She also made a promise to herself to never let her temper get the best of her again.

* * * *

The last day of Euric's seven days arrived all too soon for Petra. She'd woken up that morning with a sense of dread. The night before he'd broken the news to her that he still intended to return to his time to fight in the *munera* one last time. She didn't try to argue with him to make him change his mind. After their argument earlier that week, she didn't want to start another one that could possibly cause their relationship to break down.

So Petra did her best not to show her anxiety while she and Euric went about their day. They went to work and did their best to act as if that evening he wouldn't be leaving her one more time. It was hard for her not to think about what could happen to him. She found herself distracted and lost in thought so many times Greg had had to repeat himself more than once when he talked to her. The worst part was yet to come, though.

At the end of the day as she drove Euric and herself to what she now considered their apartment, her stomach tightened into knots. She was glad he'd told her not to make him anything to eat before he left since there would already be a meal waiting for him when he arrived in his time. As it was now, she doubted she'd be able eat at all.

With only a few hours left until Euric had to leave, Petra knew she couldn't watch him walk through that window without making love to him one more time. She needed that closeness only lovemaking would give them. She kept telling herself it was only for one more day, but she couldn't stop herself from wanting to cling to him and never let him go.

She waited until after Euric had showered. Once he went to the bedroom, she came up behind him and wrapped her arms around his waist. "Euric, make love to me. I know you said a warrior shouldn't the night before he has to fight, but I need you."

He turned in her arms so he faced her. "I need you as well. Touch me, Petra."

Since Euric only wore a towel around his hips, it took a single tug for Petra to have him naked. She lifted her face toward him as he lowered his lips to hers. His hand worked on the buttons of her blouse while she ran hers caressingly along his chest and abs. He kissed her demandingly, shoving his tongue into her mouth and using it to stroke hers. Once he had her blouse and bra off, he undid the button and zipper on her skirt. It fell to the floor to pool at her feet. She stepped out of it and kicked it away.

She lowered her hands down Euric's body until she reached his fully erect cock. She wrapped her fingers around it and pumped it up and down his length. He moaned into her mouth. He pumped his hips in time with her strokes. Wetness leaked into her panties. The more aroused she became the more desperate she felt to have him deep inside her pussy.

As if he sensed her need, Euric stripped her of her panties. Once she was free of them, he ran a hand up the inside of her thigh. A finger brushed against her slick opening before it thrust inside her. Petra squeezed him harder while she continued to work him up and down his shaft. When a second finger joined the first, he pumped them in and out of her in time with her strokes on his cock. She couldn't hold back a whimpered moan.

She pulled away from his mouth. "Come inside me, Euric. I want you."

In response, he lifted her and carried her to the bed. He followed her down as she came to rest in the center of it.

Petra opened her legs wider when his hips settled between them. With one stroke, he sheathed the full length of his cock inside her pussy.

Petra pushed her heels into the mattress while Euric set a slow and steady pace. The feel of him moving inside her, making them one, had her clutching his biceps. It felt right having him so deep inside her that she didn't know where she ended and he began.

Keeping their bodies joined, Euric rolled onto his back so she ended up on top. He plucked one of her nipples. "Take me, Petra. Ride me until we both cannot hold back any longer."

She braced her hands on his wide chest, lifted onto her knees, then pushed back down on his cock. They moaned in pleasure. She set a faster pace than Euric had. She arched her back, positioning his shaft so it rubbed in the spot that gave her the most pleasure. His cock grew even harder inside her. Petra tightened her inner muscles around him, feeling the tip of him butting up against her cervix with each stroke in.

As she rode him, Euric said, "Open your eyes, Petra. Look at me." After she'd done as he'd asked, he spoke again. "I love you. And I *am* coming back. Nothing is going to stop me from making you my wife and making our own family together."

Petra nodded, unable to speak, knowing if she did she'd just start crying. She rode him faster, harder, and when her climax washed through her, she finally managed to say, "I love you so much, Euric." He surged into her one final time, and with a loud moan, he came deep inside her.

She collapsed onto Euric's chest and held him tight. He had to come back to her. She loved him so much she doubted she'd be able to live without him.

* * * *

The time for Euric to leave arrived. Petra watched him dress in his tunic. She wasn't ready to let him go, but letting him go was what she had to do. He tied the rope belt around his waist and turned to look at her where she sat on the bed. She'd hoped never again to see him wear it.

Dressed in a pair of shorts and a tank top, Petra went to Euric and stepped into his open arms. She buried her face in his chest, fighting the urge to break down in a flood of tears. He didn't need that from her. She needed to stay strong.

Euric kissed the top of her head. "I am all ready to go. The window has opened. I can feel it slightly pulling at me. It is not as strong as it was the other times."

She gave him one last hard hug before she lifted her head. "I guess you still have the choice to stay or go."

"I guess." Euric let her go, but took her hand and led her to the living room where the window stood open. "I want you to wait until tomorrow evening to open the window. I should have been presented with my rudis by that time and will be back in my cell. My *Lanistae* will expect me to spend one last night at the *ludus*. Come morning, he will find me gone."

Her throat tightened as she fought to stop the tears that burned behind her eyes. She lost the battle when a single tear rolled down her cheek. She wiped it away. "Even though it'll probably kill me having to wait a whole twenty-four hours to see you again, I'll hold off." Another tear and then another spilled over.

Seeing them, Euric pulled her to him one last time. "Do not cry, Petra. It is not forever. It is just a single day. Keep telling yourself that."

"I know," she said on a sob. "I'm still going to worry about you. I can't help it."

He pushed her out of his embrace, gave her one more kiss, then turned to face the window. His shoulders lifted as he took a deep breath. Euric stepped through to his side.

He turned and put his hand against the window. "I will miss you, Petra. I love you."

As the mist thickened around him, Petra said through her tears, "I love you too."

The window closed between them. No longer able to hold back the rush of tears, Petra sank to the floor and sobbed her heart out.

* * * *

Fourth Century Rome

Euric turned away from where the window had been and stood really not perceiving his surroundings. Seeing how upset Petra had been, he had started to have second thoughts. Walking through the window had been one of the hardest things he'd had to do. The seven days he had spent with her had shown how right she was for him. Yes, they'd had one bad argument, but all couples fought like that at some point. During the rest of the week, they had grown even closer.

Now back in his time, it really did not feel as if it were his anymore. Petra was not there for one thing, but he had become used to all the modern conveniences of the future. He had actually started to take them for granted. He felt as if he did not belong there.

He did not regret his decision to come back, though. If he had not, Euric had a feeling at some point down the road he would have regretted it. He never wanted it to ever become between him and Petra. And if he ended up with regrets, that would have happened.

The scent from the tray of food sitting on the small table drew Euric over to it. Even though he really had no appetite, he took it and brought it to his bed. He sat and methodically ate. The food tasted good, but he really did not pay much attention to what he put into his mouth. The knowledge that he had to eat to keep his strength up was the only reason he ate.

Once he finished every morsel of food, he put the tray on the table and then stretched out on his bed. He lay for what seemed like hours, staring at the ceiling of his cell, only able to think about Petra. With no real idea what time it was since there were no clocks like the ones in the future, Euric forced himself to close his eyes and go to sleep. It was only for one day, he told himself. Only one day.

* * * *

The following morning Euric woke up with pains in his stomach. At first, he thought maybe he was not used to the food from this time anymore. As the hours went by and they worsened, he wondered if something else caused them.

By the time the guards came to his cell to give him his armor, Euric had vomited more than once and his bowels had come loose. The bucket he had been given to relieve himself while locked in his cell was filled with the stinking mess.

The guard who handed him his armor made a face when he looked from Euric to the offensive bucket in the corner of the cell. "Are you feeling unwell? Should I tell the *Lanistae* that you are not in any condition to fight today?"

Euric held his stomach against the painful cramps that still plagued him and adamantly shook his head. "No. I can fight."

The guard shrugged. "Have it your way then. I will have one of the slaves come and get rid of that bucket." The guards left Euric alone.

Feeling weak and shaky, Euric buckled on his armor, determined to see this through to the end. A slave came and took away his bucket. By the time he had returned with it emptied, Euric had to use it again. Something was terribly wrong with him. If he did not know better, he would think he had been poisoned, but that could not be possible. The food from the night before had come from the *ludus'* own kitchens and only slaves worked there. They would have no way of getting their hands on any poisons.

Once a guard came to collect him to lead him through the tunnel to the *Amphitheatrum*, Euric started to have serious doubts as to whether he would even have a chance of winning his match. Only the thought of receiving his rudis and being able to get back to Petra kept him putting one foot in front of the other. At the entrance to the arena, he put on his helmet, and with shaking hands, took his sword from the guard. Feeling as if this were the last thing he wanted, Euric stepped out onto the sandy floor.

The mob cheered as he walked to the center of the arena. Calix entered a few seconds after he did and came over to Euric. He gave Euric a smile that said he knew something was wrong with Euric and was pleased to see the condition he was in.

Euric and Calix gave the salute to the senator and mob, then turned to face one another. With his stomach cramping, and fighting the urge to vomit when there was nothing left to throw up, a chill ran down his spine. Calix looked too sure of himself.

The Roman made the first strike. Euric blocked it, but in his weakened condition it seemed to go right through him. He staggered out of range when Calix's sword came swinging at him again. The third strike he was able to block with his shield, but it just about drove him to his knees.

Euric was able to get a strike in, but he could not put enough strength behind it. His sword glanced off the surface of Calix's shield, leaving Euric wide open for the Roman to get a strike in of his own. The blade caught Euric across the ribs. His armor protected him from being cut, but the blow still hurt.

After backing away from Calix, Euric circled him. The Roman lunged in and pushed Euric across the floor with blow after blow. Euric felt himself getting weaker. With his stomach cramping painfully, he could do nothing to stop them.

Calix laughed as Euric tried to block his hammering blows. "Did your last meal not agree with you, Goth?" Euric's eyes widened with understanding. Calix laughed again. "From the look of you, I would say the little something extra I arranged to have put in your food is doing its job. Nothing like a death cap mushroom to help rid one of one's enemies.

Hearing that he had indeed been poisoned, Euric stumbled and fell. Calix quickly moved in and placed the tip of his sword against his throat. Euric froze in place. He looked up at Calix. The mob shouted *missum*, mercy.

"How?"

The Roman gave him an evil smile as he pressed the tip of his sword harder against Euric's skin. A trickle of blood rose to the surface and pooled in the hollow of his throat. "Being popular with the mob does have its benefits. I have become the favorite of one of the women who come to visit me. A very well-to-do woman. It did not take much convincing on my part to get her to bring me the mushroom, and the slaves in the kitchen are easy to manipulate."

As the mob's chanting grew louder, Calix looked away from Euric toward the senator who presided over the *munera*. Obviously, given the signal to spare Euric's life, the Roman removed his sword from his throat and stepped back. Euric painfully stood. Guards rushed forward to surround him and Cailx. Two of them took their swords away. Calix and Euric took off their helmets.

The senator, accompanied by the *summa rudis* and his

assistant, walked out onto the floor and headed toward them. Once he reached Calix and Euric, he took a palm branch from the assistant and presented it to Calix. The mob roared their approval.

The senator took the wooden sword the *summa rudis* carried. His face showed some concern when he turned to Euric, but he said a few words about Euric's capable fighting abilities as a gladiator. He handed Euric the rudis that symbolized his freedom.

Euric accepted it and almost dropped it when he could not stop his hands from shaking. He managed to cross his right arm over his chest and nod at the senator. The mob roared loudly again while Calix and Euric were led away by the guards who surrounded them.

Once they were partway through the underground tunnel that would take them to the *ludus*, Calix slammed up behind Euric. "I know you are already a dead man, but I want to make sure it is a for-sure thing."

Seemingly out of nowhere, a small knife appeared in Calix's hand. Sick and growing weaker by the minute, Euric could not stop what happened next. With a quick sweep of his hand, Calix ran the sharp blade of the knife across Euric's throat, slitting it almost ear to ear.

While blood gushed from the wound, Euric fell to his knees. As if from very far away, he heard the guards grappling with Calix. His body going numb and his sight dimming, he fell the rest of the way to the floor. With his rudis clutched in his hand, his last thoughts were of Petra before death claimed him.

CHAPTER FIFTEEN

Present Day

For Petra, the day Euric was to fight seemed to be never ending. She'd dragged herself out of bed before her alarm went off after she spent the night tossing and turning. She thought of not going to work, but figured sitting around alone in her apartment all day, waiting for the time when she could open the window, would make her a basket case. At least at work, she'd have something to help make the time go by quicker.

The first thing she did when she arrived at the mansion was inform Greg that Euric wasn't feeling well and had stayed home. Greg had her tell Tony not to expect him. That taken care of, Petra immersed herself in the work Greg had for her. It helped a little, but the worry she felt for Euric only seemed to intensify as the day went by. She couldn't shake the feeling that something had gone terribly wrong. It wasn't something she could put her finger on exactly. It was just a feeling of wrongness.

By the time she left work, Petra felt almost frantic with

the need to see Euric. Finally home, she changed out of her work clothes and into a pair of shorts and a t-shirt. It was still too early for her to open the window, but she no longer could take the not knowing.

Standing in the middle of her living room, Petra took a deep breath in the hopes it would steady her nerves. It didn't. "Window, show me Euric so I can bring him over to my time, where he has chosen to stay."

Petra waited for the familiar misted window to appear, but nothing happened. She waited a full five minutes before she tried again. "Please show me Euric so he can come back to me."

When it still didn't appear, Petra told herself to stay calm, not to overreact. After all, she'd promised Euric she wouldn't try to open the window until that evening. Maybe it wasn't opening because it was still too early. It had to be that. She didn't want to think it wouldn't open again. She stayed clear of that way of thinking before she really lost it.

She was about to sit on the couch and turn on the TV, hoping something would be on that would distract her, when a small circle of the window opened. It grew in size until it was the shape of a large beach ball. Petra slowly stepped closer, trying to convince herself that it didn't mean anything that the window had returned to its original size and shape.

She nervously fisted her hands at her sides as the mist inside cleared. Instead of showing her Euric's cell, the window showed her the view of what appeared to be a kitchen from that same time. A man worked on putting a tray of food together. There was some kind of meat covered in gravy and a green leafy vegetable that had been steamed. There was also another item of food added that looked like a sticky bun.

Petra silently watched as the man fugitively glanced around before he pulled what looked to be a mushroom out of the pocket of the apron he wore around his waist. It was one she'd never seen before. It had a large white cap, about two inches across, which was rounded. The man took a small knife out of the same pocket and quickly cut the mushroom before he added it to the meat and gravy. He used the knife to mix it together before it disappeared back into his apron pocket. The way the man acted, she had a feeling the mushroom wasn't supposed to be part of the meal he prepared.

Once the man lifted the tray and left the kitchen, he took it to a familiar-looking door. She'd never seen the outside of Euric's cell before, but the door looked the same on the outside as it did on the inside. A feeling of dread washed down her spine when a guard let the man inside the cell and he placed the tray of food on the familiar table before he left again.

Petra went closer to the window when Euric appeared in her line of sight. He didn't look at her as he went to the tray and brought it over to his bed. Having seen what she saw in the kitchen, she knew she couldn't let him eat the meat.

"Euric, don't eat that," she said loudly. He didn't lift his head in her direction, or even act as if he'd heard her. "Euric!" she shouted. Petra tried to put her hand through the window to stop him, but it didn't work. Shouting his name once more, she pounded on it. He still didn't hear her. With sickening dread, she helplessly watched as Euric ate all the food on the tray.

The scene in the window seemed to fast forward. Euric lay on his bed, moaning while he clutched his stomach. He suddenly threw himself out of it and rushed to the corner where there was a bucket. Helpless to do anything to help him, Petra watched him throw up.

The scene skipped ahead again. Two guards arrived at Euric's cell, carrying armor. After an exchange of words, where Petra only understood what Euric said, they left him alone. He donned the armor, looking pale and extremely sick. His hands shook while he did up the buckles.

After Euric left his cell once the guards returned, Petra realized the time had come for the *munera*. She wanted to yell at Euric not to go, that he was in no condition to fight, but instead she bit her lip and whimpered to herself, knowing he wouldn't be able to hear her.

By the time Euric reached the Colosseum, there wasn't any doubt in Petra's mind that the kitchen slave had slipped a poisonous mushroom into Euric's food. Not sure of what kind it was, she visualized what the mushroom had looked like. Once Euric crossed back over to her time, she'd have to rush him to the hospital and the doctor would more than likely need a description of it to determine what Euric had been poisoned with.

Having to watch Euric fight when he was in such a weakened condition, had unshed tears burning behind Petra's eyes. Even though it didn't do any good, she pounded on the window, hoping it'd let her get to him, but it still kept her out.

Petra sucked in a sharp breath when the other gladiator, Calix, said something to Euric that caused him to fall. Calix placed the tip of his sword at Euric's throat. The sight of it made Petra grow cold inside. Of what Euric had said about how defeated gladiators were killed rose to the surface of her mind.

She breathed a sigh of relief after Calix stepped away from Euric, who came slowly to his feet. Petra's concern for him grew even stronger as she watched him grimace in pain, and at the paleness of his face. Somehow he managed to stand straight and tall when three other men came out to the Colosseum's floor. As Euric was given his rudis, she smiled as a tear ran down her cheek.

Euric and Calix were escorted by two guards through an underground tunnel. Knowing he'd be brought back to his cell, Petra anxiously watched their progress.

What happened next Petra would forever be imprinted on her mind.

Calix suddenly shoved into the back of Euric. He said something in Latin, and with sickening horror, a knife appear in his hand. A silent scream stuck in Petra's throat as the other gladiator used it to slit Euric's throat. It had happened so fast even the guards didn't have time to stop him.

Finally finding her voice, Petra screamed, "No! No! No!" over and over again as blood gushed out of Euric's throat with each pump of his heart.

He collapsed to his knees, then slowly fell forward onto the floor. The angle his head was turned, she had a perfect view of his face. With her hand fisted to her mouth while great, gulping sobs rose out of her, Petra saw the life leave Euric's eyes the instant death took him.

Wanting to get to him, needing to get to him, Petra used both fists to pound on the window. To her horror, it filled with mist and slowly shrank in size. She screamed at it not to close, but it continued to shrink until it disappeared.

Petra collapsed in a heap on the floor. Knowing Euric was now lost to her forever, she sobbed uncontrollably. Inside her mind she screamed that fate couldn't be so cruel as to take away the man she loved. He couldn't be gone, but seeing him lying lifeless on the floor said it all.

Lost in her sorrow, she lay there for hours. Her apartment grew dark as early evening turned into night. Still she didn't move. At some point, the phone rang, but she didn't answer it.

When it rang over and over again, she finally dragged herself to it and picked it up just to make it stop. "Whoever this is, stop calling," she said in an emotion-choked voice.

"Petra? What's wrong?" Lia said on the other end. "Talk to me."

Another rush of tears rose to the surface. She said

barely above a whisper, "He's gone, Lia."

"What do you mean by gone? Euric left you to stay in his time?"

She made a noise that sounded between a hysterical laugh and a heart-wrenching sob. "I wish he'd only done that. He's dead."

"How do you know? Has the window opened? You can't be sure unless it has."

"I'm more than sure. It wouldn't open to let Euric through, but it let me watch him die."

"I'm coming over."

"No!" Petra fought back another sob. "No. I don't want to be around anyone right now."

"Petra, you shouldn't be alone right now. We—"

She hung up the phone, not letting Lia finish what she was going to say. Sick at heart, feeling as if she'd never get over the loss of Euric, Petra managed to drag herself to the bedroom. She climbed onto the bed and curled up in the middle of it. After grabbing the pillow that had been his and still held his scent, she buried her face in it and cried herself to sleep.

* * * *

The next morning Petra didn't get out of bed. She didn't get up to shower or eat. She didn't even bother to call Greg to let him know she wouldn't be coming into work. She just lay there, clutching Euric's pillow to her chest and stared at the wall. He was gone and her life held no more meaning. She had nothing to look forward to. There would be no husband or children in her future. No man would ever be able to take his place in her heart.

When she could no longer ignore the demands of her bladder, Petra got up only to relieve herself and then went right back to bed. And that was where she spent the rest of the day and night. The phone rang a half-dozen times, but after it'd rung the first time, she'd turned off her cell phone. She slept, but when she did, she dreamed about Euric and the time they'd spent together. She woke up sobbing, calling his name.

Petra must have fallen asleep again, because the next thing she knew it was morning and Lia stood over her, shaking her and calling her name. She looked up at her friend who stood in her scrubs.

"Lia?" she croaked. "How did you get in?"

Lia held up a set of keys. "You gave me a spare set, remember? And a good thing too." She took Petra by the arm and tried to pull her up into a sitting position. Petra fought her. "Oh, no you don't," Lia said. "You're not going to lie in bed like this anymore. You're going to take a shower, change your clothes and going to eat something even if I have to sit on you and force feed you."

"Just leave me alone." Getting up to face the world was the last thing Petra wanted right now.

"No, I won't. I just got off a night shift at the hospital and I'm not in the mood to put up with you telling me to go away. I gave you some time, now you have to stop feeling sorry for yourself and do something about it."

"Feeling sorry for myself?" Petra asked with some anger. "Having to deal with Euric never coming back to me is hardly feeling sorry for myself." She choked back a sob when she said Euric's name.

Lia put her hands on her hips. "Good. You're getting angry. That's a start. Now maybe you'll start using that head of yours and think. You can still get Euric back."

"No, I can't. I watched him die."

"Yes, but you watched him die in the fourth century. You're forgetting one little thing—the window. You can save Euric. Just get it to open before he dies, to a time when you can stop what's going to happen. You already know how he's going to die so you can make sure it doesn't turn out that way."

Petra pushed herself into a sitting position while she thought over what Lia said. Could she stop Euric from dying? A small spark of hope formed inside her, but it quickly became extinguished.

"I could do what you say, but what if the window won't open for me again? The last time it opened, it only showed me scenes of the past, as if I were only an observer. Euric couldn't see or hear me."

"Then you force it to open and let you through. It's about time you played hardball with it."

"It never worked when I made demands of it before. I doubt it'll cooperate when I need it to."

"Do you want Euric back or not?"

"Of course I do," Petra wailed.

"Then make it do what you want. If it won't open for you when you tell it to, we'll get the thing that started all this between you and Euric in the first place."

"The rudis?"

"Yes. I have a feeling it's responsible for the window opening to the past. Somehow we'll get it to work for you again. Now get your ass out of that bed and into the shower. You look like shit, and I doubt Euric would want to see you like this."

Realizing Lia wouldn't relent, Petra got off the bed and then took a shower. What Lia suggested, in her heart of hearts, she hoped it worked. She was willing to rail, scream, threaten, do whatever it took to get the window to open for her. Even if she had to steal the rudis from Greg, she'd do it.

Feeling her resolve strengthen, Petra stood under the shower and let the water wash away the evidence of her hours of crying. She wasn't going to shed any more tears. It was the time to fight to get her man back.

* * * *

After Lia watched Petra eat every last bit of food on her plate, they drove to Greg's mansion in Lia's car with the intention of taking the rudis. Petra had tried to open the window once she'd finished her shower, but it didn't appear even when she'd pleaded with it. If not for Lia being there with her, Petra would have felt it was hopeless. Lia hadn't allowed her to sink back into despair. Instead, she bullied Petra into eating and then said they were going to try the rudis next.

Once they arrived at the mansion, Lia parked her car in front of the garage. When Petra didn't try to get out, she said, "Let's go, Petra. No second thoughts."

"It's stealing."

"No, it isn't. You're just going to borrow the rudis for a little while."

Petra took a deep breath and nodded. "All right."

They left the car and went to the front door of the mansion. At Lia's nudging, Petra opened it and walked inside the foyer. Trying not to think of what she was about to do to a man she respected a great deal, she led Lia to Greg's study. Luckily for them he wasn't in the room.

Seeing the rudis on its shelf had Petra fighting back a wave of grief. The sight of it brought the image of Euric, lying in a pool of his own blood with his rudis clutched in his hand. With a shaky breath, she reached out and picked up the wooden sword. Something sparked slightly where her fingers made contact with the wood, but it was nothing like what she'd felt when she'd touched it for the very first time.

Lia passed her the large duffle bag they'd brought to put the rudis in. Petra had unzipped it and had one end of the rudis inside it when Greg walked into the study. His gaze went from the rudis in her hand, then up to her face.

"Petra? Since you didn't come to work yesterday, and you didn't answer your phone, I was worried about you." His gaze lowered once more to the wooden sword she held. A frown creased his brow.

She swallowed, knowing she'd have to say something. "I need the rudis, Greg. It's a matter of life or death."

He moved closer. "Whose?"

"Euric's."

"I don't see how my rudis could be that important to Euric. What's going on, Petra?"

"Petra," Lia said, "tell him. Tell him the reason you need it."

Petra shook her head. "He'll think I'm crazy."

"You told me and I didn't have you taken away to the nut house."

"Only because you saw with your own eyes that I told the truth."

"Just do it, Petra. Try using the rudis. If it works, he'll have all the proof he needs."

Greg, who'd been silent until now, said, "You can tell me anything, Petra. No matter how bizarre you think it may be."

She kept her grip on the rudis as she let the duffle bag drop to the floor. Petra stepped to stand in the middle of the room to face Greg and Lia. "What I tell you will probably be more bizarre than you think it is."

"You can trust me, Petra."

She shifted the wooden sword so she held it flat in both hands. She looked down at it and tightened her fingers around it. "When I touched the rudis for the first time after I brought it to you, something happened. The only way I can describe it is somehow a window that let me see into the past opened. To fourth century Rome to be exact." Petra looked up to meet Greg's gaze. So far, he wasn't looking at her as if she'd lost her mind.

"Through the window, I met Euric. You asked if he'd been part of a recreation group in Rome, well the truth is Euric was a real gladiator. He was a Visigoth warrior who'd been captured during battle in what was

Germania." When Greg didn't say anything, she continued. "It worked out that I could bring him through the window to our time. To make a long story short, we fell in love. Euric decided he'd permanently stay in our time with me, but he found out that during the next *munera* he had to fight in he'd be given his rudis, his freedom. Two days ago, he went back to fight for the very last time, then he would have come back to ours and never return to his." Her throat closed up and Petra had to clear it. "Instead of opening to allow Euric to cross over from the past, the window showed me his death. I want to go back to save him, but the window won't open."

Greg nodded. "So you decided to see if you touched the rudis again if it'd open for you?" His gaze went to a spot just over her right shoulder. "Well, I think it worked."

Petra turned around to see the window opening into its beach ball size. Greg and Lia walked over to stand on either side of her as the scenes that lead to Euric's death start to play out. Petra's tears streamed down her face as she watched the inevitable happen.

She looked away when Calix shoved into the back of Euric. "I can't watch this part," she said in a tear-filled voice.

"Ah, Petra," Lia said a short while later. "I think you may want to see this."

Petra looked up to see a new scene forming in the window. In it she saw herself dressed in what she thought looked to be a Roman-style dress in a room she didn't recognize. She glanced quickly over at Greg when she saw that he stood beside her dressed in the same type of clothing. He wore an expression of rapt astonishment. She quickly turned back to the window in case she'd missed something.

To her astonishment, she and Greg stepped through the window to what had to be fourth century Rome. The scene jumped ahead. They were inside the Colusseum, watching two gladiators who weren't Euric and Calix fight. It fast forwarded the scene again. This one showed her and Greg with another man who wore the same tunic Euric wore, rushing an obviously ill Euric through the underground tunnel. The window filled with mist and disappeared.

Lia gave a little shout of joy. "I knew it. You're going back and save Euric. And it looks as if you're going to have a little help too."

Petra turned to Greg. He was still staring transfixed where the window had been. "You'll help me?"

He turned toward her and smiled. "Of course I will. How could I pass up the chance of actually seeing ancient Rome for myself? You'll need me, anyway. I understand and can speak Latin, remember?"

Petra returned his smile. "I guess that makes you invaluable to me. There's only one problem—I have no idea where we were when we stepped through the window into the past."

"I do," Greg said enthusiastically. "That room was the living room inside the villa I just bought in Italy. It looks as if we'll be flying there, Petra."

"As will I," Lia said. "In all likelihood the mushroom that was put in Euric's food was poison."

Greg nodded. "It was. I thought it looked familiar, but when the gladiator Euric fought called it tectum mortis, death cap, I knew exactly why the kitchen slave was putting it into the food. The death cap mushroom is deadly, but it takes many hours before a person who has ingested it starts feeling the effects of the poison, which is what Euric went through."

"Then I'm most definitely going," Lia said more firmly. "Euric is going to need to be treated for the poison as soon as you get him to our time. I'm a nurse. I can look after him. And I can get everything I need to help save his life. I know a doctor in my hospital who has made a study of learning about poisonous plants. I'm sure I can convince him to tell me how to treat someone who has eaten that type of mushroom and give me the medicines to treat it."

As Lia and Greg discussed what else may be needed to take with them to Italy to ensure Euric would recover, Petra let herself hope that there was a real chance she would get him back. She looked down at the rudis she still held and sent up a silent prayer to whatever god may be listening to let them succeed. If she had to watch him die a second time, it would destroy her.

* * * *

The next day, Petra found herself on a private jet with Greg and Lia, flying to Italy. They had everything they needed. Lia had scored, as she put it, and had more than enough medical supplies to treat Euric when they got him to their time. The doctor she knew had even told her exactly how he had to be given the penicillin. It had to be given intravenously until the person who'd eaten the mushroom no longer had stomach pains, vomiting and diarrhea. He also stressed that it had to be administered as quickly as possible after the person ate it. And that there was a chance the penicillin wouldn't stop the liver from being permanently damaged. If that happened, Euric would need to have a liver transplant. She hoped they'd catch it in time before that amount of damage occurred.

As for the Roman clothing she and Greg had to wear, Greg had arranged to have it brought to the villa the day they'd arrive. He'd found a store in Rome that rented authentic-looking ancient Roman garments.

During the flight, which would take twelve and a half hours for them to reach Rome, Petra had more than enough time to think about what they were about to do. It had to work. Even though the window only showed her and Greg with Euric, and he was still alive, it'd never showed them actually getting him to the future. The other man who helped them had to be another gladiator, but not one who'd competed in the *munera* since he hadn't worn any armor. Whoever he was, she'd recognize him when she saw him. She hadn't been able to stop replaying those new scenes over and over in her mind.

Lia, who'd been sitting on the opposite side of the jet, shifted to sit in one of the seats next to her. "How are you doing?"

"I'm holding up. I'll feel much better once we have Euric in our time. The window had better cooperate."

"I don't think you have to worry about that. It showed what you had to do. I doubt it would have done that if it was going to stop you from stepping into the past to save Euric."

Greg, who sat across from Petra, spoke up. "I have to agree with Lia. I think you and Euric are meant to be together."

"You sound so sure about that, Greg," Petra said.

"Because I do feel sure. Since you showed me the window, I've done a little research into my rudis. It may be an exact copy of a Rome rudis, but it's said to have powers of its own."

"You mean like magical powers?"

"That's what has been said about it. Supposedly, whoever owns the rudis, it'll bring them together with whomever they're destined to fall in love with, bending time and space if needed."

Lia chuckled. "It sounds as if it's some kind of paranormal matchmaker."

Greg smiled. "A magical matchmaker."

Petra shook her head. "I don't own the rudis. You do."

"Maybe so, but you were the first to touch it. Maybe that was all that was needed to get the ball rolling, so to speak."

Petra liked the idea that Euric was always destined to be hers, her soul mate. "Did you find out how the rudis got its magical reputation?"

"No. It's very old. No one knows who made it or why. Before I purchased it, it'd been sitting for years in storage in Italy. It was found by the previous owner when his father passed away and he wanted to sell off his estate. Luckily for me, I'd been on the lookout for an antique rudis for years. I had my antiques dealer purchase it on my behalf through a dealer's auction."

Petra mulled over the rudis' supposed magical properties. There had to be some truth to the story. How else could the window to the past be explained? If she'd heard what the rudis was reported to do before she'd been through what she had with Euric, she would have laughed and said it sounded like nothing but a bunch of mumbo jumbo. She'd never believed in all things paranormal actually existing. She didn't even believe in ghosts — even though she liked to watch the reality shows that followed people who investigated supposed haunted places. Now she had to question her beliefs.

She reclined her seat while Lia and Greg continued to talk. Her gaze looked across the plane to the seat that had the duffle bag with the rudis inside it. They'd decided to bring it to Italy with them just in case Petra needed to hold on to it to get the window to open.

Petra let her eyes drift shut. They still had too many hours to get through before they reached Rome.

CHAPTER SIXTEEN

Greg's private jet landed in Rome at four in the morning Italy time. Once they arrived at his villa, it was after five thirty. Even though she'd slept some on the plane, Petra was tired enough that all she wanted to do was roll into bed and sleep for a few hours. Lia and Greg looked as tired as she felt.

The outside of the villa was just as beautiful in real life as it'd been in the pictures Petra had seen of it. Unlike Los Angeles, and being close to the Italian countryside, the sky was clear and free of smog. After collecting her luggage from the trunk of the limousine Greg had arranged to drive them from the airport to the villa, Petra looked around her while the sky grew brighter with the dawn. In other circumstances, she would have loved to roam around the grounds, or go wander through the medieval town of Braccian that the villa was located closest to. She would have even liked to go to nearby Tuscany and do some sightseeing there as well, but until she got Euric back, she wouldn't do any of those things.

Greg let her and Lia into the villa. The sun had lightened enough that they didn't need to turn on any lights to see. Petra looked around the open foyer. It appeared clean and well maintained. The terracotta-colored ceramic tiles on the floor shone as if they'd been freshly washed. The walls had been painted a warm orange-brown color that was more orange than brown.

"I suggest we head upstairs and get some sleep," Greg said as he shut the door behind them. "There are enough rooms for us to each have a room to ourselves. I had the caretaker I hired prepare the villa for our arrival so there should be fresh sheets on the beds. Pick whichever room you want."

Hefting her heavy suitcase, Petra followed Lia up the stairs while Greg brought up the rear. At the first bedroom, Lia mumbled a weary goodnight and went inside. Petra took the one beside Lia's. She said goodnight to Greg as he continued down the hall.

Petra only spared the room a quick glance before she went over to the king-sized bed. The same ceramic tiles that'd been downstairs in the foyer were on the floor. The walls of this bedroom had been painted in a warm sunny color that seemed to match the rest of the color scheme of the villa.

After she put her suitcase near the single dresser, Petra only took the time to take off the skirt and short-sleeved blouse she wore before she pulled back the covers on the bed and climbed into it. In a matter of minutes, she fell asleep.

While she slept, Petra dreamed. Maybe it was because she was in Italy, knowing she was that much closer to getting Euric back, because for the first time since she'd seen him die, she dreamt about the future they'd have together. For some reason, she dreamed about them living there in the villa. He was hale and strong. His bronzed skin glistened in the sun as he swung a real-looking sword outside on the back lawn. He lowered it when he saw her and gave her a smile that warmed her to her soul. He held out a hand.

When she took it, he said, "Nothing will ever separate us again." Euric lowered his mouth to claim hers.

Petra awoke with her heart beating hard while she ached to hold Euric in her arms. Knowing she wouldn't be able to sleep anymore, she got up and took a shower in the bedroom's en suite. She dressed in a pair of shorts and a tank top before she went downstairs.

She followed the smell of fresh-brewed coffee to the villa's kitchen. Lia and Greg were already up. Lia turned away from the stove where she was cooking eggs and bacon to greet Petra.

"Well, look who finally woke up. I was thinking I was going to have to kick you out of bed."

Petra went and sat at the table next to Greg. "I guess I was more tired than I thought."

Greg put a coffee mug onto the table. "You probably needed it. While you slept our outfits arrived. They're identical to what we saw us wearing in the window."

She nodded. "I guess all that's left to do is to eat, then we can go."

Lia placed plates of eggs and bacon in front of Petra and Greg before she went and got her own. Once she joined them at the table, she said, "I'll have the IV and penicillin all ready when you return. I'll get Euric hooked up as soon as you get him through the window."

Now that the time to save Euric was almost there, Petra was anxious. She took a deep, calming breath.

As if sensing how she felt, Greg reached over and squeezed her hand. "We'll get him back for you, Petra."

She gave him a half smile. "I know we will."

After they finished eating, Petra and Greg went up to their rooms to change into their Roman outfits. Her light blue linen dress, or long tunic, was sleeved and basically two pieces of wide material that had been sewn together at the top. She had to do up a series of buttons to make the dress fit. The belt she wore around her hips also helped to hold the material close to her body. The last piece she put on was a stola, a loose equivalent of a toga. It was the same color as the tunic and resembled a sleeveless tunic that she had to strap at her shoulder. It also was gathered together at the waist by a girdle and fell to her feet, on which she wore a pair of soft leather shoes instead of sandals. According to Greg, married Roman women were required to wear the stola when out in public. He also figured having Petra appear as a married woman would afford her more freedom than if she was perceived as being unmarried if they had to interact with too many of Rome's citizens.

Dressed correctly—at least she thought she'd remembered everything Greg had told her about how to put everything on—Petra went downstairs. He was already there, waiting for her with Lia. He wore a short-sleeved tunic with a classic-styled toga over it. His tunic was dark blue while the toga was off white. He also wore a pair of soft leather shoes that enclosed his whole foot and were very similar to the ones Petra wore.

He nodded in approval. Once she reached him and Lia, he held out the last article of Petra's outfit. It looked like a large shawl and was two shades darker blue than her tunic and stola.

Greg put it around her shoulders and looped it around her arms. "This is called a pulla. You pull it up to cover your head and the rest of you. Women wore these when they were outside."

That done, Petra said, "I guess we're all ready to go?"

"Yes. All that's left is for you to open the window."

After Petra went to the spot in the living room where she was supposed to open the window, Lia came to her and gave her a hug. "Go get your man. And kick some Roman butt if you have to."

Petra chuckled. "I'll do my best."

"Let's get the show on the road," Lia said as she let go of Petra and moved aside.

With a nod, Petra waited for Greg to come to her side before she said out loud in a steady voice, "Window, I want you to open to a time before Euric dies, before he fights, so I can bring him to my time to stay and never go back."

As requested, the window appeared before her. Unlike the last few times, it opened in the shape of a large doorway that would allow two people to walk through it side by side. Once the mist cleared, she found herself looking at what appeared to be the back of a large open space of ground. On one side of it were rows of doors — cell doors. High stone walls enclosed the rest of the space. The man who the window had showed would help them get Euric away stood nearby, swinging a wooden sword. She looked past him and saw there were only a couple other men dressed in the same tunic, practicing with wooden swords as well. Petra figured this had to be the *ludus'* training ground. A guard stood closer to the cell doors, looking bored. He didn't seem to be able to see them, same with the others, but that would change as soon as she and Greg stepped through the window.

The man who stood alone closest continued to swing his wooden sword in sweeping arcs. Lia walked over to stand beside Petra and put her hand against the window. "Well, hello Mr. Hunky Man With The Sword. I thought he looked hot when we saw him before, but he looks even better now."

While Lia had spoken, the man her friend had been ogling lowered his sword and looked right at all three of them. With a look of surprised shock on his face, he cautiously came closer. He had sandy-blond, shoulder-length hair and blue eyes a few shades darker than Euric's. He also stood as tall as Euric and had the same muscular build. His similarities to Euric got Petra wondering if this could be the warrior who had recently been captured from Euric's village.

The man looked around him before he put his hand on his side of the window to match up with Lia's. They both jumped back at the same time as if they'd been jolted. He said something Petra didn't understand. And it didn't sound like Latin to her, either.

"For some reason, he can see us," Petra said. "I also have no idea what he said to us." She turned to Greg. "It wasn't Latin, was it?"

Greg shook his head. "No, it wasn't."

"Great. Now how are we supposed to make him understand us?"

Lia put her hand back on the window and said with wonder in her voice, "I can understand him. He asked if we were ghosts, or some kind of gods."

Realizing what it meant that Lia understood the man on the other side of the window when she and Greg didn't, Petra stopped herself from telling Lia she'd more than likely just found the man destined for her. Now wasn't the time to dwell on it, though.

Instead, she said, "Then you'll have to be our interpreter, Lia. Ask him what his name is and see if he understands you."

After Lia did that, Petra recognized the name he called himself—Gerritt. She'd been right in her assumptions. He was the warrior from Euric's village. It meant he'd be more than willing to help them find Euric since Euric counted Gerritt a friend.

She had Lia to explain to Gerritt what they wanted to do. It was weird hearing Lia speak in English, and Gerritt obviously replying in Goth. It seemed even weirder that Lia understood it perfectly. That must have been how she and Euric had sounded when they'd first met, before the window had allowed him to speak and understand English.

A few minutes later, Lia said, "All right. Gerritt understands what's going on. He sort of gets the concept that we're from the future and that Euric knows about us. I also told him what Petra means to Euric. If it was anyone else but Euric, I don't think he'd be so willing to help out. The man hates the Romans."

"I don't blame him," Petra said. "The Romans killed almost all the people in his village and burned it to the ground before they took him as a slave to fight in the Colosseum. I'd be a little bitter if I was in his situation as well."

Greg shifted beside Petra. "Not to interrupt, but I think now would be a good time for us to go through the window. The guard is a little busy at the moment and it'd be an ideal time for us to slip past him."

Petra looked for the guard and found him trying to break up a fist fight between two of the other men who'd been practicing. "I think you're right."

Taking Greg's hand, Petra walked him through the window. Gerritt moved to her side and said something. She looked back at Lia, who quickly said, "He says to hurry and follow him. He knows where the tunnel is that leads underground to the *Amphitheatrum*."

With a nod for Gerritt to go ahead, Petra and Greg followed him. She kept her gaze on the guard, but he was having a little trouble getting the two gladiators separated and didn't once look their way.

Once they reached the row of doors, Gerritt led them to one at the very end that opened to a hallway that had another row of cells lining it. At the end of that, there was another door. It stood open, but there was a guard in front of it, blocking their way.

"What are we going to do about the guard?" Petra whispered to Greg.

"I'm not sure."

Before Petra got a chance to say anything to stop him,

Gerritt snuck up behind the guard, grabbed him by the shoulder and spun him around. His fist connected with the guard's chin and the man collapsed like a stone. Gerritt took hold of him under his arms and dragged him into one of the empty cells before shutting the door.

Petra smiled as Gerritt came back and motioned for them to go inside the tunnel. "I guess he took care of that problem," she said as she hurried down it.

Greg clapped Gerritt on the shoulder. "I guess he's a good man to have around."

The roaring of a large crowd grew louder the farther they headed down the tunnel. After they reached the end, Gerritt cautiously pushed opened the closed door. He poked his head around it, then signaled them to follow.

Greg took a sharp breath behind her. She glanced back to see him staring in wonder. He met her gaze and whispered excitedly, "We're actually inside the *hypogeum* under the Colosseum's arena. It's used to bring animals and gladiators to the arena above."

Gerritt turned and shushed them. Greg stopped talking and put his hand over his mouth to show he wouldn't say anything more. Seemingly satisfied, Gerritt nodded and motioned them to follow him down one of the maze-like tunnels. At the end of it, Petra found herself looking out at the Colosseum's arena where two gladiators fought, who weren't Euric and Calix. Seeing they'd arrived at the right time to stop what would happen next, Petra breathed a sigh of relief. Now all they had to do was wait for Euric to arrive.

Once the match ended with both combatants still alive and able to walk away, Petra clutched Greg's arm as Euric stepped out from one of the other entrances and slowly walked to the center of the arena. At the sight of Calix coming through another, she felt a rush of fury. If he'd been closer and she'd had a sword, she would have gladly stuck it through his heart.

It was more painful to watch Euric fight in real life than it'd been to watch it through the window. More than once she had to bite back a shout of warning. Not that he would have been able to hear her over the roar of the crowd. She wasn't the only one who found the fight hard to watch. Gerritt muttered something angrily in Goth quite a few times while he fisted his large hands at his sides. Petra had a feeling if he ever got his hands on Calix, the Roman would get the beating of his life.

Even though the match only lasted a few minutes, it seemed to drag on for Petra. Knowing she could do nothing to stop it made it that much harder on her. As Euric fell and Calix placed the tip of his sword at his throat, she knew they had to get into position. The plan she, Lia and Greg had come up with was for her and Greg to get into the tunnel that led to the *ludus* ahead of Euric, Calix and the guards. From the window, they knew approximately where in the tunnel Calix would launch his attack. Without his element of surprise, she figured the guards would be able to disarm him before he did any damage.

Lia had briefly outlined their plan to Gerritt when she'd spoken with him. Giving him a nudge, Petra used her hands to motion that they should return to the tunnel. He seemed to understand as he nodded and turned away from the proceedings taking place out in the arena.

Feeling a sense of urgency, Petra wanted to run back to the tunnel, but Gerritt kept the pace not too fast as to draw attention to their passage. Not that the people down in the *hypogeum* paid too much attention to them, anyway. There had to be other fights planned for the *munera*, because they saw more gladiators being led through the *hypogeum's* tunnels.

After they finally reached the underground tunnel that led to the *ludus*, Petra entered it as her heart raced. With Gerritt accompanying them, she had a feeling even if the guards couldn't stop Calix, he would. They had to get this right the first time, because she wasn't at all sure the window would give them a second chance.

Reaching the spot inside the tunnel where Calix would slit Euric's throat, Petra stopped Gerritt. He turned around to face her, and she said, "Stop. We wait here." She pointed to the floor at her feet. "Euric and Calix will be here soon."

To make sure he really understood what she meant, she said Calix's name and made the motion of a knife being drawn across her throat, then said Euric's name.

At Gerritt's nod, Petra turned to Greg. "I think he understood me. Now don't forget when they come you have to yell in Latin to the guards that Calix has a knife. Hopefully, that will keep them busy enough for us to get Euric to the training ground and the window."

"It'll work, Petra. I think I hear them coming. You'd better put the pulla over your head so Euric doesn't see you until we're ready. We don't need him to do something unexpected like running to meet you. That will only cause the guards to go after him instead of Calix."

Petra doubted Euric would be in any shape to run for any distance in the condition he was in. She did do as Greg suggested and tugged the pulla over her head so it half concealed her features. She went still when she heard the sound of movement behind them.

Gerritt pushed past Greg and Petra, putting him in front to confront the group that headed their way. Once the guard in front of Euric and Calix spotted him, he continued walking, but asked something of Gerritt. Greg shifted to stand beside him and then yelled something in Latin that she figured meant Calix was armed with a knife. As the guard in front turned to Calix, the Roman had picked that moment to slam into Euric. The blade of a knife flashed in the light of the torches that were fixed on the walls.

Petra screamed Euric's name. Unlike what she'd seen when he'd died, this time the guards were able to react more quickly. The front guard shoved Euric out of the way as the one in the rear grabbed Calix from behind.

Weak from being ill, Euric stumbled and went down onto his knees. Petra and Gerritt reached him at the same time. Gerritt didn't waste any time in putting Euric's arm around his shoulders and hauling him back onto his feet.

As they ran, Euric kept looking from Greg, who ran up in front, and then to Petra, who ran at his side. "You are here. I am not just dreaming that you are?"

Petra tugged down the pulla. "I'm really here, Euric. The window showed me that you were poisoned and what would have happened in this tunnel if I hadn't come to your time."

Just as they reached the end and arrived at the *ludus*, Euric stumbled, and if not for Gerritt supporting him, would have fallen. His face had grown even paler. Petra put his other arm around her shoulders and helped Gerritt get Euric moving again.

Euric looked at her. "I am going to die, Petra. You should not have come."

"No, you aren't," Petra replied sharply. "We just have to get you to my time. We know what mushroom it was Calix had slipped into your food. Lia is waiting to give you the medicine that will counteract the poison."

They ran down the hallway that led to the training ground. Gerritt barked something in Goth to Euric, who said something in that same language. Petra wanted to ask what Gerritt had said since it'd made him run faster when just a short while before Euric had been about ready to collapse.

Still running, they burst out into the training ground. The window stood open where they'd left it. The guard there bellowed something, but they kept running. Just before they reached the window, Petra yelled at Greg to slow down. Once he was within reaching distance, she grabbed his hand and positioned herself so she'd have the lead while she still helped Gerritt support Euric's weight. She had enough time to see Lia move out of the way as she jumped through the window, taking everyone with her.

Out of breath, Petra fell to her knees as Euric's legs seemed to give out on him. He collapsed onto the floor, his labored breathing filling her ears. They'd done it. They'd gotten Euric to the present.

Lia rushed to Euric's side and yanked at the armor he wore. "Help me get this off him. Then we'll get him to the couch so I can hook up the IV."

Petra tried to undo one of the buckles that held the armor to Euric's chest and back, but she only ended up struggling with it. A pair of strong male hands batted hers aside and deftly undid the buckles one by one. She sat back on her heels, shocked to see who was now peeling the armor off Euric's chest. Gerritt threw it aside and shifted to remove the armor Euric wore on his legs. She looked at Lia, who sat with her mouth hanging open while she watched Gerritt. Petra then looked to where the window had stood open. It was no longer there. For better or worse, it looked as if Gerritt would be staying.

Lia told Gerritt to get Euric onto the couch once he was free of all his armor. Greg went to Euric and took something from his hand and then passed it to Petra. She blinked down at the wooden sword she held — Euric's rudis. After putting it on the coffee table, she turned back to watch Lia insert the IV's needle that was attached to a fluid bag into Euric's arm. She taped it in place, then attached another smaller bag — that Petra guessed was the penicillin — to the tube and started them dripping. She put both bags in Gerritts hands and got him to hold them up. She pulled a coat rack she must have found somewhere in the villa closer to the couch next to Euric. Taking the bags one at a time from Gerritt, she attached them to two wire hangers that hung upside down from the top of the coat rack.

That done, Lia pulled off the latex gloves she wore and stepped back, allowing Petra to move back to Euric's side. "Now all we can do is wait and see if the penicillin does its job. I'll give him until tonight. If he doesn't start feeling better by then, we'll have to rush him to the hospital."

Euric blinked open his eyes and looked around the room. "We made it back?" When his gaze fell on Gerritt, he said, "You took Gerritt with us?"

Petra gave him a shaky smile. They may have made it back, but Euric still looked extremely ill. "It wasn't a conscious thought on my part. He just happened to come along for the ride."

"I am glad. I did not like the thought of leaving him behind as a slave." Gerritt said something in Goth to Euric, who replied. At Petra's questioning look, he said, "Gerritt wanted to know where exactly here was. I told him he should be more concerned with what year it was."

Lia took Gerritt's arm and led him away. "Leave the explaining to me since I'm the only other person here who understands him. Euric needs to rest."

Once they disappeared, Greg said, "Euric, I'm glad we got you safely back. I have to say that was the most excitement I've had in many years, and it'll be one experience I'll never forget. I should leave you two alone." He pulled at the toga he wore. "These may be fine for your time, but I much prefer my slacks."

After Greg left them alone, Petra sat on the couch next to Euric and bent down to kiss him, something she'd thought she'd never get to do again. She brushed the hair off his forehead.

"I thought I lost you forever. When I tried to open the window and it showed me you'd died..." She let her words trail off. "You'll never leave me again like that, do you understand? Never again." Her eyes burned with unshed tears.

Euric cupped the back of her head and pushed it down until their foreheads touched. "I promise. When Calix said he had poisoned me, I thought I would never see you again. I could not stop thinking the poison would kill me before you could open the window. I should have listened to you and never gone back."

Petra put a finger across Euric's lips. "You didn't know something like that was going to happen. At least you got what you came for." She shifted to sit up before she took the rudis from the coffee table and placed it on his chest.

He looked down at it. "I risked my life for a piece of wood."

She took his hand and closed his fingers around the pommel. "Not just any piece of wood—your rudis, your symbol of freedom. You're no longer a slave, no longer a gladiator. You can now live your life the way you want to."

Euric met her gaze and looked deeply into her eyes. "I get to live my life with the woman I love."

Petra gave him a watery smile. "And I get to live my life with the man I love, who just happens to be an ex-gladiator."

She kissed Euric, knowing she'd never have to watch him walk through that window and leave her ever again. Today would mark the start of the rest of her life with the man who came through time to be hers.

EPILOGUE

One month later

Petra watched Euric and Gerritt practicing with their swords out on the lawn as she stood outside on the patio. The hot Italian sun beat down on her, and she had to shade her eyes with her hand to better see the men. They were shirtless and each only wore a pair of athletic shorts. The sound of their metal blades hitting together carried on the slight breeze toward her.

She turned to smile at Lia when her friend stepped out onto the patio to join her. "They're at it again."

"Figures," Lia said with a snort. "When are they not at it? I think those swords have become permanently attached to them. I don't know what Greg was thinking when he bought them for the guys."

"I think he was thinking that those two Visigoth warriors over there would feel more at home if they had their own swords. And you know how he wants them to never forget their lives in the past."

"Of course he doesn't. He enjoys picking their brains

about the fourth century. I really shouldn't complain since he has given us a place to live rent free and pays us to do next to nothing."

Petra chuckled. It was true. Greg had allowed the four of them to live at his Italian villa for however long they wished. All they had to do in return was maintain the grounds, which the men took care of. She still worked for him as an assistant, though now long distance. He'd returned to the States the week before, but he'd said he'd come to the villa at least once a month to check in on them. She knew Greg just enjoyed being around Euric and Gerritt.

Lia and Gerritt had grown very close and were perfect for each other. Lia could mouth off at him all she wished and he took it with a smile before he mouthed right back. He was also slowly learning how to speak English. With Lia's and Euric's help, he was picking it up a lot quicker than Petra had expected. She and Gerritt could now have short, stilting conversations before either Euric or Lia had to act as interpreter.

Petra followed Euric as he twisted away from one of Gerritt's swings. He was now fully recovered from being poisoned. It'd been touch and go in the very beginning, whether or not he should have been taken to a hospital, but Lia had watched over him night and day, keeping him hooked up to the IV until she felt he was out of the woods. She'd also used his illness as an excuse to quit her job at the hospital and stay with them.

Giving her friend a nudge in the ribs, Petra said, "Should we interrupt them?"

"Hell yes. Seeing my man swing that sword is making me hot and bothered."

Laughing, Petra and Lia walked across the grass. Euric turned and gave her a look that made her heart beat faster. As she closed the distance between them, Petra knew her life couldn't get any better than this.

The End

ABOUT THE AUTHOR

Marisa Chenery was always a lover of books, but after reading her first historical romance novel she found herself hooked. Having inherited a love for the written word, she soon started writing her own novels.

She now writes young adult books and erotic romances.

Marisa lives in Ontario, Canada, with her boyfriend, Steve, four children, four grandchildren (she's a young grandma in her fifties) and rabbit and dog.

www.marisachenery.com